AMERICAN QUEEN

AMERICAN QUEEN
Written by Ginger Moran
Copyright ©2020 Ginger Moran

ISBN: 978-1-970071-08-5

Published by
Bluebullseye Press
A division of Bluebullseye LLC

Edited by Ginger Moran

Cover and book design
Copyright ©2020 John H. Matthews

Cover photo by IsaaK KaRslian on Unsplash

AMERICAN QUEEN

GINGER MORAN

bluebullseye press

ALSO BY
GINGER MORAN

The Algebra of Snow

CHAPTER ONE
Labor Day 2018

The thing was that when I told someone I wasn't sure when my husband would be home I knew I was telling the truth about the first part, but the second part was always up in the air.

I didn't know when Clint would be home—hell, I didn't know *if* he would be. Most of the time I didn't know where he was or what he was doing. I couldn't call him and getting a message through was iffy.

Other than knowing for a fact he'd been home long enough to father five children, I was pretty vague on everything else.

Clint was a spy.

I knew that when I married him.

Sometimes I wondered if I had wanted to be single-married. I was old enough to have settled into the habits of a single person and told myself at the time there was nothing I wanted more.

But if single-married was what I really wanted, I might have been better off with a doctor—or even a long-haul trucker.

Because Clint could be doing anything at all out there and I would never know. He could disappear and I would only know what the CIA told me about what happened. The government might not tell me anything—or they might not know either.

I was hostage to the needs of my country.

"Couldn't we be one of those spy couples?" I asked him.

It was the Saturday of Labor Day weekend and he was home—as in the country—and home—as in in our house. An absolute rarity.

He raised up on one elbow and looked at the destruction on and around our bed in which—temporarily—all of our children were not.

"We have a demolition crew in our house—I'm not sure it would be safe to have us both gone."

"And we even gave birth to it," I said, looking ruefully at the natural chaos that came with five children.

"Want to make more?"

Clint threw a leg over me and that was the end of that discussion.

The thing about having five children was that they formed a sort of tribe. It practically was its own system within the larger system of the family—with rules and agreements, hierarchies and methods of communication that had a life of their own. This was the benefit of having a Ph.D. in behavioral economics from Georgetown

University—I was a keen observer of the small, chaotic economy I had birthed.

If I'd thought about it ahead of time I might have spread them out so that the older could take care of the younger.

But I'd always been better at theory than at application.

Our children were stairstep—starting now at age five years old, the next one four, a set of twins just turned three, and the baby about to be two—and so formed a small band of brigands in which no one could really take care of himself.

Did I mention they were all boys?

In a few years they would be a soccer dad's dream—the bulk of an entire team all to himself.

But to coach it he would have to have a different job.

And, more fundamentally, he would need to survive physically, and we would need to survive domestically. Most CIA marriages did not.

There were rumblings from the kitchen below us that clearly signaled the end of civilization if we didn't get down there.

By the time I arrived in the kitchen, more or less ready for the day, Clint and Molly were mass-producing eggs, toast, and plastic cups of orange juice. I knew if I didn't dress first I never would after I'd entered the jetstream of my life.

"Who wants a kiss?" I asked.

I was piled on by all of them except the baby.

He was ambulatory now so he could have, but he was

my most independent child. He was eating, which he did with single-minded focus. He sat happily observing from a distance, high up in his chair, from which he could easily have escaped if he wanted. Red-headed, self-contained, consuming calories, Dylan wasn't party to the clamor of the other four.

I gave my other ones their kisses, carried Isaac, one of the three-year-old twins, on my hip over to the Dylan's chair and kissed the baby on top of his head, which pleased him even if he hadn't demanded it.

"I think we've got this, Molly, if you want to take off," I said.

"I think I'll get while the gettin's good," Molly said. She liked using Americanisms, though they always sounded funny in her Oxford English accent. She set the last plate of toast and eggs on the table, washed her hands, and skedaddled to her room past the kitchen. We heard the back door close during a break in the action.

Her improbably red Vette roared past the low kitchen window, attracting the four older boys who flocked over to wave and gawk and then flocked back to the table, Molly forgotten in their absorption with the sticky stuff they were spreading on their toast, mouths, fingers, tables, each other, and their parents.

"She looked like she might be fleeing," I said.

"If I had brought work home I might wonder what state secrets she was making off with," Clint said.

"Molly?" I said. "She couldn't be less spy-y."

"The best ones aren't," Clint said. "What better disguise

than someone's English nanny and housekeeper?"

I looked at him more closely. He had that glint in his eye that said he was working, whether or not he'd brought anything home.

"No, no, not today. No suspecting Molly. Her only irregularity is the Vette. Plus, she has security clearance. And I might die without her."

Clint returned his attention to the chaos.

"Can't have that," he said. "Who would entertain me?"

The boys were installed in front of *Beauty and the Beast*, which, inexplicably, given how utterly different they were from each other, all the boys loved. We had, of course, taken them to the park after breakfast and run them ragged.

The problem was always whether or not I would need a nap before I could move on to any project of my own. There were reasons why a woman's fertility peaked in her teens and twenties. Mothering wasn't for the tired late thirties.

"Entertain you, eh?" I mumbled, harkening back to the breakfast conversation with Clint. "You mean entertain *for* you."

Clint wasn't there. I had long since fallen into the habit of conversation with his ghost.

I looked at the array of lists on my desktop. There was a party in the making—our annual Halloween bash—

and with six weeks to go, we were getting into the final details of the planning. The guest list was done and the details of the menu needed to be finalized by the end of the holiday weekend. I glanced beyond my desk, strategically placed between the business and family entertainment ends of the big kitchen, to be sure the boys were entertained or asleep. Then I dove in.

I reviewed the guest list.

It was easy to say that Clint benefitted from my parties. In a world that survived and thrived on information, where politicians, statesmen, journalists, lobbyists, and spies all traded in gossip, there was nothing like a slightly lubricated group of them for spilled beans. It didn't happen very often that the spilled beans were both true and useful, but it happened often enough that I felt like I was contributing to my husband's career when I fulfilled my inherited destiny as a hostess.

If I had to be completely honest, Clint would have been happy if we never entertained. He was most content either working or hanging out with me and our own gang.

And if I had to be completely completely honest, it was I who insisted on the parties.

After a lifetime of rebelling against my mother's métier, I had swan dived right into it a couple of years earlier, as I finished my dissertation and my last baby was about to arrive. I was born to the social world and, with no chance of going on the academic job market with a trailing not just spy spouse but also five little ones, I was moving nowhere.

My mother was a socialite, as was her mother before her. Mother's years as an ambassador's wife had only taken Mother's art to an even more glittering distinction. If she didn't have a party on the horizon, she didn't know what to do with herself.

"American royalty," Clint called us, descended from the early Virginia landed gentry, steeped in power and politics for generations.

Born to land, wealth, and political power, Mother's father, a man who uncannily resembled Thomas Jefferson (naturally, a distant relation) indulged her and gave her cover from her mother's demands. Her mother was straight-out-of-England upper class. He did encourage Mother to learn the social graces and how to create events from her mother so that the maternal unit would not combust and so that she could provide her own cover later. But, when Mother had fulfilled her social duties, Grandfather let his youngest daughter into his enormous library where they read together side by side, studied the enormous map on the wall together, researched a topic among his library books together—each finding pieces of an intellectual puzzle—or discussed politics.

Mother's parents were, of course, conservative—her mother a Tory—but conservatism could take some wildly-veering party affiliations in Virginia.

Mother was quintessential First Family of Virginia. As

the youngest daughter of one of the oldest Albemarle County, Virginia families, old wealth, she too was descended from the progenitor of all Virginia old money, Robert "King" Carter. Mother had grown up among the foxes and the hounds. She had a keen intelligence from the beginning. Her mother's attempts to groom her for the horse set and hunting life were simply never going to take.

Mother and Grandfather staked out opposite political views for the sake of argument and also because Mother was by nature and intellect irredeemably liberal. But to be Southern with a mind and heart was to embody contradictions. Their arguments were not acrimonious because Grandfather, like any old Southerner, had lived too long and seen too much—and no one's heart was bigger or intellect deeper than Grandfather's—to be rigid.

Mother had gotten an excellent education at St. Margaret's and had been a fierce hockey forward in high school and college. She met my father when he was at the University of Virginia and she was at Mary Washington College. At the time women weren't admitted to U.Va. unless they were majoring in Nursing or Education or, in the rare case of having a father on the faculty, Engineering. My mother's interest was political science. She did her first two years at what was widely considered the women's branch of U.Va. , met Father on one of his rare departures from the Grounds, and married him the summer after her sophomore year.

My father was excruciatingly correct in his own way. He was descended from a long line of northern Virginia Quakers and he had not just good manners but moral rectitude. He was a handsome man, and a serious and promising student whose ability to understand global and historical complexities caused his professors to steer him toward the foreign service.

Grandfather couldn't appear to approve of the match with a Quaker headed for a foreign service career—overt approval on his part would have caused Grandmother to become shrill rather than just stiffen her posture as she planned the large and elegant wedding at their Virginia estate for their youngest daughter. But Mother knew how to appease the grande-dame who had given birth to her. She played along with the tasteful ostentation of the event. But she knew that her father was secretly pleased that his girl was going to escape the confines of her class and county—even her country.

She found her father during her wedding reception, gazing at the map of the world on the wall in his study. She stood next to him and felt the warmth of his arm around her back.

That didn't stop Grandfather from looking daggers at Father as he shook his hand before the couple ducked into the backseat of the family Rolls as they left for their honeymoon.

Mother described that look as, "If you won't kill for her, I will kill you."

She had transferred to the University for her last two

years and would graduate summa cum laude in political science while Father finished his degree in history.

Mother and Father lived in student housing after they married, much to their parents' combined disapproval. My father's wealthy northern Virginia Quaker family would also have disapproved of an ostentatious, large house, but a discreet, ivy-covered home on Oxford Road would have been gladly and easily purchased by either family.

Mother and Father would have none of it. They charted their own course from the beginning, which you might have credited to Father's Quaker background. But I had long ago come to believe it was Mother's iconoclasm that informed the moral choices they made, including her renouncing her Episcopalian heritage and joining the Florida Avenue Friends Meeting soon after she married.

I might have said that contributed to the emigration of my grandmother back to England, but Grandmaman began that campaign as soon as she concluded her final successful marital sendoff. At first it was for visits, then it became clear that she had taken up permanent residence in her family's home in Knightsbridge. For a while when we were very young, she would visit us occasionally in DC, then, later, when we lived in Europe, we would be summoned to visit her in England.

From choosing to live with people their own age rather than their class to sharing babysitting responsibilities with other student wives who quickly became mothers to the unquestioning support Mother gave Father throughout his diplomatic missions no matter where he was, to the profound and unquestioned acceptance of my brother's being gay—Mother was not a typical child of Virginia's monied classes.

It wasn't exactly a rebellion on her part. She always appeared impeccably dressed and behaved excruciatingly correctly. She tried to shape me in the mold to which she was born. But in the end, I thought she was probably faithful more than anything to the long tradition of fairness and honor within the bounds of culture that bespoke a loyalty to the Commonwealth of Virginia that extended beyond Jefferson more than to any other tradition.

After they finished college, my father began his Ph.D. in Foreign Affairs at Georgetown. My brother and I arrived in pretty quick succession. When they moved to DC, my parents accepted the gift of living at Mother's other family home in Georgetown, Evermay, and that became our landing pad for whenever my father was between postings.

My father was posted mostly in Europe, from Belgium to Austria, and my mother became known as one of the finest hostesses in Europe, bar none. She looked and acted like the lifelong Virginia gentility turned Georgetown socialite and ambassador's wife she was. Smartly dressed and well-read, she always looked like she came from the very best of Virginia lineage. As correct as she was, she was also very feminine and just a little flirty, so many of the young men in State or indeed around the world were drawn to her. She was both motherly and amusing and the men she encountered thought she was soft, receptive, feminine, albeit very proper, right up until she made a joke or two and they found themselves caught in the net of her absolute, unpredictable charm. They might have thought her a lovely flower—so might some men have thought Mata Hari. Feathery and evanescent on the surface—charming, gracious, flirtatious—I knew she had the whole shebang, herself and everything and everyone around her, bolted together with the strongest possible bolts of steel underneath.

I went to school in Switzerland then returned to America for college, getting my BA in English at Sweetbriar. My brother Jamie did most of his schooling in England, near our grandmother, and then came back to the States to go to the Naval Academy.

After college, I traded places with my brother and went back to England to live with Grandmaman in London, working in the City, and eventually getting a Masters at the London School of Economics.

Meanwhile, my parents were finishing their ambassadorial career and planned their retirement to Evermay.

The world was changing and, thanks at least in part to America's interference, the fragile structures put in place to keep what peace there could be seemed to be falling apart. It was anyone's guess what the outcome would be. Father's old-fashioned form of diplomacy depended on a set of shared values which, in a world increasingly ruled by factions, was less and less workable. There was no common ground when even the sanctity of life or the preservation of land held no meaning but only tribal beliefs held sway.

Father had been in the business for 40 years, posted mostly in Europe and, there, mostly in Austria where eastern and western Europe met. It was time for him to come home. He wasn't a naïve man and his idealism was an informed one. Still, when he stopped in London to visit me on his way home I saw a bewilderment, even a despair, I'd never seen in my distinguished old man. Though he would never say so aloud, I thought it possible that Father might have started to see the upside of dictatorships.

My parents had both lived all their lives in wealth and Mother in society. Their foreign service had always kept them at a high level of staff and service. Foreign service itself did not necessarily pay well, though at Father's level, it carried the trappings of wealth with it—the home, staff, chauffeur, the acres of glittering crystal, china, silver at state dinner, the greenhouses of flowers.

But if you didn't have your own money the return from service could be a real come down. The remains of that day could be very scant.

That tradition by itself would have demanded that Father live more modestly—a nice home in Chevy Chase, a fresh Prius every other year, hosting events at excellent restaurants with his good, grey wife. But Father had his own family money and he had also hitched his wagon to Mother's star. Good and grey were not to be found in Mother's vicinity.

On an ordinary day, Evermay would knock your socks off.

One of the biggest pieces of property in Georgetown—in all of DC—it was built in the 1800s for the most political member of Mother's family at the time—a vice president.

Retirement at Evermay with Mother seemed to have restored Father to his good humor. He enjoyed the bustle of Mother's events and the (endless) committee work Meeting roped him into. Mother understood on a deep, ancestral level that a happy, contented marriage was a much better backdrop for a successful social life than an unhappy one or even one in which the partners only tolerated each other. Her own parents achieved that contentment by living on different continents, but that bar was too low for my ambitious, smart, energetic mother.

Much of the china, crystal, silver, furniture, and many of the servants who could still stand had moved from Grandfather's Virginia estate, where he had mostly retired to his beloved, dusty library, to Evermay. They looked right at home there, a dazzling and tasteful display throughout the house, the servants bustling if I was there early, but later to fade into the woodwork as if trained on an English estate, as Delany, the butler, indeed had been.

Through no fault of their own, my parents had lived lives of privilege. Neither of them had taken it for granted. Like English royalty, they had been taught that wealth conferred responsibilities. Mother took up her social life in DC with a vengeance. She had regular dinners that rivaled the White House for state affairs, their names were on the standing White House invitation list, and she knocked everyone else out of the Thanksgiving dinner competition her very first year back. Father was lionized at Mother's dinners. Young politicians and diplomats in training were always eager to hear his tales. Her dinners always served some purpose, though it wasn't always apparent to me what it was.

She had always entertained like that, all my life. Whether we were in DC or Vienna, she had been a hostess beyond most people's touch. I mostly loved her affairs, but occasionally, unlike Mother, I was worn out by the life.

I'd known Grandfather as a little girl, a most solid presence behind Mother's glittering social presence—her fairy dust and magic so dazzling it was sometimes hard to see how she grew up with him, so at home on his Virginia hilltop. But when the high of Mother's events, her chiffon and glitter, the dizzying array of food platters and servants, the shine and clink and hum of silver service, bone china, and Waterford crystal, the slide of the silk she dressed me in, her precious red-headed fairy princess daughter, the little high heels and the hair carefully dressed by her hairdresser's assistant while Mother had hers done beside me—when all that excitement got to be too much, I would beg to go to Grandfather's house and run to his dark wood-lined study and sit quietly beside him in my own leather armchair, while he sipped Laphroaig and discussed history with me quite seriously.

I might have learned to love economics from him—not in his study but outside, in good weather with me barefoot and wild-haired beside him, or bad, wax coated and wellingtoned, walking with the dogs through the gardens or riding the estate as he discussed what was growing there, what used to grow there, and the market forces that drove it all.

I might have nurtured my rebelliousness there—and quite possibly my wild sense of color. It might have been in reaction to my beautifully tailored mother or her constant "encouragement" to conform, to succeed by the standards of society. There was little she could do about my intellectual hunger, or my tendency to drunken philosophical arguments in several different languages with distinguished diplomats from around the world, my love affair with layered language, or my extravagant embrace of color.

Grandfather was still there, holding the Virginia estate together, entertaining my wild horde on a summer weekend, and maintaining cordial relations with Grandmaman across the pond.

Luckily, Father's willingness to kill for any of us had fortunately never been tested. I'm pretty sure Grandfather had my brother Jamie sized up pretty quickly as equal to the task and took it upon himself to teach my brother all the farm arts of trapping, shooting, garroting, and body disposal. Jamie put all this to use in his service as a Navy Seal, I was afraid.

Jamie could easily have avoided military service even if there had been a draft. There wasn't and he had quite a few closed-study-door chats with Father and then enlisted, Father's lips pressed firmly together. Grandfather, faded in old age but no less formidable, was quietly proud and he nearly busted his waistcoat with pride when Clint joined the family.

Clint had no doubts. I'd never seen him dither. He might never have seen a ditherer either until he sat next to me. It's quite possible that I was squinting at the pigeons the day we met, trying to figure out if it was morally wrong to feed them. It was so satisfying to see them flock to the crusts flung, yet they were pests whose over population was only intensified by people like me. I was the most overly-intellectual bold person I knew.

I had been home from London for a year, working at the State Department, while I applied for and was accepted to the Ph.D. program in Economics at Georgetown. I stood out from the run of the mill ambitious young worker at State in that I was built more like Marilyn Monroe than the whippets who ran the fast track to success there, and I dressed in Anthropolgie dressses and cowboy boots on a regular work day.

Clint sat next to me in his crisp white shirt and tie, sleeves rolled, immaculate and trim grey pants, and smart black tie-shoes and began flinging crusts from a bag he'd brought on purpose. The pigeons were instantly attracted to him and, I could tell, flew in from miles away.

"I think some of these are from Delaware," I said.

"Southampton wouldn't surprise me," he said.

"Not New York," I said.

And then he looked at me.

When they say love at first sight I'm not sure what they mean.

Is it that you look at him and there is a chorus of song or an aurora of lights as you feel warm?

Because it wasn't like that at all for me and Clint.

We hadn't said anyting clever or even very interesting, yet I felt gunned down, like a bomb had gone off in front of me. His eyes were the clearest, most shocking ice blue I'd ever seen, almost silver in their purity. He lasered me with them and, as if I'd been shot, I fell forward into his eyes, going deeper and deeper in a free fall that was terrifying on one hand but so inevitable, so impossible to stop or even slow, there was something reassuring in it.

When all the decisions had been made, all the alternatives eliminated, there is an acceptance of what happens next, even the fear that comes with it.

I wondered at the time if this was what death felt like.

And yet this was so clearly not death but life, an opening up of undreamed possibilities, of hope that was exponentially greater than anything I'd known before in my orderly, high society life with equally wealthy, well-educated, intelligent girls and boys—accomplished, well-traveled, andon the fast track to success in the corporate or legal or medical or political worlds at the highest level. We were poised for a trajectory to more and more ambitious levels in our careers, larger and more distinguished houses, more exotic foreign travel, modest-sized but highly accomplished families and one step after another after another to life stardom with barely a stumble, rarely a fall, even if the occasional affair or fast divorce or corporate indiscretion or child not quite fitting the mold sometimes provided a manageable speed bump.

I didn't just step off the track. I leapt off.

If anyone were watching, they wouldn't have seen much, two people, one in tie and shirtsleeves, one in a flame and turquoise dress and cowboy boots, who leaned toward each other inexplicably, slightly, as they were feeding the pigeons.

Clint looked at me. I looked back. We both turned to the river. I took a bite of my sandwich. He tossed another handful of crumbs.

"Melbourne," I said.

"Not Florida," he said.

There were formalities to be gone through. Courtship was one, which we mostly dispensed with by sleeping together that night, though not a lot of sleeping was involved.

Clint's working-class West Virginia family had gone against the grain in almost every way, remaining steadfastly Catholic when to be so in the South was second only to being black in undesirability.

His parents were well-meaning people who had done a lot of harm to themselves and each other through living too large or repressing their love of life too much, bad marriages, drink, drugs, and violence.

How Clint had survived was a sort of miracle, the strength of his will and personality overcoming the odds. His mother had loved him, ultimately giving him the gift of letting him go. Teachers recognized his extraordinariness early and, like a diamond in a dark West Virginia mine, they had dug it out, gotten him into the Naval Academy, and then let him go, the one who got away.

We never went back to visit. Clint helped his nieces and nephews when he could, but always circumspectly and from a distance. If I had to, I couldn't have found his hometown on a map.

Clint met my parents. There were not amused, though they were excruciatingly polite. It was clear to them from the start that this marriage was a fait accompli and the most graceful thing they could do was simply start making the arrangements.

We were married in August, a scant five months after we met. After my mother got over being appalled that the largest social event of her life—her only daughter's wedding—was going to be denied her—and that none of the city's desirable hotels—certainly not the Mayfair—were available—she settled into planning the event as elaborately as she could at her father's Virginia estate. We were married by an Episcopalian priest on the little mountaintop of Grandpapa's home, among the grapevines and bean towers he loved so extravagantly.

I heard my father mumble, "CIA" and "West Virginia" somewhere in the father-daughter talk. All I could do was pat his hand and tell him I thought it would be okay. I wasn't sure he agreed, but he did waltz Clint's small, factory-worker mother around the ballroom floor after the dinner with all his usual stately dignity.

Grandfather was deeply gratified by Clint's steely absolute ability to kill for us—for Mother, Father, Molly, and of course the seniors—along with me and the boys. Hell, I was pretty sure America counted when it came to what Cint would take a bullet for—which was a considerable worry that I had to put out of mind so my hair didn't catch on fire.

I'm not sure my parents' worst fears weren't realized when over the next seven years I completed my Ph.D. and had a baby or two almost every year.

Mother looked pretty bewildered after the first two and, by the time Isaac and Jack came, she just reached out a well-bred hand for Molly. She loved the boys, for sure, but sometimes, she said, we were better served by her dropping off new, clean outfits in stairstep sizes and taking me out to our favorite bistro for lunch and a polite glass of white wine a half-hour with my brood made her just a little too thirsty for.

Father was glad when grad school was over. He said something at graduation about something being in the water at Georgetown that assisted in the grandson-or-two-a-year phenomenon.

They both were relieved when their dangerously fertile,

slightly gypsy daughter seemed to settle into her society role and began entertaining more regularly. They could sort of imagine that I'd fit into the mold—if the boys weren't visible all at once and the blade my West Virginia husband carried in his eyes were sheathed.

Mother's rebellion lived on in her rabid interest in politics and her ability to go deep, to analyze the facts at hand and arrive at an understanding that seemed iconoclastic at first, even harebrained, and very often proved to be exactly the way it really was, when it all came out.

She was a favorite of Clint's—who did not like many—and he often marveled at her layers. She didn't like him at first—or she couldn't understand him—but she'd seen his value over time and now she paid careful attention to him, as if solving a mystery.

If her rebellion lived on, mine seemed to have completely died out. I was faintly ashamed of the success of my parties, once I started having them, but I was most often too tired to feel the binary opposition between what seemed to be my born instinct to fight and the social expectations of my class.

A Ph.D. in Behavioral Economics took me only as far as the park bench where I met the love of my life and the unbelievably fertile ground of our marriage and landed me a block and a half away from the house I grew up in.

And so, when I fell into my destiny, I too drew up lists, worked hand in glove with my caterer and party planner, knew their staff well enough to give them all Christmas gifts, and my housecleaners were listed on my phone among the favorites. Molly was both and nanny and social secretary and we worked together like a well-rehearsed social ballet.

Not only because I was married to a top spy or my father an ambassador.

Because I was monied class, a socialite by birth, never mind my Georgetown University Ph.D. or my excessively large brood.

Hell.

I had never wanted to be this. Had worked all my life to escape it. My proper mother with her correct posture and excruciatingly correct manners and her fine sense of what others expect. That was not going to be my life—better to live in a gypsy caravan.

I looked around my big kitchen, with its butler's pantry and scullery beyond, thought about the feature done in *Architectural Digest* on the renovation we did of our historical Victorian home, and watched the caravan ride away from me in my mind.

At least I didn't sheepishly follow the crowd to the National Cathedral on Sundays.

For all my mother's correctness, she had decidedly taken a turn when she got married.

Not that my father wasn't excruciatingly correct in his own way. He was descended from a long line of northern Virginia Quakers and he had not just good manners but moral rectitude. My mother had renounced her Episcopalian heritage and joined the Florida Avenue Friends Meeting when she married.

She rarely actually attended Meeting, though she worked hard on the committees and the building itself met her standards, having been constructed purposely to attract the Quaker president at the time—Herbert Hoover. The other Quaker president, Nixon, was never invited. His politics were abhorrent plus, of course, he was part of the California and thus corrupted offshoot of the religion.

The children and I were all members of Meeting and we regularly attended Meetings where nary a preacher called, nor did members respond with a song of praise.

There did seem to be a few conflicts of interest in my life—two came quickly to mind.

One between my wealth and my religion. Another between my husband's job, which necessarily involved violence from time to time, and my religion, a peace church.

But Quakerism, especially in DC, was a large tent and the saying that Quakers came to do good and stayed to do well was manifest at Florida Avenue Meeting House where many a diplomat's Lexus was parked on Sunday and every Democratic President with school age children necessarily sent them to pricey Sidwell Friends School.

Plus, my husband would be the first to point out that he was by nature a peaceful man and used violence only in the defense of peace.

We had had many a philosophical debate over this when we first met, but I had long since secretly harbored a gratitude that he would and could kill anyone who tried to harm me or the boys.

Along with a tiny, tiny wish for a small, ladylike handgun of my own.

When my phone buzzed I knew better than to pick it up within the boys' hearing—that was a guaranteed way to instantly cause them to need my attention—so I checked to be sure they were either mesmerized or asleep—my eldest was building a Lego tower that would be higher than is possible in the world of physics and give him both great satisfaction and great anxiety—and took the phone into the butler's pantry, closed the door, and answered.

"You sound so quite—what is the word, muzzled?" Ana said.

"Muffled?" I said.

"Yes, yes. Muffled. Are you captive?"

"Only by my own doing," I said.

"What do you say?"

"Only that I'm fine—not captive. I don't want to wake the baby," I said.

"Oh, I understand. No, babies must sleep. How is the tiny one?"

"He's fine—thriving." I rarely admitted to anyone other than my inner circle that I had five not-so-tiny babies because it not only seemed to be but actually was a bit excessive. I didn't know Ana well enough yet to know if she'd be shocked. She was eastern European, Montenegrin by birth, the Speaker of the House's wife, and mother to one discreet little boy.

I went on: "I called earlier to say I'd love to have you come to the Halloween party."

"But of course, dear Agatha, we will be there. We would not miss it for worlds!"

I laughed, hoping not too loudly—I didn't want Ana to be insulted. But I suddenly saw all the little worlds of Washington spinning through the air, which was funny, and how a wind from Ana's presence could blow them all away, which wasn't funny, I wasn't sure why.

"I'm so glad," I said. "Could I ask you a special favor and get you to stop by that afternoon to help with the flowers? I know it's weeks away, but I'm sure your calendar gets full."

Deeply conversant with the ways in which to build alliances, I knew asking for help was a way to create one with a woman. Interestingly this was one thing that crossed cultures. She agreed with enthusiasm and I let her know what time and we said good-bye.

It might be a long time until the party, but a good hostess nailed down the corners of it—the most important guests—long before the invitations went out by calling the chosen few.

I wanted to know Ana better. She was married to one of the most powerful Congress people and he was a bit of an outlier while she maintained a strict adherence to society's most traditional role for the spouse of the Speaker.

He had risen to power uncannily quickly from working class Pennsylvania roots to Speaker. If I were a snob, I would have said he was nouveau riche, his father having made a fortune through questionable steel manufacturing practices. He was on the wrong side of the political aisle for my family and, on top of that, we simply didn't like him. But for some reason I just liked his wife. Lovely and private, she reminded me of a fairy tale princess, maybe Rapunzel, held captive in a tower by a troll.

"Yes, of course, I will," Ana said. "I have put it on my calendar already."

We hung up.

"Though you couldn't say Adam Trent looks like a troll," I said out loud. I had his press photo up on my laptop. He was a genuine hunk—movie star good looks and something else a little wild around the edges.

Clint opened the pantry door.

"There you are," he said. "I think the bomb is getting ready to go off in the kitchen and I couldn't find you. Did I hear you talking to yourself?"

"Yes and no," I said. "Mostly I was just hanging out in the butler's pantry."

"Nothing wrong with that," Clint said. "I don't think."

"'Mother of five loses wits and is found mumbling in large closet,' reports the Post," I said.

"'Doctors consulted say perfectly normal taken in context,'" Clint finished. "I say let's take the bomb to Udvar-Hazy and let it go off there."

"Good plan. The space shuttle has withstood the nuclear blast of the sun."

"It can absorb the firepower of five hooligans," their father said.

As it happened, Mercedes had a SUV that functioned as a mini-van while looking a bit like an armored vehicle and we had all five strapped in after a mere hour's preparation. A miracle given that diapers, snacks, meltdowns, and one inadvertent nap all intervened—and all without the miraculous hand of Molly to bring it together. But I could see that dinner was going to involve Udvar-Hazy chicken nuggets. There was no way either Clint or I would have one atom of energy left by the time we got home.

"Where next?" I asked as we zoomed around the beltway in our minivan disguised as an armored car.

"Udvar-Hazy," Clint said, a little puzzled.

"I know where we're going, you idiot. I meant where are you going next?"

"You know I can't tell you that."

"I thought maybe if I caught you really tired and surprised you, you might tell me."

"Better for you not to know. How about you? What's next?"

"No going inside the Langley gates ever when I drop you off, having my entire family, our staff, and, yes, even my children's friends vetted for security—that's what's happening. Never knowing where my husband is when he's gone or when he's coming back. Calling someone who *may* be able to contact you if there is an emergency. Never even knowing where you've *been*, so no 'Remember when you were in Marrakech.'"

"I can sometimes tell you what I ate," Clint said. He had a sheepish, pleading look that was so out of character for me, I had to laugh.

"Too late to rue the day I met you," I said. The boys broke out in even louder clamor, if that was possible, a reminder and a breather in one burst of noise.

"The party is coming together. You'll be there, right?" I couldn't quite let go of the tired, old bone I was worrying.

He was quiet and I knew he was wondering "what party?"

"Halloween, dahlink. It's only been on the calendar since January."

"I knew that," he said. "As far as I know I'll be there. Who are your targets for this one?"

"I'm still curious about the Janes'. He seems to be pretty content to have followed her to the Supreme Court and be taking care of home and hearth."

"Do you find a lack of ambition suspect?"

"In a Supreme Court Justice's husband, yes. Generally, the women on the Supreme Court aren't married, and most political husbands seem also high-powered. But Mr. Janes seems like a really nice man—a homebody."

"Jealous?"

"No, not really."

We had arrived at the space center and began to deplane. I had three of them holding hands and running in a circle on the grass while the eldest oversaw them. I helped Clint unload the baby, put him in the backpack, and put it on.

"I was talking to Ana," I said once we'd gotten everyone inside and established a more or less regular pattern of herding them from one historical plane to another. I had never been interested in the mechanics of planes—or anything else involving metal and moving parts—but mothering five boys changes the fundamental composition of your likes and dislikes. Even I had a deep sense of awe for the black, sleek spy plane that once flew below the clouds without a sound. It could easily have been a work of fiction but wasn't.

"Ana—Adam Trent's wife?" Clint said. We had gotten really good at picking up conversations after intervals of physical activity.

"That's who I was talking to the in the closet. Along with myself."

"Ana Trent doesn't strike me as one of your lifelines."

"If you're referring to the absolutely essential few people without whom I would perish, then, no, Ana doesn't qualify. Though she might one day."

"As motley a crew as ours is, I can't see the eastern European Speaker's wife as one of them. She also doesn't strike me as much of a woman's woman."

"She's definitely not that. And, in case you hadn't

noticed, my cabinet isn't made up of too many warm and fuzzies."

"And, actually, not all that many women."

"True—most of my longtime girlfriends were scared off around the twin wave of Pampers," I laughed. "Besides, I like men."

"That works out well," Clint said, leaning over to kiss me. The baby slid perilously close to his father's head and got the surprised and angry look on his face I'd never seen on another child. He was born with a natural sense of indignation.

"I can't see me getting too buddy-buddy with Adam, though," Clint went on after the baby was righted.

"Whoo-boy, I can't see that either," I said. But something niggled at the back of my mind—some idea that Clint himself had suggested the invitation to the Trents. I made a mental note to ask him about that, which, like all mental notes for a mother of five, went straight into the mental trash can.

Adam Trent was, if anything, supremely superficial—all talk and no principles—and my husband was the least superficial person I'd ever known. They would have nothing in common—though it might be interesting to see Adam try to get information out of Clint. And find out the real meaning of the word "stonewall."

In a town that thrived on gossip—indeed was powered

by it almost exclusively—my husband was expert at getting people to talk without giving one iota of useful information himself. I had no doubt he could lie very professionally when he needed to, but I had a deep reliance on his integrity, his honesty. In a world where language ruled and what you said or didn't say could open doors, be held against you, exalt you, or bring you crashing down, I relied on what Clint said to me utterly. If it is possible to say there is a singular, recognizable thing called truth, Clint was the man to speak it.

He had looked like that from the start—like someone who could cut to the chase, who held strong views and would defend them, whose commitment to integrity was so bone deep it would not be mediated even in death.

Well, first he looked like a super-cute guy who for unknown reasons had decided to sit next to me when he sat down on one of the many benches along the Potomac.

My Father and I usually attended Friends Meeting together, as we were the Sunday after the Saturday trip to Udvar-Hazy which ended in a predictable fog of fatigue that proved why autopilot bedtime routines were so valuable. Father happily shepherded the boys off to First Day School so my silent meditation wouldn't be disturbed.

He might have been a little disturbed that my thoughts were more often on the shenanigans Clint and I had been up to that morning than the Inner Light, but It's important to shield parents from that kind of insight.

For me, living as the misfit I was with all I'd been raised to had become infinitely easier since Clint.

In him I had my partner, my mate, my justification, my vindication. Not a mirror because there was nothing reflective or reactive about the man whose blade I had taken into my soul. No, he was all decision and action. While I could really get confused.

Yet we were a match.

And that was all there was to that.

When Meeting broke up Father brought the boys back from First Day School, carrying Dylan on his shoulders and shepherding the rest of them by moving side to side behind them, much like an Australian shepherd might, creating a cohesive unit where none existed in nature.

"Thanks, Father," I said, taking the baby and moving the boys along the pew beside me in no particular order, hoping the wooden seat would contain them. Futile. The boys, even the baby, eeled under the seat, escaping both forward and backwards, clean white shirts scooting across the floor, and out the other, open end to disappear in the crowd of Meeting-goers, Jules holding Dylan by the hand and guiding his young steps.

"Someone will grab them," I said.

"Are you saying that in hope or confidence?"

"It would be an empty hope except I know there are doughnuts in the basement."

"The perfect lure," Father said, his worry lines smoothing.

"You can't fool me, Father," I said. "You pretended like you liked good behavior all my and James's life, but you actually like these scoundrels of mine."

"They are awfully tiring," he said.

"You do look a little exhausted," I said. "Let's go tank up on whole wheat doughnuts and fair-trade coffee."

We made our way to the dining hall in the basement where, sure enough, the boys were bellied up to one end of the long, paper-covered table, each one eating in his chosen fashion, from Jules just delightedly diving in to the youngest, held up by a helpful Quaker, taking a careful inventory of each possible choice with maddening care before pointing one out, to every other possibility including Theo improbably enough looking everywhere for a carrot and giving up before taking a sugary round out of desperation. Theo, my second born, was sometimes lost between his gregarious older brother and the racketing twins. But when it came to eating, he stood out as the only natural vegetarian in the bunch.

"What's ahead for you today?" Father asked.

"Not sure. Naps all around. Then maybe the Zoo."

"You Mother might want to go with you. She has a thing about the red panda. Clint in town?"

"Yes. And there is the party coming up so there is planning for that."

"It's Halloween, right?" He looked a little confused.

"Surely you've lived with Mother long enough to know party planning starts a long time ahead. I'm counting on you and Mother to hold down two corners of the living room."

Mother had long ago taught me the full court press approach to successful party-giving—first, make sure the people who will make your party go have accepted well ahead of time. Then, during the party, have an anchor person in each corner of the space to make sure conversation, drinks, food, and traffic flowed there. She had had to incorporate Clint into her party plans as, ordinarily so restrained, he turned out to be an unexpected firecracker at parties—saying something explosive, just on the edge of good taste, just to see what would happen.

"We'll be there, of course."

"And the Trents will be, too. Ana confirmed just yesterday."

Father allowed a conversational pause to open up by which I knew he wanted to make a point. I'd learned long ago that Quakers use silence as a weapon.

"Something about Adam Trent I should know?"

"No, no, not at all."

"By which you mean yes. Give, Father. What does State have on Adam?"

"Nothing," my father said. He was both constitutionally and by religious persuasion given to tell the truth, so he amended his statement. "Nothing I can say, at least."

"I don't know how you ever did any spying, Father. You really have a hard time fudging the truth."

"Who says I did any spying?" he said indignantly. "I was a diplomat."

"Same difference, half of the time. But I've never

known how much spycraft you were involved in all my life, so there's not much sense finding out now," I said, lifting Dylan up onto my hip.

"That's a fundamental problem with this town. You can't tell when someone is leaking classified information or spreading wild gossip," he said. Theo and Jack attached themselves to his hands—both by fingers and by sugary meltdown—while I could see Jules across the room taking Isaac toward the bathrooms. The twins' potty training was happening mostly in the wild.

"You should ask your mother about Trent," Father said.

"Because she is the keeper of the pure gossip?"

"You can rely on her to know the latest."

"I've often thought how effective it would be for the ambassador's spouse to be the spy."

"Your mother is a very knowledgeable person," Father said.

"That's an expert non-answer, Pop," I said. "I'll call when I get home and see if I can't get anything more satisfying out of her."

"Do that," Father said.

Jules steered Isaac back our way and we seized the moment of having everyone in one place to leave.

On the way home, I wondered if there was a threat in his command.

I thought about my mother, taking advantage of the sugar-stun in the back to have a thought.

"Knowledgeable" might not be the word I'd use for her. I thought of her as layered, more like. And driven.

Before I called her, I'd try to get clear with him what

I wanted to know from her before she dazzled me with other information. She was a central source of information in DC power politics, though what she said could easily fall either into the category of reliable fact or wild speculation. Was it some State Department secrets about Adam Trent that Father wanted divulged or was it the latest gossip about him? How would I know?

"Clint!" I called as we barreled through the front door. "We're home!"

But the house rang with my husband's absence and I knew before Molly said it.

"He's gone," she said, coming to greet us and scoop up the boys so that I could be stunned again, alone.

CHAPTER TWO

The Zoo

My husband's sudden, unexplained absences were as much a part of our married life as the boys. When duty called, Clint went.

It was his job. Its very nature. He had told me so from the beginning. He had tried to warn me.

But there was no stopping the tsunami of our love for each other. And there was no stopping the terrible, life-sucking undertow of his sudden, awful absence

I sat on my bed for an undetermined time. When I could get up I made my way to the bathroom.

The first time it happened I was literally sick. I had no idea that a disappearance could have that effect. No one had ever left me or even threatened to leave. The lovers I'd had before Clint had all been part of a polite, orderly affair—even the Europeans—and the temporary absences when one or the other of us was on a trip were predictable, punctuated by predictable, reassuring calls and emails that prevented any alarm.

Even the final leave-taking had been calm, orderly, well-explained, and reasonable.

Not so these rippings-away.

If I had ever lost a child—had one torn from my body or my arms—it might have felt like this.

Or if anyone had done a heart transplant on me without anesthesia—just cracking open my rib cage and taking out the still-beating one but forgetting to put in a new one—maybe that would compare.

To be fair, the first time it happened and I promptly threw up I was also newly pregnant, so that could have explained it. But I was never sick in any of my pregnancies. I have a theory, however specious, that boy fetuses have less hormonal conflict with the mother's system so cause less havoc, so I leave that conclusion open.

Clint's absence felt like the onset of a terrible illness I was unlikely to survive.

I got into my huge open spa tub and soaked in hot water and Epsom salts until I felt some of the physical ache ease a little.

I got out and toweled off. I lingered for a moment hands over belly, aware that, at another time in my life, there might have been the earliest stirrings of the assault of a swimmer in the receptive mermaid arms of the egg and then the nuclear explosion of cells as their union led to something that couldn't be stopped or controlled. We still did nothing to prevent it. There was a brief, quickly forgotten, mixture of the usual consolation and trepidation at the idea.

What if anything went wrong? What if Clint never came back? What would be the point of going on without him?

The point, of course, would be all those young 'uns. Five of them—they would be the reason.

I moved like an old woman getting dressed. My joints were stiff, my fingers fumbled.

I would not know where Clint was—ever. I wouldn't hear from him while he was gone—ever. I wouldn't know when he was coming back until he was there.

Oddly enough, it was Delaney, the butler at Evermay and Molly's cousin, who had taught me the finer points of marriage. Mother had schooled me in being head of a household, for sure, but there was little in her nature that allowed her to be subservient and Delany knew that too many bosses were combustible. So, he taught me the art of assessing power, not to always be the star, which came in very handy in being Mother's daughter and was absolutely crucial when it came to marrying Clint.

Being a stone-cold, bossy feminist had worked well to get me through graduate school and had won me not a few high-level publications and consultancies. But knowing when to be on and when to turn down the volume had been a really useful skill in my marriage.

Clint wasn't a prima donna—he didn't want or need attention or his way. He held power by nature, intellect, and training. His ability to understand a situation and make a good decision fast had no doubt saved his sweet ass regularly, mine several times, and, as far as I could tell, that of the country more than once.

But, by God, if playing second fiddle to him meant letting him go, I wanted my mother.

"There he is, see?" Mother pointed to some opaque bushes. "Isn't he darling?"

Luckily, she had my oldest boy by the hand. He would agree to anything to keep his grandmother—or anyone—happy.

He nodded solemnly, though he also caught my eye while my mother rhapsodized about the red panda. We silently acknowledged that Mother might be a bit over the top when it came to the red panda.

Neither of us could see a thing. As far as I knew, the panda, who looked more like a fox in pictures, had never been recovered after his last escape and was living happily ever after in the Cathedral dumpster. Jules and I would spin that yarn together later.

"Adorable," I said.

"You don't mean it," Mother said. "You're just saying that. Jules loves him, though. Don't you, dear?"

Jules did the best imitation of enthusiasm I'd ever seen. I began to suspect he actually *had* seen the panda and maybe was flattering me? Kids—no one was more wily.

"I love him, Grandmaman," he said. He had adopted the convention I used to refer to my grandmother and his accent was excellent.

She let go of his hand and he ran ahead to the sea otters.

"He is a real prize," Mother said, beaming after him. "When he isn't bullshitting. I haven't seen the damned panda for months."

"Mother!" I said. "I'm shocked. You don't mean you don't see him either?'

"Of course not. Do you think I've gone do-lally? Now move along with that wagonload before they all swarm out and disappear like that rotten red panda."

I yanked the wagon handle to get the wagon moving again—four little boys could provide quite a lot of inertia—while Mother sauntered off after Son #1.

"Where is he this time?" Mother said when I caught up to her. "Never mind. You can't tell me."

We both knew we weren't talking about the animal anymore.

"That's because I don't know, Mother. I never do. You know that. How do you know he's gone?"

I hadn't mentioned Clint's disappearance when I called her.

"Because you looked poleaxed. Like someone extracted your spirit and left your body behind.

"Zombification by CIA," I said. "Anyway, there's the party to organize. I'm afraid no one will come."

I knew from long experience that Mother wouldn't offer me any motherly sympathy—she wasn't that sort of feminine—but she would distract me.

"Oh, you think no one will come to a DC power couple's party? That would be different," she said.

"I don't think Clint and I count as a power couple."

"I meant your father and me," she said, deadpanning.

"Yes, for sure, Mother. People will come to my party to see you and Father. He has been in State for years and your own parties are famous."

"And you're coming along in the family tradition of remarkable social events. And Clint is—well—striking. And mysterious. People are drawn to him."

"I thought you didn't approve."

"I'm capable of questioning the choice of him as a husband while appreciating his charms as a man."

"Good lord, Mother. That is Jesuitical."

"You clearly have a similar response," she said gesturing to my wagonload, getting restive now even though we were moving, and sweepingly included the polite little deceiver she had by the hand again.

"Guilty as charged," I said.

"Let's go over the guest list," Mother said.

My mother was the sort of professional socialite who had the guest list memorized this close to the event. It was one of the banes of her existence that I could never remember who I'd invited.

When she had reminded herself of how this was she hustled us through the rest of the zoo—nothing else gripped her imagination like the red panda so she didn't believe anyone else would have a favorite and, magically, the boys seemed to fall in with her belief—not just the pliable Jules but even the most independent-minded of her grandchildren. There was just something about a forceful personality—someone who, underneath, had no doubts, no hesitations.

"But I like the poison frogs," I said. We were settled at the outdoor café, the boys happily consuming nitrates and UV rays.

"What?" Mother said. She had my phone in her hand and was reviewing my Evernote guest list.

"I sort of like the frogs—"

Mother looked like I'd spoken an alien tongue.

"The ones inside. We didn't go to the Reptile House."

Without putting the phone down, Mother said, "First, they are frogs. Second, they can kill you instantly just by touching them. A touch you might have died of anyway just because they are frogs."

I laughed. "Mother, you have such a royal disdain for frogs!" She looked so upright, even to her zoo-going elegantly casual grey suit and string of uncultured pearls. "What happened to the little girl who grew up wild in the Virginia countryside?"

"Just that," Mother said. She looked for one split second wistful, as if she saw the Virginia estate farm where she grew up, the hayricks she would have climbed on, the high barn doors leapt from. "She grew up. She went to the city." Mother looked at me then. "And you mustn't fool yourself about things that are dangerous. Just because they are beautiful does not mean they aren't fatal."

"I think there is a story behind that, but I'm going to have to wait for your tell-all to come out to know what it was."

"My tell-all?" Mother laughed—and would have politely snorted if it had been lady-like. "Hardly. Besides, what makes you think I mean me?"

"Are you trying to tell me Clint is dangerous? The man I've tied my entire life up with? And the lives of my children?"

By then said children had hared off to the complex world of tunnels and slides built just for such energy.

"Clint?" Mother said. "Yes, he is rather beautiful, isn't he? Maye dashing is the word." She looked girlish for a moment, her classic features animated as if she were about to leap from the barn again.

"Mother! I never really understood you had a taste for the piratical!"

"Me? Perish the thought." She took the opportunity to give my bohemian rose Anthropoligie top and ripped jeans (albeit not ripped artfully by the maker but by some son testing out his scissors skills) a once-over. Her face composed itself again. "Now let's get back to this list."

She read out the names of Clint's boss, the head of the CIA, my parents' close friends from State, the Congresspeople from northern Virginia and southern Maryland, the four senators which had been expanded to include West Virginia's two in honor of Clint. The Monsignor was a friend of Clint's though when they saw each other it must have been clandestine because Clint didn't go to Mass.

"The Vatican and the CIA," Mother observed. "Where could there be a more secretive pairing?"

"I'm pretty sure Clint and the Monsignor don't talk business."

"Probably not, though I would imagine the Monsignor would like to reclaim Clint, given the evidence of his faithfulness."

"Mother, you know I'm not going to discuss our views on birth control—"

"Or lack thereof," she murmured.

"—with you," I finished.

"Nor would I want to," she said. "Now, who else?"

"Father Bream, of course."

"The jolly Irish priest?" Mother said and she sparkled briefly at the memory of all the times she and my dissertation advisor had matched wits.

Father Bream, my dissertation advisor from Georgetown, was a regular party attendee at my events and Mother had recently begun to include him in hers.

"Of course. I think Molly would invite him if I didn't."

Mother had a very quick look of "no better that she should be" at the thought of Molly competing successfully for Bream's attention.

"The Speaker is coming," I said.

"Adam Trent? What an odd choice. You surely have nothing in common with him." Contempt radiated from her skin, poisonous as any colorful frog's.

"I'm not entirely sure why. I think Clint might have wanted him on the list."

Mother's classically plucked brows went up.

"Plus, I've gotten to know Ana."

"Ana," Mother said. "Now there's a walking mystery."

"What do you mean?"

"No one knows exactly where she came from, do they?"

"Everyone knows she's from Montenegro."

"Everyone knows that," Mother said, giving me her most impatient, "slow learner" look. "But what else?"

"I don't know that you have to know everyone's whole history to invite them to a party," I said, on defense as so often with Mother.

"Oh, don't think you have secrets from me, my girl. I know when you're getting close to someone."

"That's a thing I find really annoying, Mother."

"That I always know what you're up to? Well, it isn't that hard. I'm your mother. And you are incapable of hiding anything. It all shows on your face."

"Good thing I don't have to make the family's living as a spy," I said.

"You'd be shot at dawn practically every day. Now tell me about how you got to know Ana Trent."

I knew for a fact that Mother wasn't interested in the subject for my welfare—she wanted what intel I had on Ana to add to her store. But I wasn't going to get any from her if I didn't give what I had.

"We met at someone's birthday party," I said. "Don't ask me whose because I won't remember. A friend of Theo's probably—they are the same age."

"I didn't know they had a child," Mother said.

"Adam has several from previous marriages—they're all pretty much on public display."

"Not a savory lot, though attractive enough."

"But no one talks much about this boy," I said.

Mother's interest was really picking up now. I suddenly imagined her peering through a lorgnette. Like many Southern women of her generation she was all fluffly femininity only on the surface.

"You're such a gossip, Mother," I said, suddenly laughing. "But, really, I forbid you talking about this to anyone." I was serious about that.

"You have my word," Mother said solemnly.

"The boy is quite sweet—but I think he might have special needs."

"Clearly not Down Syndrome?"

"No, but something," I said.

Mother looked thoughtful for a moment and then we both looked over toward the play structures. My five were all in sight, each playing according to his nature. Jules was shepherding, boring several of his brothers plus some unrelated ones explaining something, while my second one worked on a fairly elaborate sand castle in the sand box—elaborate for a four-year-old anyway—while the twins held hands and spun around while my baby looked on, a bit puzzled by the unnecessary activity.

"They are as different as could be and several handsfull," Mother said. "But none seems to have a disability other than an excess of personality."

She looked like she might just consider this a disability.

"Now tell me about Ana," she went on.

"She seems very buttoned-up, very controlled. She

came here in the late 90s, met Adam soon after she got here, and they married soon after that."

"As I recall, he was still married to his third wife when he met her."

"Yes, but they've been married the longest of any of his marriages."

Mother filed this data in her mental cabinet. "What else?"

"Not much. She came on a work visa—UN, I think—and stayed. She got citizenship after they married."

"What did she do?"

"Translation. She doesn't work outside the home now though."

"Good lord, what a baroque phrase that is—'work outside the home.' In my day we all understood how much work there was inside the home. It wasn't shameful to do that necessary, high level executive job."

"That does seem to have escaped the notice of the 60s women's movement. There was a great rush to get into the workplace."

"Leaving all the work at home undone."

"Or double-duty. As the economics evolved to demand two-income families."

"Not a great long-range strategy. But let's get back to Ana."

"She does seem to escape like smoke, doesn't she?"

"I can't see that you two would have that much in common."

"The party was at a farm—there were hayrides and such. We ended up on one together. She wasn't particularly friendly with the other mothers, but she seemed to like me. We just started talking—about the kids, mostly."

"What do you know about Montenegro?" Mother asked.

"Nothing at all. And I'd like to."

Mother gave me a very dubious look.

"Can't I be interested in learning something new about the world?"

"Oh, yes," Mother said. "You are nothing if not a hungry intellect. But you have decided interests—and eastern Europe is not one of them, despite doing a lot of your growing up in Vienna."

"I don't even like to travel much anymore. Too many airports in my life."

"Air travel *has* become increasingly unpleasant. Surely Clint can help you get business class."

"Clint doesn't get business class himself. I'm sure he travels as anonymously as possible. He'd go inside the luggage if he could."

"He'd have to, to be anonymous. He's noticeable under any circumstances." Mother smoothed back her perfectly coiffed hair and I had to laugh at her inveterate flirtatiousness, even toward my husband. "But we digress again. What interests you about Ana?"

"Tell me what you know about Montenegro."

"Well, where to start? It's a very old country, part of the highly contested area between Europe and middle East, sometimes more European, and for a very long time part of the Ottoman empire."

"Cut a little to the chase: how about post-World War II?"

"Part of eastern Europe, behind the Iron Curtain, though not a part of Soviet Russia. It was governed by Marshall Tito for a very long time—fifty years or so—as the coalition of countries that was named 'Yugoslavia.' When the Soviet bloc fell to pieces, the country of Yugoslavia did too—splintering into many, often warring nations. After the Balkan Wars, Montenegro seemed to go mostly toward the European Union, becoming part of NATO. But lately it has been drawn back toward Russia some, as that country's leader extends his reach as far as possible."

"Especially if it will disrupt NATO," I said, just to show I hadn't been completely newspaper-free for the past seven years.

Mother nodded her approval. "Now you tell me what interests you about Ana Trent," she said.

"She seems so alone, I guess," I said. "She doesn't seem to have any connections."

"Least of all to her husband," Mother said.

"Quite true. She doesn't talk about him readily."

"Not that there aren't plenty of marriage of political convenience." Mother seemed to be adding up the ones she knew.

"But what would be the advantage in this case?" I said.

"She's beautiful. He's rich. The usual," Mother said.

"But why the huge international gap? Surely she could have found a wealthy European who wouldn't have dragged her in front of the political Kleig lights."

"She does seem profoundly uncomfortable there,"

Mother said, rolling her mental videotape footage of the Trents. "He had his pick of American prizes. Maybe it helps that she doesn't completely understand what he's saying."

"Not because she doesn't understand the language—and several others. She was a translator, after all."

"Maybe she could pretend like she doesn't understand?"

"That wouldn't be too hard to fake—no one seems to understand what Adam Trent is saying."

"Or they understand it too well—he speaks in such crass overstatements."

"One does wonder how he got elected."

"Or how he gained so much ground there. He has quite a following."

"Maybe people like unintelligent belligerence?"

"Maybe it was preferable to unintelligible double-speak."

"He does have a sort of genius for saying what people want to hear."

"An evil genius."

"What does your discipline have to say about people like him?"

For a second, I couldn't see what in my life could possibly be considered a discipline. Then I remembered my Ph.D.

"Economics has to do with choices people make mostly about money, not politics."

"But your area has to do with irrational choices, right—buying or spending that is bad for you."

"Not exactly irrational so much as governed by mental structures over which we have little control or even access into. Some of us call it "bounded rationality." Like gobbling snacks before a full dinner you know is coming. It has to do with forces you aren't aware of that drive choice."

"Adam Trent is nothing if not a bad choice," Mother said. "And it will cost money and a lot of it."

I wasn't used to considering Mother a seer so I paused to wonder what she knew that she wasn't telling and that gave her time to go back to scrolling through my guest list.

"I still don't see why you're so interested in Ana," she said. "She seems vapid at best to me."

"I suppose I feel sorry for her."

"Sorry for all her wealth, pampering, and haute couture?"

Mother's exquisite wardrobe didn't give her a lot of room to talk there, but I let that go by.

"It seems like a gilded cage. Sometimes she looks trapped."

"I can't imagine Clint holds any sympathy for the Trents. He must despise Adam."

"Oddly, I'm having a very slight suspicion he was the one who added them to the list."

Mother paused to consider. "Clint adds people to your lists?"

"Sure. Doesn't Father?"

"No. The parties are entirely my realm."

"I guess that's one thing that differentiates State from the CIA."

"I suppose I can see that," she said without conviction. "But I would think Clint might not want someone with deeply evil intent in his home."

"Not that spies can't find out everything about you without going in your actual house."

"Well, it wouldn't be that Clint has a huge family," Mother said.

We looked toward the playground where an uproar had broken out, all five of mine suspiciously close to the center.

We were both by then too experienced to intervene as long as there weren't any long silences—much more ominous than clamor could ever be—and didn't bother to get up, unlike a flock of mothers and grandmothers nearby. Even they subsided back to their seats as the rules of playground engagement were internally applied and the normal level of chaos restored.

My phone buzzed. I looked at the screen and put it away.

"Any word from the man of mystery?" Mother asked.

"None," I said.

She put her hand over mine, offering what consolation she could.

CHAPTER THREE
Misbehaving

We made it through Labor Day without incident and to bed.

It was hard to feel lonely when you had five children, I'd found. They might all start out in their beds—all except the baby who never quite made the transition out our bed into his own—but one by one they found their way into our California king throughout the night. If Clint and I had the privacy for shenanigans in the morning, it was because they'd woken up and gone back to their rooms to play.

Jules sometimes tried to tell us that he just came in because he was checking on the other three who weren't already there, but he also gave himself away as the most gregarious of us all—and thus the one most easily made lonely. The house was big enough for each to have his own room, but Jules had never wanted to move to his. So when Theo climbed down the bunk ladder and made a beeline for the parental bed, Jules, in the lower bunk, was on alert. It would be a matter of minutes before he shadowed his brother into the parental boudoir. The twins never lasted long in their room.

I shifted over, moving the baby with me all night long until by morning Dylan and I were on the last few inches and someone was draped across the foot of the bed, sleeping where the dog would, if we had one.

I always wondered, when Clint was home, how we would all fit in. Clint wasn't large, but his body was like a coiled steel spring, making up in density and intensity for any girth. I had a suspicion that he just packed us all in, like an efficient sardine packer, so that we all fit precisely and securely in the great whole.

"Tiny, two smalls, a medium, one large, one extra large," Theo was saying as I woke up.

"What?" I said.

"Our sizes," he explained solemnly. "Dylan is tiny, Isaac and Jack are small, I'm medium, Jules is large, and you are extra-large."

"What does that make Dad?"

"Gigantic," he said. After a little thought, he added. "He's this big." His arms sketched a giant in the air above the bed. Theo was our grammarian and word *meister*.

"He's working," I said, though Theo hadn't asked out loud. That was what we had decided to say, at the risk of putting them off employment later on.

"Oh," Theo said. He considered this, as he considered everything and made a decision, as he so often did, to be more thoughtful.

"Would you like coffee?" he asked.

"I would. Would you like orange juice?"

"I would," he said.

We slid out of bed, leaving the others in a heap. It would be mayhem soon enough getting everyone ready for day care and school, but my little buddy and I would have our peaceful moment in the kitchen. Of course, he didn't actually know how to make coffee, but he could happily and companionably pour his own orange juice. His question about coffee, I knew, wasn't about *his* making it but his polite way of suggesting that I make breakfast.

Molly appeared soon after we'd settled at the kitchen island, me with the Post and Theo with a comic book. No one in my house could stand electronics that early.

"Morning," Molly said. She was not, in truth, a morning person. "Coffee," she added, a little desperately.

Armored with a brief interlude of quiet, we were ready when the horde descended, clamored for food, and then, having gone through breakfast like locusts through a wheat field and flailing into school clothes and shoes, thundered into the Mercedes with more or less what they would need for the day, Molly bringing up the rear with the baby.

I remained stubbornly attached to dropping off and picking up my kids from school and camp. I preferred to think it wasn't because I didn't want people to see my housekeeper doing it, but even Quakers, as accustomed to acts of rebellion as we might have been, weren't immune to approval addiction.

The boys had all, naturally, been on the Sidwell Friends waiting list from before birth—eventually filling the blank space the school saved for a "Wells." The boys weren't birthright Quakers because Clint remained Catholic and had never joined Meeting, but it went without saying that they would be accepted at Sidwell thanks to my family's standing at Florida Avenue Friends Meeting.

Even the baby and twins went to the day care attached to the school, so my heroic pickup and drop off was actually one stop.

I went home after sloppy kisses were exchanged—or not, in my standoffish baby's case—and fortified myself with another cup of diesel-strength coffee in order to resist the temptation to go straight back to bed—to sleep or to weep, I wasn't sure which.

Molly knew better than to ask—about Clint or about bed. There were certain subjects best left unspoken lest the dam break. She had the party planning equipment spread in front of her on the table when I got home, inviting me into the project.

I sat at the scrubbed kitchen table across from her.

"I'm thinking four different savories, two cheeses, a ham, a rib roast, and four desserts," she said. She had the most recent party binder open to the menu section. Neither of us liked to do this work on the computer. Even the iPad had the wrong feel for this hands-on domestic work of old.

"The mini-quiche is always a hit. And what about a crab dip?"

"Too many people allergic," she said.

"I guess it wouldn't do to bump off a squadron of CIA," I said.

"Even one would be frowned on," she said.

We laughed.

I loved and depended on her dry English humor.

The truth was that no one from the ranks of the CIA would be there—they didn't party with people who didn't have top clearance. I was never invited to the parties beyond the Langley gates—no wonder so many CIA marriages wrecked.

"You know, for some reason, I'm thinking about something different—I don't know what," I said suddenly.

"Maybe little tacos?" she said. "The next day is *Dia de los Muertos*," Molly said with an impeccable Spanish accent. Brits loved to travel.

"Maybe. What about the crackers with spinach and artichoke dip?"

For some reason I suddenly felt really tired of menu-planning. I noticed Molly just put a little check mark next to the artichoke dip—she already had the menu drafted and was just pretending she needed me.

"Petit-fours, of course," I said.

"Naturally," she said. Another little checkmark.

"What do you think about the wines?"

"I don't like to choose if Clint will be back," she said. It was the closest she would come to asking if I knew where my husband was or when he'd be home.

"Why don't you go ahead and choose—you have a great sense of what our guests would like," I said, the closest I'd come to answering.

Molly would finalize the menu and have the caterer on board by the end of the week without my help. She'd already cleared the path of destruction left by the boys getting up and the breakfast chaos was no more.

I went up to my room and had a moment of "huh?" That was what my brother and I called those times of sudden and complete consternation about what to do next that come upon one quite regularly—unless you're my mother—without heretofore having a name for them.

I didn't have a child to attend to, the party was motoring along under Molly's stewardship, Mother was at her house. For a brief flash I looked into the abyss of Clint's absence. I realized I was holding the shirt he'd worn the day before he left. I put it down quickly.

That rabbit hole would not do.

I was angry suddenly—in a flash of heat that went through my body.

It was all Clint's fault I had no job—nothing to help me through his terrible absences.

My life as a socialite wasn't enough.

God help me, having five children wasn't either.

I started to laugh.

Clint had certainly done his best to fill the chasm of his absences. It was probably physically impossible to create more distraction.

And now it seemed, as the hot flash receded, I might be headed for early menopause, so that would end pregnancy as an avenue of distraction.

Better find something else.

But what?

It couldn't be anything too demanding—not even a volunteer job where they depended on me. Because this was an unusual day in that nothing had gone wrong yet. Molly could handle a catastrophe or two, but if things went off the rails with the house, the party, and more than two boys at once, even the marvel of Molly had a limit.

I found my phone under a pile of Clint's shirts destined for the cleaner and called Father Bream.

It was a matter of minutes before I was dashing past Molly as she commanded the caterers on the phone—"Hold the catering order," I said as I ran past her. "I have an idea."

The cleaning ladies were in the living room and I said hello as I galloped past them and out the front door. I was pretty sure the phrase "cleaning ladies" was no longer politically correct, but it was hard to think that way when you felt like getting outside and down the street was an emergency.

"Going to the University," I said by way of explanation. Which would explain nothing to them.

It was an intellectual emergency.

"Father Bream, is it?" Molly called out from the kitchen as I opened the front door. "Give him my greetings."

I didn't bother to wonder how she knew. There might be a British Isles telegraph no one else can hear. Or maybe it was a Catholic one.

I'd given up wondering about such things when my two lifelines tuned in to each other for the years I gestated and worked on my degree.

When your degree is in an area like behavioral economics, where business, psychology, and human nature collide, the tendency to do wrong despite the desire to do right is your area of fascination.

I hadn't started out in this particular area of economics. I started in straight economics, as I had studied them in London. I wasn't entirely sure how I'd gone from a BA in English to a Masters in Economics, as there was surely nothing mathematical about me whatsoever, but somehow, I had made that leap. The leap from straight econ to behavioral might have seemed shorter, but, in fact, it was at one time considered a radical shift.

If economics was the study of the science of the distribution of wealth, then behavioral economics, when it came into existence in the late 20th century, showed exactly how soft a science that was. In short, it was a rebellion against its parent discipline.

Economics studied the ways in which people, companies, and governments made and distributed money. Behavioral economics studied the ways in which each of them failed at this.

Economics was based in rationality, in the belief that the said entities made choices based on utility and the maximization of profit.

But said entities so often failed completely at this.

Witness countless personal and corporate bankruptcies,

the failures of, actually, most governments to be solvent, never mind profitable.

Enter behavioral economics.

The early behavioral economists began to look at the irrational choices made very frequently if not routinely by everyone, everywhere. It started out looking like there was just chaos behind it all—impulse and greed drove most choices. And it wasn't only in the area of wealth but also in choices from food to sex to power.

I had always been a rationalist myself as a young person. Mother and I often argued about this. Although I looked and acted like an anarchist, to her way of thinking, I actually believed in rational thought and, like many a young person before me, had been attracted to the heroes in Ayn Rand's work. Why not be ruthlessly driven by logic and personal responsibility? Mother, despite her relentlessly traditional appearance, had too much experience to believe that such rigor could ever come to pass—or was even desirable, in the long run. After I had been through a few rough patches, a few unaccountably disastrous relationships, I began to know the predictability of unpredictability and came close, once or twice, to despair until the example of the struggle between chaos and order in literature like Hemingway's, Fitzgerald's, Faulkner's, and the French existentialists gave me comfort and a framework for understanding the anguish of freedom.

My London School of Economics experience had coincided with the last of my rational phase and, early in my marriage and as the babies began to arrive, I found myself more and more at odds with the very concept of order. I was already well into the Economics program at Georgetown, though, and had no intention of bailing out. Luckily, Father Bream, whose Ph.D. was in Economics but whose faculty home was divided between Theology and Economics, had begun to teach some classes in the area of Behavioral Economics.

Behavioral economics, was, at first, a bastard child of standard economic theory—ignored and unwanted. But the leakiness of pure economic theory—that people made choices freely and appropriately and, by extension, free market economies were the best way to achieve economic stability—was woefully inadequate in explaining what happened, particularly in times of economic stress.

Over time, I shifted my area of specialty to Behavioral and Father Bream took me in for my dissertation.

In Behavioral Economics I found something of a balance. Though I remained steadfastly on the side of economics as a science, I could see the influence of chaos in choice. Behavioral Economics recognized the chaos but went further, to see not sheer anarchic chaos at work, but a pattern—a predictability to the unpredictability.

It turned out that people, and thus larger entities, have a gift for being both bad at taking and at avoiding risks. Because of built-in heuristics in the human mind, we are actually not very good at making decisions, and, in short, take too many risks in the short term and not enough in the long.

In that dicey area, where the mind is busy making choices based on the wrong things, other influences can quite easily be brought to bear. Witness all of marketing.

Although my area of research during my dissertation had been on the use of language to influence market choices, I had fallen, in my off-time, into a fascination with the way in which evil can emerge when people's thinking is actually so full of slippage.

That was where it became very good to have a Jesuit priest as your dissertation advisor. And if you get just the right Jesuit priest, you got one that is both logician and exorcist.

But that, of course, was not what our department was interested in, so much of our conversation happened offline, in Bream's office.

The rest of the department was involved in exploring the science of profit.

I had made some headway in studying the importance of language in using the strongly and sometimes embarrassingly wrong-headed heuristics we use to make decisions that land us in hot water. My central argument included a study of the ways in which Macbeth was manipulated by Lady Macbeth into killing his king because he had *said* he would, a decision both of them would come to regret deeply and, while briefly promoting them, would ultimately kill them. Lady Macbeth had been an expert "framer," choosing the one way to frame the argument to kill the king—the use of Macbeth's word of honor—that would make him follow through on the statement.

It had not taken us long, given the nature of the play, to begin to transfer the thought experiment to politics and, then, to the ways in which the worst of human nature can show up there, even though it seems irrational, wrong, historically condemned. What does it take to steer clear of the idea of some sort of evil appearing from time to time, to take over human decision-making?

Father Bream and I had many a conversation on the issue of evil—not only the classic problem of how can people continue to believe in a benevolent God when there is poverty, hunger, wealth disparities of such stunning proportion, women and children beaten, people routinely murdered but also and especially the evils associated with late capitalism.

As far back as I could remember, I'd had to struggle with my good Quaker secularism that dictates there is a human cause for human behavior: neglect or cruelty spawn the same.

But I had an innate sense, perhaps born of living in Europe so much of my life, that American naivete was actually a serious—possibly tragic—flaw when it came to dealing with the evil afoot in the world.

So much malevolence transcended the Quakers' logical explanation. It ran rampant, animating people who didn't *want* to be cruel but who could so easily be turned to the purposes of the devil.

And what allowed otherwise good people to be fooled into making decisions that went against their own interests? Bream and I visited the neuroscience and experimental psychology faculty to find an explanation. But that had brought us, ultimately, back to Bream's original home, theology.

There seemed to be something in the human soul—a terrible, possibly fatal, weakness—that longed to be fooled, no matter the cost.

"How are the young men?" Father asked me after a bear-like hug. It had been months since I'd seen him and I'd forgotten how life-giving that hug was to me.

"From anyone other than you, I'd be really annoyed that you ask about my brood first," I said.

"Ah, but I am me," he said, with the authority only he could, if without grammatical correctness. "And you secretly long ago converted to Catholicism and have been 'confessing' to me without knowing it for years. I know you love those babies as much as you ever did your career—and you loved your career quite extravagantly."

Tears suddenly stung my eyes—the tears only being understood brought.

"I didn't mean to give up my work," I said, wiping my eyes with the big clean hankie he handed me. "I meant to go on with my career."

"Just because you aren't galloping around a narrow and often petty tenure track somewhere doesn't mean you've given up your work."

"Well, I'm not sure how that would happen," I said. "Though Clint and I seem to have put the baby machine on hold for the moment—and Mother Nature seems to be bringing it to a full stop—I can't see much scope for a

Ph.D. in behavioral economics where I am at the present moment."

Father Bream broke into such hearty, wrinkle-creasing laughter that I started laughing with him.

When we finally stopped and he wiped his eyes with another enormous white handkerchief, I said, "What was that about?"

"Look around you," he said, starting again at the chuckle level. "Why would you possibly need a degree in the mechanics of why people lie?"

I looked around the large, comfortable, book-lined room that was shabby in a good way, involving leather-bound books and single malt whisky. A man's room in the best sense—given to the life of the mind in the interests of helping the vulnerable and deluded—intellect in the service of justice.

I looked back at Father Bream.

"I can use my work in your study?"

"My dear girl," he said without the least hint of disdain, "you live in Washington, DC."

"Of course," I said, wondering what took me so long—lingering effects of baby brain. "I suppose I could do some sort of consulting for political groups or service for worthwhile lobbyists."

"You could always write," he said

"I meant to—only I thought it would be as part of an academic career."

"But there is certainly plenty of scope outside of academia. Your work, used correctly, can be a sort of ethical exorcism, an opportunity for people to shape their behavior toward better ends. I'm thinking there may be areas of research even closer to home."

"My children act like little devils sometimes, but I don't think they need an exorcism yet. Clint is his own ethical Dyson. And all I do otherwise is give parties. Besides, you know I resist the idea that our work could or should be used to pursue particular ends, even benign ones. It's one thing to study the heuristics behind choice. It's another to use that knowledge to shape behavior."

"We have certainly had this conversation before," Bream said and moved the conversation on. "Is there anyone in your social realm you have your eye on?" Thus began the catechism.

"I was starting to pay attention to Adam Trent."

There was little about Father Bream that could be considered cloistered, either by means of his academic position or the cloth. He loved the rough and tumble of politics.

"Interesting. What about him?"

"There is a quality to his rise that seems artificial—unnatural, if you will. He seems to gain influence at a pace that can't be explained by his policies or his personality."

"He is propelled," Bream agreed. "His unseating of Ryan certainly seemed improbable."

"Besides, he's such a smarmy SOB. There is nothing real or genuine about him. He's a failure in every way that ought to count."

"He didn't make his own fortune, has failed at every business he's tried, is well-known as a serial philanderer and misogynist."

"And yet here he is in a position of power."

"Might call for a re-read of Machiavelli."

Father Bream paused there and gazed through the leaded windowpanes, out toward the Capital would be if you could see it from there. But his eyes cast upwards after a moment, the blue in them reflective of the light blue mid-day late summer sky.

"A parvenu," I said with quite a lot of vitriol.

"Spoken like true old money," Bream said, only a little admonishing.

"They're coming to the Halloween party," I said. "You're coming, right?"

If I'd tried to distract Father Bream with my rapid fire second question then I had indeed gotten baby brain and completely forgotten his attention is indestructible.

"You are having Adam Trent to your house?" he said. "Correction: Adam *and* his wife?"

"Yes. I know Ana, his wife. Or I'm getting to know her. Her son is Theo's age."

"I know for a certainty that Trent's child wouldn't be at Sidwell. Neither the politics nor the intellectual capacity line up. Where did you meet Ana Trent?"

"At a kid birthday party. Theo was invited to a pumpkin patch party, which meant that all of mine went. Her boy was playing by himself and Jules took him under his wing. Ana came over to thank me. Not that Jules' nature is my doing. I was just staring into space, I think—not talking to other mothers but using all that noise to give my brain a space out. So she wasn't interrupting much."

"I'll have to have a talk with my godson. It's not always wise to be so generous," Father Bream muttered. He was a great advocate for the limiting of choice if it made bad choices possible or even likely.

"What's wrong with befriending Ana Trent? She seems sort of lonely, bereft. She gave up a career, too."

"I think you too may need to be more cautious with your kindness. There is such a thing as leaving things too wide open. What does Clint say? That he would welcome the Trents into his house comes a real surprise."

"Because he's neither kind nor generous?"

"No, no, that's not what I meant."

"Well, he may be the one who put their name on the list."

"I wonder what he's thinking. He's never not strategic, several moves out ahead of most people."

"Maybe he thinks it would be good for me to have a girlfriend. My other women friends seem to have fled before the child tidal waves," I said, surprisingly close to a teary temper tantrum. "Are you men suddenly in charge of everything we do just because we bore your children?" I added, completely nonsensically.

I didn't tell Father Bream that Clint was gone again—maybe he understood that, or maybe he didn't need to know. I kept that information to myself as much as possible.

"Now, now," he said, producing yet another enormous clean white handkerchief, soft, sweet-smelling and astonishingly comforting. "Of course not. You and Ana Trent have a lot in common. You're both very smart women who have chosen to focus on mothering. Both married to strategic men."

"Do you mean manipulative?"

"I suppose that's another word for it."

"I thought you liked Clint."

"I do. Very much," Father Bream said.

"But that doesn't mean you don't think he's manipulative." I put the hankies in my tote, with the other clothes bearing marks of humanity that would need hot water laundering.

"Sometimes manipulation is necessary," Father Bream said, looking back out the window.

That led us back to our area of study. We had a friendly debate about the wisdom of leaving choices free and open or limiting them based on a benign architecture. We talked about what was new in the field—I did keep up with the research when I could, but my eyes tired easily and I preferred listening. Father Bream had a gift for taking the most complex, wordy, academically expansive ideas and putting them in clear language without losing any of their layers.

He was wrapping up just about the time my breasts started feeling heavy. Though Dylan had weaned himself at precisely one year, sometimes they forgot.

"I think there is plenty of scope for your specialty," he said." There is no lack of poor choices that have no basis in logic."

"But that doesn't seem to be particularly new in this town. It has always been a center for malarkey. What interests me the most, now, is the willingness to believe—what seems to be an active desire to be swallowed up by lies."

"From the latest videogame to the shiniest political movement—the human capacity to believe in what they wish for seems practically limitless."

"In America, the naivete borders on the dangerous. It seems like child's play to dangle hope as a lure."

"That devil," Father Bream said.

"And the ability to tell what is real hope from what is patently false—that seems almost completely lacking."

"Discernment is indeed a most precious commodity."

"The problem being—who makes the choices? And the manipulation isn't harmless, is it? Or the naivete without terrible, real costs. Who helps to shape the choices, and by what standards?"

"As we know from our field, poor choices don't cost just your money."

I was starting to get too heated, I could tell—a hot flash was starting to roll through my soul.

"That is indeed a port of entry for the Seven Deadlies—the gullibility gateway," Bream went on. "The belief that the fat and sugar on the plate before you won't kill you, no matter that you have consumed quantities of it before and after." Father Bream patted his cassock, under which was a substantial belly. "And then there is always faith," he added.

"Which no one can see either." The hot flash was reaching a dangerous degree. There was something deeply personal at stake in this conversation, but I didn't know what it was.

"And marriage," Bream added.

I felt consumed suddenly by volcanic waves. Marriage, I thought bitterly to myself. How absurd.

CHAPTER FOUR

Seaglass Eyes

It was unusually hot when I went back outside.

And muggy. Only in this swamp of a city, I thought, as heat flashed through my body and I felt my age again—or the proximity of the fires of hell—could it be this awful in September. And, despite all of its intellectual power and deep store of rationality, the campus at Georgetown always had, to me, an aura of something medieval, a castle within a plague city. Or possibly an aura of things even more ancient and primitive, a raw form of good and evil, unadulterated by polite society or politics.

The Exorcist had been filmed there, hadn't it?

But that of course was a movie and thus not real. The profundity of its effect, though, didn't come from the artifice but from the human mind's most primitive understanding of right and wrong, good and evil, safety and danger. The bedrock of the mind *was* primitive— and gave rise to the institutions, laws, religious structure, the social mores—all the abstract persiflage of academic disciplines, including—perhaps even centrally—my own behavioral economics.

I was grateful to hop in the Mercedes and feel the

solid slam of the door and the instantly cold stream of conditioned air that very rapidly became too cold.

My phone bluetoothed in and the display told me I had two messages. One number was unrecognized and the other Molly. I called her and we went over where we were with the party. Molly was anxious to meet with the caterers. I was tempted to say, fine, whatever you want is fine with me, but I was having an uncharacteristic rebellion this time.

"I just want to think about it a little more. I got a wild hair when we were talking about tacos and *Dia de los Muertos* and thought about having the whole party have a Moroccan theme."

Molly was silent. I could hear her mentally wondering if I'd entirely lost the plot. Who had ever heard of a Moroccan Halloween Party in Georgetown?

"Wild hair?" was all she said.

"A crazy idea," I explained.

"Indeed," she murmured.

Molly knew and liked the formalities, but I could imagine her calculating the risks of my craziness in party theme versus the risks of my not having enough to do in Clint's absence. Clint's absence came out on top.

"I love that," she said. "We'll take a look when you get home." There would be a mutual eye rolling between Jane the party planner and Molly, but they would get the job done.

I had no excuse whatsoever for this idea. How did one little taco get me there? The Dia de los Muertos and

Ramadan had nothing in common. Tacos and tabouli—no relation. And yet this was the vision that had come to me, even to tasting the food in my mouth. Could I be having some weird shadow of a craving as my ability to have babies faded?

When enough silence had passed for all that to have settled in our respective minds, Molly said, "You got a call on the home phone."

"That's weird," I said. "No one ever calls the landline. I don't think I even know the number."

"I answered. It was Ana Trent. Here's her number."

I punched the number into my phone as Molly gave it to me—and realized it was the unrecognized number on my phone.

"Got it," I said. "She called the cell too. Any message?"

"No, she just said to call back at your convenience. Pretty formal."

"That's Ana. She follows the old ways."

I called Ana who answered as quickly as if she'd been waiting for my call.

"Agatha, can we have coffee?" she said breathlessly. "I mean, I know you are very busy with the boys, but maybe sometime?"

"Sure," I said. "They all go to school or day care, plus I have a marvelous nanny. So, I usually have time. When would you like to get together?"

"Now?" she said.

There was real urgency and, of course, I had nothing I really had to do.

"I'm in Georgetown. What's a good spot for you?'

"Can you come to Dean & DeLucca?"

I hunted for a parking space closer to M Street and found one miraculously.

Ana was already there, sitting at a table in the café and I wondered for one second how she happened to be in Georgetown too just at that moment.

She sat elegantly upright, her powder blue suit and smooth silver jewelry cool and untouchable. She carried an air of absolute inviolability around her, an incapacity to be disturbed. It could be self-confidence, but had seen this same aura around survivors of terrible trauma too—so I knew it did not necessarily bespeak security but could also come from the will not to be disturbed like that again.

"I got you an espresso," she said. She indicated a tiny, pristine white cup on the table with a wisp of steam still floating from the top. "If you'd like anything else, I'd be glad to get it for you."

"This is perfect," I said. I sat across from Ana and had a sudden fear the chair might collapse. Then I realized it was Ana.

She had one-upped me—by being there already, ordering the coffee I would have ordered for myself, and having the timing exquisitely, mysteriously right. And her offer to "run get" me something else was clearly a dodge, a false face of servility. She would send someone to get me something—if there were a servant nearby. There were none, not even Secret Service. As wife of the

Speaker she didn't qualify for a detail—not that they would step and fetch if she did. There was just an aura about her that seemed commanding, even if her servants were invisible.

I hated to think that my class had bred snobbery into me—God strike me down if I turned out to be a Quaker snob—but there was something there—a competition—that both rattled and didn't reflect well on me.

"What is up?" I asked her as I made myself sit more securely in the chair. I unfortunately had the day before's scissored jeans still on. Had makeup touched my face that day? A brush my hair?

"Oh, you are funny, Agatha," she said, "You use those funny American sayings. That one always makes me think about the rabbit." She was twinkling, her long slanted eyes bright above her high cheekbones.

"You mean Bugs Bunny?" I said, starting to laugh too.

"It's not right, the Bugs Bunny?"

"It's completely right," I said, laughing harder. "It's just that it's become so much more gangsta—'whazzup?'—that I forgot it came from a cartoon."

"Gangster?" she said.

"Gangsta—like in rap music."

"Oh," she said. She thought for a moment. "Or the app: whatsapp."

"You've done me one better," I said.

At that moment my sense of wary competition suddenly fell away and I enjoyed being with a verbal equal, even appreciated one who might be able to out-do me, and in a second language. Or third or fourth, in Ana's case.

As the merriment faded from the air, her concern—just a hint at the corner of her eye—returned.

"So, Ana, it's great to visit with you. I'm glad you called," I said. "I think you had something on your mind?"

"Yes," she said. "I'm worried." She looked less worried than puzzled—but maybe that was a function of her militantly smooth brow.

"About Adam?" I said—more declaration than question.

"No, not Adam—he is always fine."

There was some shadow in her face—something below the surface—that I couldn't read. But I could read an absence—no affection, no respect—perhaps an exasperation. They had been married as long as Clint and I had, so there was bound to be some of that. It went with the territory. But there was no warmth there to balance it—none at all.

She had the face of a handmaiden—a beautiful one, for a fact. One with the deep indifference of someone who did a job for which she had no affection or attachment. It was an assignment, perhaps a lifetime assignment, she had to endure. And endure she would—she was meant for this role, whether by birth or grooming. She would make the most of it, get what she could.

And there was quite a lot to be gotten.

Adam Trent had been rich and good-looking before they met—born to those. After they married, he turned to politics and rose very quickly in that intoxicating world, as rich in intrigue, plot and counterplot as any royal court.

I didn't know Adam well—he was obviously of a different political stripe than my family. I knew that he had risen meteorically, but I wasn't sure by what means. Partly he had hitched a ride on the coattails of the current president—a teeth-grindingly predictable representative of the old order who had been elected in the reaction to the president before him who was seen by a swatch of the country as an upstart and far too progressive, what with wanting to take care of people whose assets might not have been as extensive as those of the people in power.

I had long ago given up trying to see reason in why those same people could be persuaded to vote against their own interest. I'd come to believe, like the good behavioral economist that I was, choices aren't nearly as rational as we might imagine. The connection between the present moment and the future is tenuous, on a good day. Very often people's *wish* to be something they weren't—rich, handsome, famous, loved—was far more persuasive than any set of dry present facts could ever be.

That or the possibility Alan Lichtman over at American University put forth that Americans just like change for its own sake—eight years of one party in the White House was all the American people could take without changing things up, like putting on a new outfit after wearing the same clothes for a couple of days, no matter how unflattering the effect.

Trained as we were from the cradle to project our wishes and introject those presented to us, and not to tolerate the boredom of sameness (go West, young people!) to always be in a state of wanting, irritated by contentment—it was no wonder we threw out clothes, cars, marriages that weren't quite right in the hope of one that would be a more perfect union.

At least the current president seemed experienced, enough not to cause tremendous uproar—his recent election had made few headlines and his VP seemed equally predictable—and so I had followed my father's lead in settling in for eight years of boredom.

Clint would serve whomever was in office—political party choices rarely affected the intelligence community—they just got on with their jobs. But he had seemed to be quite as ready to be bored as Father and I were. There seemed to be something about Adam Trent in particular that had attracted the lighthouse beam of his attention—or the gaze of the hawk.

I watched Ana for signs of disturbance at my mention of her husband, but none showed, even in the slow eddying of her thoughts back to her tiny cup of espresso.

Mine was long gone—tossed back all at once in an act of desperation that sudden energy depletion often brought one.

"It is Wolf," she said.

"Your son?" I said. Hawks, wolves—I was lost in the woods for a moment there. "How old is he now?"

"He is only five—like your Jules, no?"

"Jules is actually 100—no, he's actually almost six. Theo is almost five."

"Does he like school? Does he have friends?"

I laughed. "He has four brothers, so I think he sometimes *wishes* he didn't have so much company."

"Wolf has no one," Ana said.

I stopped laughing.

"I'm so sorry," I said. "I didn't mean to laugh about your son. My house is just so over-populated, loneliness is hard to imagine. But for an only child, it would be so different."

"Wolf is lonely," she said simply. "And so am I. Are you not also lonely?"

Her cool, long blue eyes were on me, interrogating, halting any lie I might have made up, demanding truth, on pain of pain.

"Yes, of course I am," I said in spite of my awareness of the extensive web of connection I lived in. My husband was often gone, my children were young, Molly was running the show, my parents were lovely, but their quiet, steady, socially acceptable life wasn't something I ever aspired to, and my career was gone.

"I'm lonely too."

We sat there at Dean and DeLucca, two women who had everything—wealth, stability, husbands, children—in Ana's case association with overt power and in mine I suspected I was connected to quite a lot of covert power.

We were well-dressed and our posture was excellent. Our cars on the street were luxury.

Ana was far more glamorous than I—she was truly striking and exotic, neither of which could be said about one. But I compensated with animation and character in my face and the complete inability to conceal anything.

I had always seen Ana as alone—quite probably in a loveless, virtually arranged marriage. Sometimes her distance from Adam in public made her look more like an escort than a wife, like someone dressed for the part and playing it exquisitely, giving every appearance of actually being there while in fact there was no scintilla, not a single neutrino there with him—all molecules swirling at a distance, elsewhere.

And yet she was there enough to have just nailed me.

My marriage to an absent man, the filling of my body cavity over and over with him and then his boy children, the fantastically busy life, the way people tried to get themselves invited to my parties, my lovely father and sharp-witted mother, my dear Molly—the most alive times remained the times Father Bream and I dueled with our minds, crossing and parrying at higher levels of understanding—those were the time I felt most there.

Except for possibly at this moment, when this woman I barely knew called my name in her eastern European accent, pointed out that I was lonely too.

"I am better so," I said.

Ana looked puzzled.

"A William Carlos Williams poem. 'I am lonely, lonely./I was born to be lonely./I am better so.'"

She held my gaze then, not needing time to translate,

understanding fully and instantly, like a lover.

She lifted her espresso to me and we clinked tiny mugs and drank. I realized too late that mine was already empty.

Pretty soon we were laughing. It might have been a sisterhood born in bleakness, but, as is so often the case, there is nothing to hide there. The love of loneliness is not universal and had a tinge of shame to it—talk about un-American! But, once admitted, there was a great freedom in it.

"Bring Wolf to the party," I said. "I'll have two sitters—a young couple—they're used to my five and one more won't make much difference. He can stay over if he wants."

Her smile—a rare and prized possession—lit her face and, I swore, warmed those seaglass eyes.

CHAPTER FIVE

Party Plan

The rest of the day went into shopping. Molly and I stayed in touch as if a general and her first lieutenant were preparing the battle plan.

It was a challenge to have a party in late October that didn't shade into costume. And yet that was not done. Not in my neck of the woods anyway.

It could get pretty absurd if they did, though. You could try to reign it in by insisting on classic domino figures—just black and white costumes and small, identity-obscuring masks—but that verged on Carnival. And hadn't the trope been taken over by Marvel comics?

Those of us who were permanently trapped in the swamp of Washington (and that was not a trope—the city quite literally being built on the wetlands of the Potomac River) tried to avoid showing what a Carnival the place was—always threatening to boil over. Rio and New Orleans could afford to celebrate as there was some natural limit to it there—maybe an honesty about the riot that became its own boundary.

But DC—if the evil and chaos that boiled just under the surface—if that ever boiled over—there was a world to be lost.

What in the world was I thinking? It was the next day—the one before had disappeared into the maw of post-Labor Day catch up and family and this one had already begun in the usual flurry of domestic physicality and then trajected into the strangely lonely day. I was in full party prep mode. I maneuvered into my garage and parked the Mercedes behind Molly's Vette.

I had tried not believing in evil. What rational person would? That was nonsense made up to scare the child mind. There were people who acted badly—usually made to do so by the deprivations and cruelties of their life. Take care of those conditions and "evil" would vanish. That was how we Quakers explained it.

But I had too many moments of discomfort about the vast expanse of cruelty that people seemed to perpetuate—the wars deliberately started, the famines deliberately inflicted to control people, the misuses of land, animals, children. And then there were the bad actors. The Hitlers and Stalins. And even more appalling, the people who permitted them. I had never admitted my dawning belief in evil to my father. I suspected that my mother knew all about it already.

Molly met me at the door.

"Have you thought about flowers?" she said.

No need for introduction or context. We were weeks from the party, but it paid off to think of every single thing as early as possible. We didn't waste time on niceties.

We hadn't finished the menu conversation. Once I'd said "Morocco," it came to a dead halt. It would be preying on Molly's mind. She would be wondering how my mental health was. The menu would give her a reading. Moroccan was well beyond the boundaries of taste my mother (or Molly, for that matter) would have approved of. But what was truly deadly was the idea that the menu was not given to a sit-down dinner. Was it possible that I was thinking of stations? That would be outside all the rules of decorum.

"Maybe cacti?" I said. "I bet Jane will have ideas."

"Maybe the Botanical Garden," Molly said.

There were levels of insanity to assess. The choice of Moroccan food *might* just be a momentary aberration. Not having a menu at all sometime *very* soon would call for intense therapy. And going outside one highly-vetted group of suppliers—going to the Botanical Gardens for floral display might call for hospitalization. She was testing my mental balance.

"Worth my life to try smuggling cacti out of there," I said.

Molly laughed, hopefully. "Just don't get jailed," she said. "The Department of Human Services wouldn't know what to do with all these kids. Deedee will have cactus. I hope."

Jane was in the dining room, her iPad set up in front of her. She was our long-time party planner, both Mother's and mine, and knew our tastes well, even the conflicted ones.

I had said "Morocco" to her too and that had set her imagination of fire, once she'd gotten over the shock.

I wasn't sure she was going to broach the subject of stations—Molly might have told her to hold back on that one.

She had a box of china with her to start considering choices.

"I think I never recovered from the Marimekko influence of my early adulthood," I said, tracing the big cobalt blue flower on the side of the Arabia coffee cup Molly had set out on a tray for us.

"But it wars with your Versailles impulse," Jane said. She took out the plate of Sevres china that was an example from Mother's own china, which she almost always used for her dinners.

It couldn't have been more elaborate—tiny pink and yellow flowers, wide loops of green, traced and embraced by gold leaf. It was one of Jefferson's favorites—and, not coincidentally, my grandfather's house china. I had resisted it for years, fought to stand by my Danish modern, then stubbornly stuck to white, but, around Isaac's birth, given a Boxing Day party that was full Sevres.

"You know I love the Arabia look—the order of it," I said, wistfully.

"That was your style, for sure," Jane said. I could see she was withholding judgment.

"But then chaos hit," I said.

"It almost always wins," she said.

"You mean my kids will never grow up? I'll never be me again?"

"Maybe not the me you were," she said.

Jane was older than I but not by much. Like any gifted party planner, she had experience beyond her years because her success depended on reading people quickly, accurately, and diplomatically.

"Planning a high-end party in DC requires all sorts of skills," I said.

"Practically a Ph.D. in psychology," she agreed.

"That and some soothing medication might not hurt," I said.

"Now one way to deal with complexity is to go with a look that is popular in England right now—a layered look of multiple styles."

She moved a few pieces into the setting and a few out.

Suddenly there seemed to be an order to the chaos, one layer framing the next, a color theme running through them all that brought order and structure to the jauntiness, as if Jefferson and Frieda Kahlo had made friends. How did the English understand this while Americans strove for either extreme—order or extreme, ungoverned freedom? Maybe it helped to be a really old culture, or one not driven, from its inception, to a clean slate at all costs. A need to throw the naturally flawed baby out with the bathwater.

"That's genius," I said. "What is this pattern?" I picked up a particularly brightly colored charge plate.

"It's Moroccan," Jane said.

She placed it on top of a tin plate and topped them both with a red, cobalt, and gold bread plate. Somehow, they all chimed together.

"That is going to give Molly a heart attack," I said. "But I love it."

"Molly might surprise you," Jane said. "But I'm not sure I'd tell your mother just yet."

We looked at each other, Mother's look of horror vividly imagined in both our minds.

"Best not," I said. "I'm going with Moroccan. Can Eric handle it?" Eric was our go-to caterer.

"I'm pretty sure he has contacts with a Mediterranean chef."

"Might have been the north side rather than the south," Jane said, doubt creeping in.

"Looks like we're going to go international, like it or not," I said.

"Not just international, but exotic," Jane said.

"Parties sometimes have their own nature, like they say characters in a book sometimes do," I said.

"Sail on, Captain," Jane said, gamely. "I'll follow you."

"Could you call Molly and tell her we have the china? And tell her next we'll move on the florist. I'm not sure what Deedee is going to come up with, but Molly was afraid it was going to be cactus."

"Still might be," Jane said. "Something scrubby."

"Any idea where I could find some Tuareg musicians?" I clearly had the bit in my teeth.

"Good lord," Jane said. "I have plenty of talent contacts, so, sure."

Jane already had the phone to her ear and was giving

instructions to her assistant to start collecting enough of the place settings she'd laid out for a party of 100. She waved to me as she went. I could tell by her instructions that she was already wrapping the idea of stations into the plan, though neither of us was saying it, as if delicately stepping around a subject in poor taste. She said she would come by next time with the cups for espresso now that we were clear on the theme.

She got on the phone to our florist and said "Morocco." Deedee said she'd have to do some research and would get back to us. She was English too and reassuring by nature, but you could tell there might be some shared "tsking" and concerned expressions with Molly later.

CHAPTER SIX
Church

I was headed toward the University that afternoon when I got sidetracked. I seemed to have a case of nerves suddenly and felt a bit driven, a little afraid, and afraid I might get more afraid. I'd had very few panic attacks in my life but enough to know I didn't want any more.

For some reason I found myself in the little Ignatian church near the University and took a pew. No one was there. I could easily have been mugged or murdered there—the door was open to all. But somehow it seemed safe just the same.

I let go in the light blue of the church. I found myself on my knees for some reason, tears running down my face. My hands were clasped and I was in full-torrent whispered aloud spoken prayer before I knew what I was doing.

"Thank You for my children, first and foremost. Every one of them is a nuisance and also a miracle of a boy. Please watch over them and help each be who he is meant to be in this world.

"And thank You for my parents, though Mother can be a bit of a trial." I didn't pray to anyone in Meeting and was surprised at how honest I was being. What made me think of God as someone I could be so chummy with? I went on nevertheless.

"Thank You for my home, for Molly, for my incredibly privileged life," I went on.

I went on, rushing as if the words had been dammed up all that time in silent Meeting.

The church was quiet around me, but the air felt alive, the plaster figures in the stations of the cross looked alive, as if pausing for just a moment as they went from one station to the next, doing as they must, as they were bidden—it was not an easy task they had to fulfill but they did it with joy, not resignation.

I looked up at the cross behind the altar. I was suddenly unspeakably relieved it didn't have a crucified Christ on it.

The cool blue air seemed alive with a sort of effervescence, an airy champagne, bursting with life, unpredictable life, the generation of a world, a universe, an embryo that had purpose and design and yet was also random, fragile, full of possibility and danger. The goodness and badness were both there in potentiality. The anxiety to choose was also built in, a part of the design. The ability to choose good or bad, to contribute or to rob. To give life or to take it.

And suddenly I was truly sobbing, an ugly cry, as they say. Dylan giving full voice to the misery of the world, and I was glad no one was there to hear me.

Except that, just as suddenly as the cry had come over, me, someone was next to me.

Father Bream was kneeling next to me on the prayer bench, neither touching me nor holding me back from crying in any way, just kneeling next to me while I prayed for my missing husband and hiccup-sobbed.

I got done with the worst of the cry and we both sat back on the pew, another of his big, clean handkerchiefs a ruin in my hands.

"It's Clint, is it?" the Irish brogue there just enough to warm his language. I hadn't told him that Clint was gone, but there didn't seem to be much use in what I thought of as my discretion when it came to the bunch of intuitives around me.

"He's gone again. I don't know where. I don't know why or for what. He can never tell me. The boys are at school. I have a party to put on. Everything is normal, as it should be. Except that the man I love, who holds our lives in his hands, is somewhere I can't reach him."

"Is there more to it than that?"

"He could be killing people. Or helping people kill people. Or setting up a lot of people to be killed. He could be gaining someone's confidence so he can betray them. He could, for all I know, be a double agent, and betray his own country. He could have a mistress in Serbia—and another one in Kabul, for all I know."

"'There are more things in heaven and earth, Horatio, then are dreamt of in your philosophy,'" Father Bream quoted *Hamlet*.

"Far too many for me to like or be comfortable with," I said.

"Well, here, then, is a good example of the benign limitation of choice," Bream said. He didn't rub it in. "I'm not sure we are here to be comfortable," he added.

"But to create discomfort on purpose? Uncertainty, war, betrayal, treason—surely these things are human creations—a matter of free will."

"Perhaps not as subject to reason, perhaps more what we are embodying—the war between good and evil—than, say, creating an unnecessarily 'busy' life of superficialities."

"Clint might be killing people for good reasons?"

"I don't know. But perhaps that is what he is called to do."

"You know in my religion that isn't possible—that would be a complete contradiction. Nothing violent can be of God."

"Maybe you need a new religion."

"Father Bream, are you evangelizing me?"

"Not at all. But you might be evangelizing yourself."

The conversation took us to the coffeeshop, where we lifted up into our head and discussed at length the ways in which fundamentals like life and death, good and evil—the moral battles—were translated into economic ones by various sleights of hand and how sophisticated the deceptions had become, the phishing scams in politics so specific and targeted to people's deepest fears and wishes it was a miracle that anyone resisted them. And yet how primitive we were, driven by the ancient instincts, how little time had changed the fundamental structures in our minds, the way we understood loss and gain.

There was a fundamental conflict between the way we instinctively understood time—as if everything were happening only in this minute, with no past or future—and the way our brains had very slowly evolved to understand time—with a sense of history and a future that could be shaped for good or ill by choices in the moment. In the present moment we were often glad to take huge risks—to eat the wrong food, gamble the rent payment—and in the long time frame afraid to take the big risks—like staying committed forever to one person.

By the time we were done, I had swum back up to the surface of life and went gladly back to the world of floral arrangements and place settings, restored to my life blessedly free of the deeper questions for the time being.

"I just want to make one thing clear," I said as we got ready to part. "I might have to accept that Clint might be killing for good reasons, but that line of thinking doesn't extend to his being married to someone else."

"Better a killer than a bigamist, I always say," Father Bream said, summing up. "There you have it—the beginnings of your own theology."

CHAPTER SEVEN
The Tower

Molly was quite literally up to her elbows in plates. A week had gone by. Jane had found what she wanted and had had it delivered already. Molly was giving it a quick wash before she stored in it the party staging area of the butler's pantry—which would be the whole butler's pantry by the day of the party.

By quick wash I meant sterilization.

"Hey, Moll," I called out as I came in. "What do you think?"

"I think it's *lovely*," she said. "You know I never liked a minimalist approach. What is the point of emptiness?"

"Ask Mies van der Rohe," I said. "Deedee said she'd do some research on Northern African flowers and get back to me by early next week with some choices. Eric has been asked to consider tagines—should have those choices early next week too. He said he has a chef in mind—someone really special."

"I talked to Betsy about getting the boys from school that day and taking them trick or treating in the neighborhood," Molly said.

"That one-time candy binge won't destroy their souls,"

I said. Molly was a great believer in home cooking—a regular meat and three veg for dinner.

"Hmph," she said noncommittally. She and Jane had worked out a system of stations that didn't offend Molly's sense of propriety too much, though no one had dared bring up the décor with Mother yet.

"There's going to be another boy, so we'll have to figure out how to shepherd him into the pack—maybe Betsy could pick him up too?"

"Another boy?" Molly said. Much as she adored my horde, she had questions about adding to it.

"I invited Ana Trent's little boy. What's his name."

"Wolf? Wolf Trent?" Now she was astounded, as much as Molly could be. "What on earth would Wolf Trent be doing at your house?" There was political expedience—maybe—in inviting the parents to the party—Molly clearly felt—but the child? Having a playdate with the boys implied a level of intimacy no expedient could explain.

"In DC the battle lines are always clear, but it isn't that unusual to cross them," I said.

We were sitting on either side of the island, drying colorful, jaunty Moroccan china by hand with crisply clean linen kitchen towels.

"A play date is outside the usual political calculus," she said.

"Ana asked my advice over coffee. Wolf is struggling in school socially—and I just invited him."

"You're a kind person," Molly said.

"And such an impulsive American?"

"You said it, not I," Molly pointed out. "I do wonder what Clint will say."

"He doesn't think much of Adam's Trent's ambitions."

"I'd say he thinks quite a lot about them," Molly corrected. She didn't miss much.

"He thought it was a good idea to invite them to the party."

"That's not the same as having the son among his sons."

"Well, he isn't here, is he?" I crashed a plate down on the quartz counter a little too hard for anyone's comfort. "I'm going to check the tower," I said. The ugly cry was threatening to metamorphize into an ugly temper tantrum.

"Perhaps a little lie down," Molly murmured.

I started laughing. When Molly needed me to calm down, she went all English on me.

"I'm okay," I said. "Really, I am."

"It's hard to have him gone so much, love," she said.

"I'm going to check that the leak got fixed," I said. There was a perennial leak in the tower roof.

Rising up on the north face the house above the third floor, the tower marked the house as one of the quintessentially Victorian ones in the neighborhood.

We were working hard at keeping it out of conversations that Clint was still gone. Molly avoided the subject because she didn't want to see me cry, but we both avoided it with Jane and party guests because it was part of the code of discretion in the town. Most people assumed he would be there, assumed he was just at work now. It would not do for them to know that he wasn't, nor did I know where he was, nor when he would be back.

Like most Georgetown houses, mine had the original materials outside and form carefully preserved while the interior had gotten all the mod cons—the latest in bathrooms and kitchens. The interior Victorian detail— the plasterwork and lighting fixtures had, of course, been preserved or restored, and the last time we had painted it we'd restored it to its original, intense colors through paint archaeology. Though the colors weren't quite a s deep as Federalist candlelight would have called for, they would have glowed in the Victorian gas light.

The tower room had been painted a deep teal blue in an effort to keep a calm atmosphere, but the boys used it as their pretend castle so there was much more often hot tar being thrown from its battlements than restful withdrawal from the world. They had no interest in the daily domestic duties of castle-dwellers like the cooking or gardening or tending of animals. They were above the details of getting meals altogether. Molly saved them from any such intrusion by providing a plate of sandwiches and pitcher of milk in case their boar hunt failed.

But she didn't exactly calm things down after provisioning—I had caught her more than once leaping and whooping as vigorously as the older boys, enough to knock plaster off the ceiling. Must have been some

Viking under all that stiff upper calm.

There was a leak under the eaves that opened up spontaneously no matter how skilled our roofers were, as if some Victorian spirit defied our attempts to get rid of her. I went up to the tower to check it regularly, perhaps to visit the spirit.

Mostly I went to remember my boys in peace—all their toys in the trunk, books shelved—a state of stasis that would never obtain when they were actually present.

All was peaceful—and dry. The fall rains hadn't started yet, but they would be coming before the party and it would be good to just schedule the roofers prophylactically. I made a mental note—uselessly.

I went back down to my room. I was suddenly, desperately tired. Sometimes being where they had been did that to me—the boys didn't have to be there actually to have their electricity drain mine.

I lay down on my bed and closed my eyes. Clint was imprinted on the back of my lids so vividly I sat up, heart pounding.

I must have fallen asleep—one of those sudden deep sleeps like being dropped into an oubliette. A sleep you aren't sure you can come back from.

And in that dream Clint was in trouble. He was somewhere he couldn't get out. And I didn't know what was wrong or where he was.

It took a minute to calm down, to realize I was in my own peacock bedroom, had my own things around me (if not my wits), and my own bed under me.

But that didn't restore Clint, my husband, my lifeblood. I could call his office and ask for reassurance, but that would pretty much be the definition of an exercise in futility.

They would acknowledge my concern and assure me that they would let me know if anything happened to him. The kind of freezing cold comfort that burns.

My noisy, smelly, animal children were much more comforting and soon I went under the welter—Molly had picked them up from school while I slept and they made a beeline for my bedroom as soon as they got home.

I always loved them and was glad to see them. This time I was profoundly, deeply grateful for their animal heat, their grabby hands, the way they banged into me with their little boy ferocity.

CHAPTER EIGHT
Party Day

The next weeks vanished into the abyss where time goes when you have five children and a party to put on.

Party day arrived on Halloween, as planned. For once, the boys had thundered off to school under Molly's firm hand. I looked around the kitchen from command central on the island.

I was already fully dressed and made up. This sort of day called for full battle gear from the earliest moment.

Other women faced party day in their running togs— after putting in their five miles.

I only had the appearance of energy. Late thirties and five children had taught me that my most precious commodity was my energy. I wasn't about to expend mine in shin splints and sweat on a day which, even at the end of October, was swampy in Washington.

I had on clean, pressed (Molly) jeans and a crisp white shirt (Clint's). I didn't own any white shirts. My flats were leopard. The only color on me that day was in the turquoise and coral earrings Clint had given me for Christmas.

Putting them in my ears was a symbolic gesture of

stitching him to my body, incorporating him. I hadn't heard anything from him or the company all these weeks. The code of secrecy prevailed even to my home, with neither me nor Molly mentioning that my husband, whom party guests would expect as host, was MIA.

I noticed that my hair had gotten even shorter last cut. It had shortened with each child. Naturally curly, my hair had been long when I met Clint and had none of the grey shot through it now. With Jules it had gone to my shoulders and now with Dylan it was barely below my ears. If I'd had Ana's bone structure I might have considered going even shorter, but there was nothing about me that suggested sculpted, never mind skeletal.

I had more of a Renaissance body than an Esprit one, but I'd always worn my flesh well and Mother had loved to dress me like a doll, so I had an appreciation, perhaps delusionally, of my looks. Clint's appreciation of my curves was undying. I wasn't a plus size—I was zaftig, my body made for comfort and enjoyment, like the curvy women of the 50s—Marilyn Monroe or Doris Day. In my social class, one of the pastimes was getting and keeping thin, but I noticed it was the women who were newer to wealth who obsessed over it and possibly spent an unnatural amount of time in the bathroom after a meal. My mother's generation was more comfortable with a realistic body like Jackie O's—trim but not gaunt. And I had charted my own path entirely. It wasn't just the children that drove my look—I had always tended toward the less under-control.

When Molly came back we had our task lists ready and we took off to our separate work—she putting finishing touches on the living room with Jane's crew, me and Jane in the dining room making sure the stations there were right, and giving final directions on placing the china, silver, bar ware, and vases.

Because it wouldn't be a sit-down affair, everything would require careful placement.

The overall party decorating had been done in the days before, with children banned from entering through the front door or into the living and dining rooms for more than a week.

Jane, the decorating crew, Eric, and Deedee the florist had worked together to make a fantasy land of our rooms, turning cold, end of October Washington into a desert hideaway. It was not inspired by *Casablanca*, with all its Western hotel décor and music, but by the real Morocco—the desert, the colors, the flowers.

Cobalt and gold drapes were hung along the walls to create a sense of being inside a room-sized tent, decorative tin lights hung everywhere, housing tiny bulbs of yellow light, a spice market was set up against the far dining room wall, myriad open boxes of spices and scales full of yellow turmeric and red cayenne. The living and dining room furniture had been moved out and replaced with cushioned divans with turquoise and cinnamon cushions. The Aubussons had been covered by woven desert rugs of rich color, hopefully preventing Mother, who hadn't yet seen the set-up, from having real concerns about the food from separate stations being ground into the Aubussons that were underneath.

The parking crew would arrive later, swiftly moving cars to the lot we had reserved as quickly as they arrived at the door, as would the flowers.

"I think only the dessert plates here, don't you?" Jane said.

"You flatter me by asking," I said. "Of course, you're right." I put the stack of dinner plates on the buffet.

"Perhaps Clint could help with the bar," Jane said. "I don't mean serve. Bruce will do that, of course. Just stand nearby. He's pretty decorative."

I laughed. "He is that. Sort of James Bond in his Daniel Craig incarnation. But he's not here right now. I'm not sure he'll be back in time."

Or ever. But I didn't say that.

"You genuinely don't know?" Jane said.

"That must offend your sense of order," I said, laughing at Jane's look of complete puzzlement. "It's hard to plan around an agent."

"That must be incredibly hard," she said. "And I don't mean party planning."

"I can't say I really knew what I was getting into when I married him," I said, stopping fussing with the silver, honoring her genuine concern. "But he tried to warn me."

"Well, I guess it could be worse," Jane said. "You could know what skullduggery your husband was up to. I see the Trents are on the acceptance list."

"Ana and I've gotten to know each other a little. Her son and Theo are the same age."

"She's model beautiful, isn't she? Too bad she's trapped in that marriage."

"There doesn't seem to be much good to say about him. Smarmy is a word that comes to mind."

"Conniving, manipulative, and bullying are also words I hear."

Just about when we'd done with the china my mother came through the kitchen door with Starbucks. Jane took hers and went to help Molly.

"It looks *lovely*," Mother said as her eyes flicked around the dining room.

"You're covering your shock well, Mother," I said, laughing. I had only seen her eyes open wide at the lack of a fully set up dining table and patrol the stations before she brought them under the iron control of not letting me have the satisfaction of seeing her shock.

"I know you're going to edit," I said. "So I'll pretend not to notice."

"Don't tell Jane, either," Mother said as she put her cup down on the sideboard and began to move plates and vases into different positions. "She is a treasure. But she *does* work mostly with the minimalists. And, well, we know that isn't *you*, is it?"

It was clear that she had to work to accept me sometimes.

"I wonder where I got having an opinion from?"

"I did offer my Sevres," she said. "You know it's the

same as Jefferson used at Monticello."

"Yes, but we were going Moroccan—not Federalist."

"*Versailles*, darling. Not Federalist," Mother said. "Your father doesn't approve—nothing of the Quaker simplicity testimony about it. We owned slaves, too. And your father still married me. So there you have it. Life is complicated." Mother didn't pause to make all the connections. "Did I hear Jane talking about someone who is bullying and manipulative? Not in Washington, DC, I'm sure." She rolled her eyes heavenwards.

We laughed.

"Adam Trent," I said.

"I'm still not sure why he is on the guest list—*or* why he would attend. But I know you. You wouldn't satisfy my curiosity. So I'll just have to watch and learn."

My mother had Lauren Hutton's beauty and elegance and brain. She also had a daughter who was, paradoxically, both bolder and more discreet than she was. And who had compounded the confusion by marrying a spy.

"Your brother is worse," she said as if she'd been carrying on the conversation in her head.

My brother James worked in the Pentagon and we all had a suspicion that he might be the designated survivor. But that was a state secret and James far more tight-lipped even than I.

"So annoying to have all these men in the family who know so much but won't gossip," Mother was continuing in the same vein. She was capable of carrying on an entire conversation by herself. "So, Adam Trent is coming for sure?"

"Ana is and she says Adam is coming with her. Her son Wolf is coming too—to play with the boys."

Mother's brow went up sharply.

"She said he was lonely," I said. "He's been over a few times now."

"Where does he go to school?"

"I'm not sure."

"Didn't Ana say? Don't mothers brag about which school their kids go to any more?"

"It isn't Sidwell. He'd be in Theo's grade and he's definitely not."

"Do you think Ana is as much a victim as people say she is?"

"Adam did come from gangster money—Jersey real estate, something. And gangster wives are sort of captives, right?

I could see Mother flipping through her mental Rolodex to see where everyone's background was stored.

"His father made the money—mostly on the back of Irish immigrants—stealing their property, exploiting them as workers then banishing them from their own neighborhoods.

Mother nodded, reading the story from her mental microfiche. "I'm not sure killing wasn't also involved," she said. "I am surprised Clint would have him in the house."

"Clint wanted him here," I said.

"Keep your friends close and your enemies closer, maybe?" she mused, making what sense she could of this puzzle. "But having his child over? That seems like deeper cover than even Clint would go."

"He doesn't know that part. He was gone before I invited Wolf."

I didn't know Mother's eyebrows could go that high.

"And, besides, he isn't here, is he?" I said. It came out altogether too spitefully for party day.

Mother read the spite and also Jane's very slight exasperation over Mother's "edits." She swept us out the door and to the Peacock Café.

I spent lunch in a political tutorial

And there I was hit over the head.

"Your father and I aren't sure *what* is going on, but we're sure we don't like it," she said without preamble.

"By which you mean you noticed things Father hasn't and you've brought them to his attention?"

"Your father's career was as a *diplomat*," she said. "And he became so very good at it."

"By which you mean too diplomatic," I said. "Did he see too many sides to the issue? Was he more tolerant than you could tolerate?"

"I'm not one to criticize," Mother began.

I hooted. "Sorry," I said. "Go on."

"But sometimes it's necessary just not to see things in order to remain in the jobs he had." She speared a piece of lettuce and lifted it in her ladylike fashion to her mouth. "Adam came from new money—you know what I mean by that. I know I can say that to you without sounding unforgivably snobby. It's different."

She took a sip of still water. Neither of us drank alcohol generally, though it required some subterfuge at parties and the collusion of trusted bartenders. Sobriety would be an unheard-of ostentation.

"Ordinarily, of course, he would never have been taken into the political world. For one thing, there's no reason to be interested. He makes a lot more money and wields more power in his own world. For another he's not a lawyer or the rare doctor who goes in for politics. Businessmen with money sometimes become mayors of big cities—but they don't run for Congress. It's not a very highly paid job, relative to corporate salaries."

Mother was running through the catalog of politician's attributes that she knew I knew—she was using the review to play a game of "same or different" to understand Adam Trent's career.

"Often the desire is inherited—there have been several generations in government. Of course, that isn't the case here. But what is most striking is the lack of a certain quality, a gravitas, that it takes to seem trustworthy."

"No one would say Adam Trent has gravitas," I agreed. "He doesn't even have experience."

"He's a buffoon, a con man, a barker," Mother said. Her dismissal was a near annihilation.

Antoine, our usual waiter, had delivered our espressos while Mother talked. We sipped.

"So why is he Speaker?" I asked. "There seems to be no logic, neither from his point of view nor anyone else's."

"Exactly," Mother said, clicking her cup precisely back into the saucer indentation. "There has to be something else he wants. Or something someone *else* wants."

"You mean Adam Trent is being manipulated?" I asked. "Mother? You couldn't possibly mean that. That's the most far-fetched thing I've ever heard you come up with."

"It does seem pretty far out there," she said. "But why else would he do it? The Speaker doesn't have that much power on authority. He is usually presiding over a squabbling kindergarten."

"The only thing I can think of is he is two steps away from the presidency."

"Only one, dear," Mother said, looking me in the eye. "Only one step away."

"But both the President and Vice President would have to be gone."

"Very improbable," Mother said. She took out her mirrored lipstick case and freshened her lipstick. "But he does make a very handsome puppet, doesn't he?"

★　★　★

I was upstairs staring into my closet. It was almost time for the party. I couldn't believe I didn't have my outfit planned. Wasn't Jane supposed to have that on her party planning checklist? Shouldn't Molly have asked what I needed taken to the cleaners? And Mother—Mother, for Chrissake—couldn't she have jogged my memory by *once* asking if we needed to shop?

But, nooooo. They must have all thought I was some sort of adult. Incredible.

Jane thought all she had to do was coordinate the guest list and caterer and equipment rental, plus get the house cleaned and decorated. And Molly—what had she to do other than run the whole house, take care of the kids often, and make sure Clint and I were clean and fed?

And Mother—what had she to do other than run the whole estate of Evermay and my father?

Well, she was also classy-eyebrow deep in politics too, as usual.

Handsome, indeed, I thought as I riffled through my closet. That was what she had said about Adam Trent. While she should have been thinking about what her daughter was wearing that night, Mother was turning her mind to handsome men and political analysis.

I pulled my jewelry box out, having failed to find any clothes I wanted to put on. I was still in my robe—the flamingo pink one Clint had given me before Dylan's birth—and steaming from the bath. I could hear the boys thumping up the stairs from their dinner outing with Betsy and her husband Jim. Betsy was leading, Jim managing from the middle, and Molly shoving them all along from behind with her voice from the kitchen. We were pretending I wasn't there at the moment in the off chance I could get dressed in peace.

Mostly the boys knew better than to bother me before a party. It was the one time their sticky hands and dirt bothered me. Right before a party, nerves hit, as if I were going on stage.

I pulled out rings and stacked them on my fingers. I thought about what Mother had said and reviewed the likelihood anything would happen to both president and vice-president.

Besides all the security that surrounded them—the depth of which even I didn't know—they practically never travelled or appeared together. So it would be hard to eliminate both at once. I supposed they could be eliminated sequentially and, as long as it happened before the next election, the Speaker would take over.

How likely was that?

Not very.

Plus how many enemies did the President have? He was bland, a good administrator, boring, some would say. Practically the epitome of what Mother said made a traditional politician—old money, came up through the Senate, a lawyer. Though he was of the opposite political party from my family, he was an old-fashioned conservative, with unimpeachable values and a predictability you'd have to be very young to find offensive.

If he had not moved the needle much, if nothing had changed much under his administration—given the volatility of the world—was that such a bad thing?

And the VP was even less offensive, if that was possible.

It was as if the whole electorate had gotten the same brain fog I had. I blamed mine on excessive children, but excessive cortisol from stress could be to blame for it all. The electorate might well blame divisiveness exhaustion. Better the bland than more finger-pointing and blaming.

So, Mother must have truly gone off the rails this time. She had before, I was sure. She must have this time— there was just no evidence at all.

I looked down at my hands. I had stacked every band I had on as many fingers as I could. Some were plain gold, some platinum, some had diamonds embedded, and one of my favorites was a wide white gold band with sapphires, rubies, emeralds, *and* diamonds embedded in it.

My hands looked as married as hands could look, as if all those bands could lasso Clint and bring him home.

Because it was sunset and there was no sign of Clint— no text, no call, no message from the CIA, no FB message. Well, he wouldn't do anything on social media. No agent could even have an account.

I heard Molly go up the stairs with the sounds of little footsteps beside her as she spoke encouragingly to someone made nervous by the steep, winding ascent to the tower as if he might be captured.

I remembered that Wolf Trent was coming over and that I'd asked Ana to come early. I hastily dropped my sapphire, ruby, emerald, and diamond earrings into my ears. They were a replica of a pair Jackie O had worn. Tastefully gaudy. They went perfectly with the low-necked peacock silk cocktail dress I slipped over my head. I stepped into low black velvet sling backs. Stilettos never were part of my wardrobe and the wear and tear of five pregnancies would have made them look like Minnie Mouse boats.

I spritzed Chanel #19 lightly across my shoulders and took a quick full-length look. Not too shabby, I thought. Unfortunately, the one person I wanted to impress was MIA.

Molly was coming down the tower stairs as I came out of the bedroom.

CHAPTER NINE
Halloween Night

"Best not to go up," she said as she saw me turn toward the stairs going up, drawn instinctively by my children's voices. "They are settled in with Betsy and Jim and the new one is getting folded in by Jules."

I laughed. "Plus, Ana must be downstairs."

"Yes," Molly said. "And ravishing." She looked not quite approving, though I couldn't tell exactly of what.

I went down the stairs and straight into the dining room.

My home was not among the homes of Georgetown devoted to tasteful, minimalist style on an ordinary day. I loved the layered, complex look and rich colors of the modern English designers who understood that one level living, flat rooves, and pared down décor didn't suit the human heart. More than one Georgetown modernist matron considered my house de trop.

But that night Jane and her decorators had taken it to a new level.

Deedee had made a true masterpiece of the flowers.

Everywhere—in gold and blue filigreed vases, squat tin pots, and square, textured containers were the most beautiful and gaudy flowers.

Dahlias in every bright color—red, orange, yellow— and purple orchids everywhere.

The lighting was gold and red, shot through with elements of indigo. The food was starting to appear and there was a fresh, frosty pitcher of mint tea I couldn't resist.

"Gorgeous," I said to Antoine who was a regular captain on Eric's catering crew. He nodded and smiled, already inhabiting the silent invisibility of the professional server.

"I hope you don't mind, Agatha," Ana said. She was at the other end of the buffet in shadow, arranging something next to the stack of dessert plates. She had her back to me and then she stepped aside.

She had brought a huge arrangement of poppies, lavender, red and gold giant dahlias, and black hollyhocks the likes of which I'd never seen before. There were lapis-blue delphiniums punctuating the arrangement that was stunning.

Ana smiled.

"I called Jane last week and she was so kind as to tell me you had chosen a northern African theme, so I found these. You like them."

It wasn't a question but a statement with the barest hint of interrogatory, just enough not to seem presumptuous.

"Of course, I do," I said. "They are out of this world. Speaking of which—so are you!"

Ana Trent was eye- catching under any circumstance, but that night her tall elegance, her other-worldliness, was taken to a new level. She had on an orange slub silk suit jacket with a wide collar and low neck. The skirt was pencil thin, above the knee, and black velvet. Her Jimmy Choos added another four inches to her height and her jewelry was a mix of dark amber and diamond that wouldn't have worked on anyone less striking than she was. But she enhanced everything she wore as well as lighting up her corner of the dining room with an extraordinary red gold light that seemed not only bright but volcanic.

She leaned over and kissed me on both cheeks.

"You too look lovely," she said.

And there was something about her warmth, her deep look into my eyes, that made me feel the sincerity of her comment as if I were indeed a small, rare, bright jewel next to her brilliant beauty and no less treasured.

"Wolf was so happy to come," she said.

And there again was the defenselessness, the vulnerability about her son that made me feel important, valued, unique, essential to this woman's happiness, which, at that moment, seemed like the most important thing in the world.

"The band is fantastic—a brilliant touch," I said to Molly. We were in the living room, passing by each other in our duties and shouting over the talk. Molly never considered herself anything less than an honored family member and we never did either. As a consequence, even our guests who knew she was the housekeeper and nanny treated her like a family aunt.

"That Jane is awfully clever," Molly said sagely. Molly had been the one to review the tapes from the talent agency Jane brought to consider band choices. We paused to listen past the din in the living room to the Tuareg band playing on the side porch. They were barreling ahead with their orchestrated clamor right then. The party had hit critical mass—enough people had arrived and enough vodka had been consumed to have revved them up and begun to speed past their Friday fatigue.

There was a moment in every party I'd ever given or attended—which surely by then numbered in the hundreds of thousands, including the 10,000 my debutante year (and, yes, Mother insisted on that tradition, as did most Virginia society mothers. And also regularly chastised me for my exaggeration)—where you thought it might not catch, where the inertia of ordinary life might just supersede the willingness to step outside the norm, where it would have been handy to whip out Zelda and F. Scott Fitzgerald for a wild dash to the nearest fountain for a quick dip—any excuse to step out of your skin and become what you were not—or were, and didn't care to admit.

It had never happened at my parties, but I'd seen it at others, felt the willingness to be other slip away, and, though everyone stayed on, there was no fire to it, no energy, no engine going full blast.

"You can say what you like, Miss Molly, but I don't

think this particularly jaunty Tuareg band was Jane's idea," I said.

Molly gave me a sideways smile, a very English shrug, and an air drum beat in sync with the music as she headed for the kitchen.

Jane had had the crew create a story line for the whole event, an invitation to the world of mystery, of intrigue, that was Morocco, with an actor in belly-dancer garb welcoming people at the door. And then, once in, going deeper and deeper into the secrets, the smells, the senses of that land.

The lighting was perfect—gold and red, just enough to be able to see your way through the stations and the people thronged around them, but also darkly mysterious, with folds in the curtains hiding who knows what. The smells from the food stations—one with lamb tagine, the couscous beside it, another with the chicken kebabs, interwoven with preserved lemon and olives, yet another with the sardine, anchovies, and mackerel—were heady, intoxicating in and of themselves. Saffron, turmeric, and cinnamon filled the air.

Eric's special chef turned out to be the Moroccan embassy's chef, who was glad to take a turn out in society.

I was considering my next conversational target—was anyone left out, or conversely, overwhelmed—when I caught sight of Mother expertly piloting Father from one group to another, making sure the young people paid homage to the old diplomatic lion while also gathering intel as she went without the young people's knowing.

"Another coup," someone said behind me. I turned to Robert Erghart, the foreign affairs correspondent stationed in DC for CBS.

"Thanks, Robert. Where are you back from?"

"Most Middle East but some Russia lately," he said.

"What's going on there?" I asked. And had he seen my husband, I didn't ask.

"The usual," he said.

"For a while there it seemed like the Cold War was over."

"We all thought so, but politicians, it seems, can't resist a good sequel any more than movie producers can."

"Except this one seems a little less cold," I said.

Robert looked askance. "Anything there? Off the record?"

"Neither on nor off," I said quickly. "Problem with being a spy's wife. People actually think you might know something."

Robert laughed.

"Except we probably know less than anyone else," I said. "But you can't help your journalist's instincts. I forgive you."

"What makes you uncomfortable about Russia these days?"

"Diplomat's daughter's instincts, I guess. Do things seem just a little too quiet to you?'

"That was why I went—things seem eerily quiet across the board—here and there. As if a storm is brewing, but off the radar."

"Or an animal getting ready to pounce," I said.

The room was hot, the crowd close and loudly friendly, and yet I felt suddenly cold. I put a hand on my belly in that strange, atavistic protective instinct I'd felt in early pregnancies.

"You let me know if you get any more of those feelings, okay?" Robert said.

Someone seized his attention from behind and I turned to run smack into Adam Trent.

As if I'd conjured an animal by talking about it, Adam's striking profile and black and silver hair were on full display. He was surveying the room with a Moroccan plate of chicken tagine with preserved Meyer lemon and olive on a shish kebab stick, and the leavings of lamb and coucous. He was surveying, quite unaware that his hostess was by his elbow.

There was a kind of alertness to his pose—and also the aura of a predator. He was a very solitary hunter. But not like a lion who was a fast and formidable hunter—no, one who was silent and worked in the dark.

Or in vicious packs. I looked around and saw no one—no one near enough to spring at any rate.

Adam turned toward me and I was caught in his gaze. He had dark eyes, with a glitter deep inside them, like an animal in the night. I so disliked everything about him—his politics, his personality, his treatment of his wife—his nouveau riche attitude of entitlement without the experience to use the power of privilege well—all were despicable.

And yet there he was in my living room, within arm's reach, and he suddenly seemed . . . attractive.

Good lord.

"What a gift you have," he said.

"I beg your pardon?" I said.

"You have a gift for drawing people to you," he said. "Having a successful party with all these different people is an art. You have a gift for it."

"Thank you," I said. "That seemed genuine."

"And you didn't expect it," he said. "Here I compliment you and you promptly insult me."

"Sorry," I said. "I didn't mean to. Insulting guests isn't what gifted party hostesses are known for." I felt knocked back, wrong-footed, chastised by my mother's internal voice for being sincere rather than polite.

Adam smiled—a surprisingly warm one. I felt forgiven. And, more, familiar.

"What's new in the House?" I said.

"The usual—health care, tax cuts, infrastructure, budget," he said.

"And other means of destroying the country."

Adam picked a glass of mint tea and vodka off a passing waiter's tray and toasted me. I thought he was going to find an excuse to move away from me—I was clearly erratic—one minute distant, the next friendly, then incendiary.

"Someone has to do it, don't you think? When the government is no longer serving the people, when the little guy is suffering? When the power has gotten concentrated in the few, the ones with all the wealth and power, the ones who've had it for generations?"

Adam Trent clearly knew to whom he was speaking—a member of the class he declared he was out to destroy and yet one who could be made to feel guilty for it.

"Wasn't it Loki who was the god of destruction—but a god who is there on purpose, to disrupt so that a new order can emerge?" he went on. "Has your side succeeded in any real change?"

"You might have me on that," I said. All the changes my political party made last time seemed so small, so incremental, so much injustice still around. "I guess that depends on what the new order looks like."

"Aye, there's the rub," Adam said. "Why not work with that rather than just resist?"

"Be part of the change?"

"Ana said you invited Wolf over," Adam said, abruptly changing the subject.

"Yes, I did," I said. I was glad he'd brought Ana up so I could go back to disliking him because I was dangerously close to seeing something appealing in what he'd been saying. "She said he was lonely."

"She is an amazing mother," Adam said. He looked across the room at his wife, a flame, and her sea glass eyes met his darkly glittering ones in some extraordinary exchange. "And she is lonely too," he said.

When he looked back at me again, I felt suddenly drawn to him. I felt appreciated, respected. I was glad he honored me with his thoughts, his vulnerability to his wife and his son. I suddenly, treasonously, fell into liking Adam Trent.

I was the one who excused myself.

My brother Jamie was next to the bar, uncharacteristically not talking to anyone.

"You looked parched," he said. He gestured toward the army of bottles.

"Just tonic," I said.

"I'm going to get Antoine to put some lime and sea salt in it," he said. "You need sustenance." He handed me a clean, cool drink. "What happened to you?"

"The strangest thing," I said, taking a long sip. "I was talking to Adam Trent and I fell into like with him."

"Good lord," Jamie said, taking an equally long sip. "I won't breathe a word to Mother or Father."

"Thanks," I said. "I wouldn't want to cause heart failure."

"Luckily, they seem pretty hardy. They survived my being gay."

"Even your being in the Pentagon."

"Even being the person who might be president if everyone else is obliterated didn't cause infarction."

"In either of them."

We are looking around the room together, as siblings do, looking for the people who brought us into the world, the atavistic attachment. Our powerful, stately parents who somehow gave birth to two iconoclasts—colorful, contrary, embodying their worst nightmares of military violence and excess.

We found them simultaneously and watched them, back to back, talking to Robert Erghart (Mother) and the delicate, tough PBS anchor (Father) while rings of junior Congresspeople subtly waited for the journalists to step aside so they could have a turn with the old lions. Ordinarily, the political journalists weren't invited to parties, though plenty of political business went on at them. But my parents were friends with most of them and they had become standard on my invitation lists as well.

"Even your marrying a spy didn't cause a stroke. But your liking Adam Trent could be a serious health risk."

"I might get over it," I said.

"I fervently hope so," Jamie said. "What brought it on?"

"He seemed sort of sad," I said. "And he seems to actually care for Ana and Wolf."

"You don't imagine that sympathy extends to the people who've been rooked into believing him?"

"I don't know, Jamie," I said. "He had this weird argument about the chaos that is needed to restore order."

"A cleansing flood, maybe?"

"Well, said like that it does seem ridiculous."

"Especially since, if you'll recall, God was in charge of the original one."

"But what about the fire next time?"

"There is that."

"One reason I don't drink at parties is so I don't get into conversations like this," I said.

"Let's go dance," Jamie said.

We had learned to dance from our mother in the kitchen wherever we were in the world, and we were experts by then.

The Tuareg band on the side porch was in full flood, their jaunty collaborative noise and Jamie's expert partnering lifted me out of my confused funk. Molly cut in on me as the next song began and Jamie took her around the dance floor.

I made the rounds to talk to the minority Whip and head of Ways and Means who were talking about their grandchildren near the dessert station.

"What, no budget negotiations?" I said. I saw that they both had piled their plates with the orange slices soaked in cinnamon and rosewater. Each had one of the spice cookies, nibbled, on the side.

"We have a rule that we only talk hair, nails, and children's schools when we are out of the House," Maxine, the Whip, said.

"The triumph of the important over the urgent," Nancy agreed.

The three of us went deep with our pedicure salon recommendations. They each lifted the exquisite gold and cobalt blue demitasse cups with Turkish espresso to their miraculously still lipsticked lips and I marveled, once again, at the durability and elegance of power in these women's hands. I excused myself to check on the caterer.

Eric didn't need anything at all—of course. If he had, Jane and Molly were both around to ask. Moroccan food might have been new to him and the exact recipe for mint black tea spiked with vodka had called for some experimentation and testing, but he was an old hand at the new. He had gotten the most amazing chef and crew together all by himself. He nevertheless conspired to pretend like I was essential.

Mother came by while I was surveying the side table to see how the couscous was holding up.

"It's a lovely party, dear," she said. "You look like you've checked out, though. Has your introversion taken over?"

"Mother, you are truly uncanny," I said. "Do you think anyone else has noticed? Or are you just criticizing the menu?"

"I'm not. But you might take a little break and tank up. The party is starting to really heat up."

She didn't mean tank up on drink, as she was the one who had taught me the value of sobriety at social events. I looked around the room.

After the first moment of ignition at a party there was always a second stage, like rocket lifting off. At this stage, it was either going to push beyond the ordinary atmosphere and escape gravity or fall back to earth, an ordinarily successful party but not one people talked about later on.

The party was at that critical moment—it looked like it might achieve that rare mix and air and fuel that could truly combust—Father Bream seemed to be doing a sort of Irish jig to the Tuareg twanging stringed instrument and oboe—so that antickness could happen—the sort where breakthroughs could happen—political rivals making a coalition or journalists getting an on the record, human angle on a story that changed a national trajectory—or a fistfight.

The sounds were so loud that everyone had to lean in to hear what anyone else was saying. It was hot and even the music sounded jangling.

I'd never had a party turn into a fistfight, but Mother had. Though it might have seemed like a failure, she took a strange pride in it—another feather in her social cap. Washington could be so tamped down, so boring, and Mother, for all of her dignity, had a deep wild streak.

Someone—Jane maybe but more likely Molly—had put a skeleton playing piano on the back porch. Someone had remembered that Halloween and the Day of the Dead were within days of each other and celebrated with great enthusiasm in Mexico—the two, life and death, so intertwined.

I went into the garden behind the house. It was a small, walled garden, mostly bricked in, with raised flower and herb beds near the house, roses against the back wall, and one old oak in the corner.

I sat down on the wrought iron bench and looked up into the deep recesses of the dark, resting in the depth of the shade back there, tanking up where even city light couldn't penetrate.

If I could like Adam Trent, what else was moveable, I thought to myself. Were my values that easily shifted? Could I betray everything else I believed in? Could I leave my children? Have an affair?

Something moved in the dark. Or did it? I shook my head, trying to clear my vision without totally destroying my hair-do. I saw a movement again, small, slight, almost indistinguishable.

I should have gone inside, gotten Father or Jamie or Eric or Robert, or the musicians with their heavy, portable instruments.

Or, if I didn't want there to be a strong reaction, one of the women: Molly, Jane, Mother, or even Maxine or Nancy. Women were so much more given to secrecy.

But I didn't go in.

I put my drink down and slipped deeper into the arms of the night.

We didn't talk for a long time. We kissed with that hot, deep passion that can come to the long married like a forgotten fever in which daily life and the small resentments were incinerated, even the deep fear of eventual loss, contributed to the bonfire. We came very close to ripping each other's clothes off there in the ivy dark—possessed beyond reason by our primitive need for each other. In our love, there was never much economy.

Clint lifted his mouth from my breast to ask if we were going further.

It wouldn't have been the first time. There were airport bathrooms where our reunions couldn't wait and the side of the stall as good as any five-star hotel suite. So our own backyard would have represented an almost conservative choice, even with our own party raging over our shoulder.

But the flame flickered just at that second and it occurred to me that waiting even briefly was a means of stoking rather than extinguishing it.

We still hadn't said anything as I pulled Clint's shirt back together in the front and buttoned it while he pulled by bra straps up and zipped the back of my dress. He turned me around and brushed some dying leaves off my rear end where he'd shoved me against the wall. That almost got us started again.

I turned around and pushed him suddenly, angrily. I punched his shoulder, two short, sharp jabs.

"You son of a bitch," I said. "Where were you? Why didn't you call? We were having a party—did you remember that?"

Clint didn't answer. There were no answers. We both knew that. He folded me against him, the only answer I needed that there was. I let go, curled into him like a lost child suddenly home.

When we stepped through the back door together it didn't seem possible, physically, but I swear the party paused. There was a hush that started in the dining room where we were and spread through the living room like a nuclear detonation, hushing everyone, turning the bright, glittering party to ash.

I wondered for a second if we'd managed to get our clothes back on—was that the shock? DC might be shocked by married sex, but probably not to that extent. No, there was something about Clint—as understated as he was, as quietly distinguished—that stunned—and not just me. And, of course, no one had seen him earlier in the party. He was just there, magically.

Or maybe there was something about the two of us—Cint's silvery sleekness, the sharp cut of him—and my peacock feistiness—the ferocity that no amount of intellectualism or social class could quite tamp down— that caught people off guard.

It was Adam Trent who broke the spell. He stepped forward, his hand outstretched and a huge, genuine-looking grin on his face as if he were welcoming his favorite brother home.

★   ★   ★

The party might have paused longer except everyone there was too well-bred to just gape. So the gaping went on in surreptitious glances.

The journalists, especially those born to the breed— and mostly those who survived in DC were born to it— circled in as close as they could to the silver beam of light, the torch of my husband, as he returned the grip of the barker.

Other people—especially those who didn't feel secure in their power—stepped away, found something else to do, a drink that seriously needed topping up or a dish of starters that needed recharging.

In truth I rocked back some myself, not quite clear on what was so combustible about the mixture of these two men.

But Clint did not rock back. Not at all.

He stepped forward into Adam Trent, returning his grip and clasping the older man's shoulder with his other hand, almost as if arresting him, making sure he couldn't escape. Or like a tornado chaser or a volcano researcher—going as close as possible to the seething, powerful, unpredictable whirl of debris—so close he could have been in danger, and then a little closer.

I listened to what they were saying—"How have things been at the company?"—"No complaints. How is the House?"—"Nothing but complaints."

Haha. Men's laughter about their jobs that, no matter what they said, mattered the most to them, that was so often so cleansing because they were so willing to tell the truth through banter—with these two men, the laughter was menacing—a threat, a gauntlet thrown and seized before it hit the ground.

Mother came to stand beside me on one side and Molly was on the other. I looked across the room at Ana whose eyes were riveted on Clint. Clint's gaze shifted from Trent's teeth-baring look over to Ana. And then he turned to me.

He looked at me with his alpha wolf gaze and I looked back as steadily, though whether I was the wounded elk longing for the kill as much as the hunter was or the alpha female, I'd be damned if I knew.

CHAPTER TEN

After Burn

The party went on for hours after that, but it seemed to be running on adrenaline at that point, with Robert scenting a story but seasoned enough to know he wasn't going to get it that night and other, younger members of Congress and the press just not quite sure what had happened. When it finally wound down, guests left with the exquisitely crafted, woven bags the women at the Moroccan embassy had made for the party.

Clint had wandered off into the backyard with Jamie which had nothing to do with their jobs and everything to do with the fact that they liked and respected each other and knew what it meant to keep secrets.

Molly and I were in the kitchen finishing off the spice cookies when Mother came to say good night.

"A dazzling evening, my girl," she said. "I couldn't have done better myself."

"That's some bullshit there," Molly said.

Mother and I looked at her.

"Well, it is," she said comfortably.

"Quite so," Mother said. She bellied up to the island with us and picked up a spice cookie. "Wasn't that something with Clint and Adam? Two animals charging."

"I didn't even know they knew each other," Molly said. "What has Clint got on him?"

"Nothing at all that I know of," I said. Both the women gave me a side eye. "I don't, really."

"And where did Clint come from anyway?" Mother said. "I didn't see him come in."

"He came over the back wall," I said.

Father had just come into the kitchen with Mother's shawl as I said it. He gave a disapproving frown.

Clint and I met in Jules' and Theo's room.

We each had our routines with the kids that, one way or another, resulted in both of us touching all five of them every night we were with them. We had a different order we went about it, mine usually quite haphazard, but Clint had a routine that started at the youngest and went up chronologically.

That night by happenstance on my part, we both finished up in Jules' room at the same time.

"He doesn't look like a devil child," Clint said.

"What on earth are you talking about? Jules is about as close to an angel as is available on this planet," I said.

"Oh, I don't mean him," Clint said as he looked down at his eldest son, the spitting image of one of Michelangelo's putti except no little wings. The planets whirled around Jules' ceiling. He had been in love with all things intergalactic from birth, so his nightlight, naturally, projected the galaxy.

"No," Clint said. "He is a good man." He tucked the solar system duvet along the side of the bed. "I meant his new little friend."

"Let's go downstairs," Clint said as he saw my Irish come up. "Even really sound sleepers can be woken up."

"I resemble that," I said, trying to make light of the argument when we were in our room. "I wouldn't have invited them if you hadn't asked me to."

"I know I did," he said. "I wanted to see Adam Trent up close."

"Besides, how did you even know Wolf Trent was here? You weren't home."—possibly the fuel for my fire.

"I have my ways," Clint said.

This did nothing to lower my temperature.

"I have my ways," he repeated.

"You mean you *spy* on me?"

"No, I mean Molly told me."

"Which you took your sweet time getting to. I didn't know whether or not you were going to get here at all. Surely there is *some* way to stay in touch."

"It's better not to. Just like it's better for you not to get too close to the Trents."

"What are you talking about?"

"Maybe it's a good idea not to invite the son of a political nitwit over to play with my children."

We'd made it to taking our clothes off. Clint was doing so in his usual systematic fashion, hanging each piece up on his side of the closet as he went, but when he took off his tie as he spoke, he pulled it out of his collar hard enough to snap.

I was too appalled for a moment to speak. Clint had never been possessive of the boys like that—claiming them as his—or even the slightest bit violent at home—though I was pretty sure he'd killed people elsewhere—or directed toward me—because what would be the point?

"Is it Ana?" I said abruptly. "Do you have the hots for Ana? I saw you look at her."

"No, love," he said. He took me in his arms and the temper drained right out of me, by magic. "You need to learn how to read looks better."

Had his look been desirous? Or was it suspicious? Or maybe it had been apologetic?

There was almost certainly a tinge of sympathy in it.

I was in bed already and closed my eyes and slept the sleep of the successful party hostess. But fatigue—and possibly my guilt over falling in like with Adam Trent—had stood in the way of our love-making just before I fell asleep. I realized it was the first time ever we hadn't made love on Clint's re-appearance.

It was deep in the night that I felt Clint curl over my back and come into me from behind, our bodies homed to each other.

CHAPTER ELEVEN

The Winter Begins

When Clint was home we went about our lives like any other family. He left for work in the morning like any Beltway commuter. Molly and I got the kids off to school and then settled the house.

Mother and I often had lunch or we had committee work at Florida Avenue. I'm pretty sure the structure of the place would have collapsed without her. From her high church Episcopalian heights as her birthright, she took a swan dive into the good works of Quakers when she married Father. We also did work for the Democratic Party when needed, not that the District itself needed an exhortation to vote Democratic. Outside the wealthy enclaves, it was mostly black, poor, and resolutely Democratic. We were safe from doing any Garden Society work—Mother was allergic, and not to the flowers.

That fall, for some reason, Clint took up church-going. I had been taking the boys to Meeting for years, but he suddenly wanted them to have exposure to his religion, so we all loaded into the little Catholic church Father Bream had found me in, Holy Trinity. We endured the service all together, occasionally taking refuge in the cry room when one of the kids needed to yell it out during the homily.

As November progressed, the cold came with it. And a brewing sense of unrest. Clint was at work longer and came home more intense than usual. He spent an hour or two with the boys and then either went back to the office or disappeared into his study for several more after the boys had gone to bed.

I could feel a threat.

Our house had every kind of security there was. Of course, nothing top secret went in or out from there, but Clint did seem to spend an awful lot of time in his study with my brother.

Meanwhile I carried on a clandestine relationship with Ana.

Otherwise, I never could have explained what I did during that time—I got up, the tidal wave of boys rolled over me, then it was time for bed. There seemed like a million things to do at home, for the boys, for Mother's Thanksgiving extravaganza. I was working on some articles that kept my mind busy from time to time—one I was co-writing with Bream—but they had no absolute deadlines and so got washed away in the flood of dailiness.

The article Bream and I were writing was about the ways in which behavioral economics and politics intersect—how the laws of the marketplace manifest in the political world, neither of which could be said to be ruled by reason. We weren't interested in the ways in which politicians were bought and sold—which had no natural boundary or daylight since Citizens United removed both limits and transparency from campaign contributions—but on how government, wittingly or not, used the same techniques any good marketer did to persuade voters that what they had to offer was the real thing. I had gotten interested in the question of the architecture of choice—including how having too many (libertarian) or too few (authoritarian)—affected decision-making. Although I maintained my defense of free choice, the argument was less fierce, as I came to grips with the ways in which choice is rarely if ever free—constrained as it is by inner heuristics like loss aversion, poor time assessment, and preference bubbles, or by outer—the rule of law or the chaotic, arbitrary, and self-interested rules of the authoritarian.

In short, we were getting at the methods that government borrowed from salesmen to convince people to buy things they didn't need or want. And we had begun to flirt with ways in which government could help people make good choices.

So far my best contribution to the thinking was that government, at best, could not be either free-choice—as people so often chose the wrong, self-destructive thing—or authoritarian—but I had gotten stuck acknowledging that my natural tendency to liberal choice-making, laissez-faire or anything-goes was, in practice an open door to people making immediately satisfying choices that were disastrous in the long run while also seeing government-provided choice as dicey. Who in the government would say what the choices were? Congress, in the case of the US, seemed completely unable to make any choices. And the executive branch—who was to say the president would allow good choices? Didn't that depend on the person in the presidency?

No government seemed to get this right, though representative democracy could well be the closest. It clearly didn't suit all cultures, however much we had tried to impose it: Viet Nam, Iraq, Libya. Surely by now, we had learned that the imposition of choice was not a choice we wanted to continue to make.

Some businesses seemed to have gotten a lot of it right: a benign, wise decision-maker over a group with whom loyalty was reciprocal, an ancient model of comitatus that might have been best modeled in known history by the small Germanic tribes in Northern Europe around the time of Beowulf. No one ruled without obligation to provide stability and wealth to the group as a whole; no one served without actively agreeing and clearly benefiting.

We digressed often—Father Bream and I—and often ended up in a muddle, trying to resolve the paradox of a good system having to come from and be administered by a mostly good ruler. I had presented one exception as the recovery community—the many layers of which had no ruling voice but a set of traditions and one book. Father Bream said that sounded like the Catholic Church—and look how much harm that had caused, which got us back to the relative morality of Bill W. and whatever Pope was in charge at the time.

For both of us, the matter of choice was deeply fraught.

Maybe Clint should have spent more time with Mother—rather than think like Father. While Mother could outwit me and pretend-pressure me to make the choice she didn't want me to so that I'd seize the one she did, poor Father's rational mind couldn't twist itself into such logic-pretzels. For him, the ends never did justify the means while Mother, like most women, took the pragmatic, Malcolm X approach that the right end justified arriving there by whatever means necessary.

For reasons I didn't examine closely, that fall my most rebellious self came out in my private life and took a strange direction.

For whatever reason, the cool, elegant house in Kalorama became a destination for me regularly after school drop off. I didn't have the nerve or the spycraft to take Jules there as cover because that open-hearted child was simply incapable of lying to his father about what he did or even simply failing to mention Wolf in his daily report to Clint on his activities. Though his dad was often distracted by the other boys or by something on his computer while Jules made his way verbally through his day—"and I couldn't decide if I wanted to go back to the block area or the book area this morning, but Barney needed help with his shoe-tying so I went over there. Then it was story-time . . ."

But Clint's ears, trained to listen through hours of crackling interference for the one nugget of valuable information, would have instantly picked up on Wolf Trent's name in the long stream of talk.

So I went by myself.

Kalorama is less crowded than my neighborhood, though easy enough to get to. I could have Metro'd my way over—even biked—but Ana always had room in the driveway for the Lexus and always had fresh coffee ready to serve.

Her house, in contrast to my lively, colorful, noisy, admittedly messy one, was the epitome of cool Italianate elegance—magnolia white walls, the palest of green silk curtains, no flowers or toile or Danish modern decorations, though there were orchids placed individually and discreetly on the entry tables. A Guatemalan print—a Moroccan tile—would have amounted to a decorator's fart in her living room.

It wasn't my taste, yet I was drawn to it right then, perhaps in defiance of my husband, or in retreat from the chaos of my own making in my life, or simply because Ana made me feel welcome, important somehow.

There was also a growing unease—in the city, in my house, in my husband—that meant the city was about to have one of its outbursts of political malarial fever. Things had been quiet too long, the administration too predictable. This wasn't a city that tolerated no news for too long.

"So, what do you think is going on?" I asked Ana one day over coffee. We were in the sun at the two-person seating area at the far end of the living room. Her maid had served us and left to clank in the kitchen across the hall behind closed doors.

"I don't know, but is something *very* big," Ana put her cup in her saucer with a delicate, bone china click and gestured, drawing a big box in the air.

"There is a lot of buzz," I said, "but I don't really hear anything of substance."

"You are so busy with your children," Ana said appreciatively, "and with your writing—I wish I had such things to occupy me."

"I'm sure you have plenty to do," I said. "Besides, don't tell me that you've bought into the American idea that busy is the new black."

It took her a second to sort out the metaphors, then she laughed.

"Oh no," I am European enough still not to fall for that busy busy business."

We both laughed at the verbal play.

"I sometimes wish there were more children, or work that I could do, but Adam doesn't want me translating. He thinks it might cross wires for him. And I'm not so much the Garden Club."

"I don't see you with dirt under your nails," I said. "No more kids?"

There was something about the extreme convention of Ana's home and behavior—her traditional décor, her absolute acceptance of the old-fashioned role of wife—that made me ask questions I quite possibly wouldn't have if I hadn't turned so oppositional.

"We try," Ana said, her elegant hands lifting up, dropping. "But no." There was something false, melodramatic, in the gesture.

"Doesn't entertaining for Adam take up some time?"

She made a slight movement with her mouth—nothing that would cause wrinkles. "I'm not like you," she said. "I don't like to make big parties. I like to sit like this, one person talking to one person."

"How is Wolf getting along at school?"

"He is doing some better. He has made a friend or maybe two. I think your Jules might have given him some tips."

"I'm sorry I haven't had him over again, or brought my boys over."

"I understand," she said. And I could tell suddenly that she did. "Jules is friended already with so many brothers. Plus our husbands . . ." She gave what amounted to a Gallic shrug—amazement and resignation rolled into one all-knowing gesture.

"Whew," I said. "You said a mouthful."

"They are like a bomb together, those two," she said. She put up her hands to ward off a blast.

"When they met at my party," I agreed.

She nodded. "It was like the appointment at Samarra."

"Well, I hope not, because that doesn't turn out that well."

"Oh, I didn't mean that," she said hastily. Toggling among several languages had many pitfalls. "I just mean so inevitable."

"Even if one of them tried really hard to avoid it."

"Or both," she said.

"Adam hasn't told you what is brewing? Is there anything going on in the House?"

"There is something there, for sure," she said, falling into idiom that was so funnily informal in her long elegant mouth. "But it is under wraps." She folded one, long perfectly manicured hand on top of the other, opal pink nail polish impeccable. "So odd."

"The House tends to do everything pretty blatantly," I agreed.

"I think it is in the White House, the troubles," she said.

"The President? The inoffensive, bland president?"

She nodded, then paused. "Or maybe the Vice President."

"That would be a bombshell," I agreed.

"But I don't hear this from Adam, no," she said.

"No? You and Adam don't talk?"

"Not so much," she said. She looked sheepish, ashamed.

"Not even pillow talk?"

"What is this, pillow talk?"

"When you get into bed together and, you know, well, just talk—let your hair down."

She put her hands up again, the same way she did to ward off the imaginary blast. When she realized it, she quickly ran one hand down her long, glossy, perfectly trimmed hair, then dropped them both back in her lap, the perfect lady-at-lunch posture, upright, hands pinned down.

"No, that is not something we do," she said. "We don't sleep in the same room."

She said it matter-of-factly, as if, of course not. We were living in Victorian or possibly Edwardian England, right? Where it was perfectly normal for husbands and wives to sleep in separate rooms. My mind snapped to the heat in my bed, the times we took each other with such ferocity it made my face burn in that cool, elegant room, wolves in the wild.

"Oh, I'm so sorry," I said before I could censor myself. The distance between Adam and Ana Trent in public, the way they seemed so self-contained, so alone even side by side—all of a sudden made so much sense to me, the fires never built together. No wonder there wasn't a larger brood.

"Adam doesn't sleep much," she said by way of belated explanation, "so he doesn't like to disturb me."

I wanted to reach out and put my hand over hers, reassure her that she didn't need to explain this to me, or try to make it better. But a sudden thought stopped me. She caught the attempted gesture and the abrupt hesitation.

"You and Clint—you have had a lot of the pillow talk, I think," she said with a smile, warm and—now—reassuring me.

"Well, it wasn't all talk, obviously," I said. She was still smiling. "But lately I guess he's been sleeping somewhere else—his study probably." I hadn't meant to say that.

"Oh," she said. Her look was a mirror of my sympathy.

"He's worried, I think," I said. "I just don't know about what."

★   ★   ★

When the boys were in bed Clint headed for his study. I followed him there. He sat behind his big oak desk, facing the computer on the return, fingers already on the keyboard. He looked up, at the far edge of the pool of lamplight from the desk lamp.

"So what's up," I said.

He looked at me like I might have taken leave of my senses.

"I know, I know," I said. "I can't ask that. Just—how are things going with you, yourself?" I tried to back up, leave him some space.

He turned to face me fully, pulling up to the desk between us.

"I'm tired," he said. "How about you?"

"I feel like things are off kilter," I said.

"There's nothing wrong. Everything is fine. Is there something wrong with the boys I don't know about?"

"No, they are all great. You seem to be working really hard. It's so hard not knowing what is going on with you. And there seems to be something going on. Even—" I was going to say Ana thinks so in my stream of babble, but I realized at the last second that would be a big mistake—"even Molly thinks so."

He laughed, letting me breathe. "Molly doesn't miss much. She'd probably know before anyone else."

I sat down across from him, a supplicant.

"So what is going?"

"Aggie, you know I can't tell you that." He had shut down again, locked down tight.

A wave of heat washed over me. Menopause, I thought, on top of everything else.

I slammed both hands down on the front of the desk.

"I am so sick of having half a husband," I said. "I did *not* sign up for this. I knew you'd be gone a lot. But I didn't know you'd even be gone when you are here."

Clint and I fought, for sure. We weren't built for cold formality. We yelled and occasionally I threw a paperback, once a glass. But it was always over in minutes—a cleansing storm that blew through. We always ended up in each other's arms.

"You know I'm in the service of the country," Clint said. "That was what *I* signed up for."

"And I'm supposed to be in *your* service?"

"You always have a choice," Clint said.

We had never in all the years together once talked in any way about divorce. We knew from the beginning we were in it for life. We knew we would be married forever, as if we had been before we were born and would be after death.

I *didn't* have a choice—and if Clint thought I did, then my world was indeed tilting.

I felt dizzy but stood up anyway.

We looked at each other for a long time.

And then I walked out.

CHAPTER TWELVE
Thanksgiving Prep Begins

Mother was in her element. Thanksgiving was the biggest event held at Evermay all year and she had ambassadors and cabinet ministers and heads of state flying from everywhere to attend. They weren't coming for a state dinner. They were personal friends of my parents, my mother specifically. Half the men—gay or straight—were in love with her. She saw to it they were—with her lovely Southern ways and just a hint of sauciness. Father didn't take offense at this, as he was at the front of the line of her admirers.

Molly spent a lot of her time at Evermay as November moved on. I didn't need her that much after the Halloween party as long as the kids stayed stowed at school. Mother didn't need my daughterly support—I could get really distracted with a good idea for my article and just disappear on her—as much as she needed Molly's hands-on executive assistance.

That left me with free time. Some of which I spent on research. But most of which I spent with Ana.

We became tourists, visiting the city's sites in each other's company. We took in the Newseum and the

Corcoran, spending days at the National Gallery and even had a fun afternoon at the cramped, clandestine Spy Museum.

We covered the National Mall from one end to the other, were amused by the antic modern art at the Hirschhorn and were sobered by the history at the African-American History Museum.

Our favorite was the National Botanical Garden. A smaller structure, mostly glass, we went there for the humidity in the huge tropical rainforest as the DC weather grew more frightful.

But really what we loved was the great array of terrains—the desert, the redwoods, the frigid mountains, and last but far from least, the great Victorian Christmas tree. The Botanical Gardens, being culturally accurate, did not restrain its English tree decorating until after Thanksgiving.

"It reminds me of my Grandmother's," I told Ana the first day the tree went up.

"You lived in London?" she asked.

"Yes, and everywhere else in Europe."

"Me as well, mostly Eastern, though. Not so much London."

"We were in Vienna for a long time," I said. She knew this.

"Close to us," she said. I thought she might mean the Soviet Block

, but, after Glasnost, it seemed impolite to say.

We even took a field trip out to Dulles to tour Udvar-Hazy one day.

Once again, we pretended to be vetting it for the boys—seeing if anything new had been added, in my case, but, really, we just liked being together.

It wasn't really a girl crush on my part, though Ana's beauty and elegance were a sight to behold. We made an interesting pair—her height and buttoned-up almost military bearing next to my quick rainbow gecko small colorfulness. We did draw people's stares, clearly thinking we were somebody—or at least Ana was—but not quite who. The wife of the Speaker isn't usually a media focus, and, though I'd been in the papers since early childhood, it was mostly in the international news section at Father's different postings. I would have been more recognizable as a child and teenager to Austrians and as a younger woman to Londoners.

Someone might have wondered what two well-dressed women were doing in the museum for space without kids—we couldn't have been spies without violating the first rule of spycraft: don't stand out. I might have wondered too. We were both too weary of it to be attracted to flight. We might have been drawn to the idea of space travel to Mars—the three years of it, the elemental nature of life in a capsule, so free of entanglements. And then even more so on Mars itself—life would be all about food and water and shade. There could be true freedom in that terrible confinement.

Ana approved the McDonald's for Wolf, though he usually had a vastly more refined diet. We might not ever bring the boys together, but we didn't go into that nicety. Ana understood the problem with Clint without my having to say much. She and I both treated our meetings as clandestine, secret even from our handlers, if our husbands were our handlers.

How retro that was, we both knew. It was as if we had returned to the days when Desi Arnaz controlled Lucille Ball's career—a 50's version that 60 years of feminism should surely have made a dent in it.

And yet there we were, wandering around the Space Shuttle, hiding our lives and our thoughts from our spouses as if we lived in pre-Sputnik days.

We did love the really old aircraft—Ana liked the Sopwith Camel a lot—drawn perhaps to a time when gender roles were more defined and thus seemed to be more reason for it, less arbitrariness and absoluteness in an agrarian way of life where the isolation was farm to farm—a real distance—rather than the suburban isolation house to house where the distance was imagined, imposed.

Ana had been particularly quiet the day we went there and, when we stopped to pay homage to the black spy plane, I asked her if anything was up.

"I get a little homesick sometimes," she said.

We were underneath the plane that flew so quickly and silently that, though it flew close to the ground, only its crew knew it was there.

"I don't really know that much about Montenegro," I said. "I'm afraid like most Americans, I haven't bothered to get clear on the details."

"Your father was a diplomat, no?"

"Yes, he was. He was the ambassador to Austria for much of my growing up years, so we weren't that far away. But I'm sorry to say that geography was not a strong suit when I was a teenager."

"Everything behind the wall was a—" she hesitated, looking for the word—"a blob."

We both laughed at the plosives.

"Such an inelegant word," I said. "But exactly right."

"*Le mot juste*," Ana said. "Like most of eastern Europe, we were attached to Russia after the Ottoman Wars."

"And how did the Montenegrin people like being associated with the Soviet Union?"

"You could hardly say that Tito and Stalin were best friends."

"It seems odd to me, as an American, that Russia could have so gladly gone back to being run by a dictator."

"That is something Americans don't understand. In the old part of the world, having a ruler is much more normal than not having one. There is much that is attractive in having someone else have all the responsibility."

"Believe me, I *do* understand that the conventional American view that free choice is right or even a good thing isn't universally held."

"I think you might be surprised by how many Americans don't hold with that belief."

"That sounds a bit ominous, but, oddly enough, I think there is some overlap with the research I'm doing— that too many choices overwhelm and confuse people.

Though I can't see the opposite extreme—no choice at all—as having much appeal here."

"But the progressives think that government should control the climate change, no? And the health care. So 'liberal' actually means more control?"

"While the right wingers cling to what they think of as freedom, which, in a case like the freedom to own weapons leads, ironically, to their own destruction more often than not through accident and suicide."

We watched a gang of kindergartners come through just then. The children were running wild through the open space, while the teacher and teacher's aide tried desperately to round them up.

Ana laughed at the kids—or at us.

"We are so like little children," she said. "We think that we want freedom, but, unrestricted, freedom can lead to starvation, disease, death."

"But oppressive parenting can also lead to suffering and, if it manifests as physical abuse, death."

"I'm going to have to ponder that one," Ana said.

We were arguing, but it felt good—like two smart people matching wits. We walked around the space shuttle in companionable silence.

"Your father and mother were not entirely conventional, were they?"

"No, Father was anti-Viet Nam, being a Quaker, and Mother is just conformist on the surface."

"Usually non-conformists don't become diplomats, yes?"

"Father was appointed by Bill Clinton, who, though a particularly moral person himself, was remarkably admiring of those who were."

"And I think President Clinton also liked the pretty ladies, did he not?"

"He did, indeed," I said. I didn't go into detail about the fiery flirtations Clinton and Mother could get going. "But we were talking about you and Montenegro."

"It does seem that different cultures have different tastes for choice. The Russians, it seems, miss having a tsar."

Before I could launch into a discussion of my research, I noticed that Ana had lost interest in the topic, wandered away somewhere in her mind, and wasn't listening. She looked quite wistful, maybe thinking of Montenegro, or possibly longing for fewer choices. She looked up at the underside of the great, dark Blackbird.

"They were at least mostly benevolent, the ruling families. Montenegro had a quite kind king."

"That seems to be the problem with having no choice, though," I said. "If you don't like what you get—if the ruler is corrupt—then there is no way out."

"The combination of a corrupt leader and capitalism seems an especially poisonous mixture," she said. "But," she added, turning one elegant palm up, "it still beats starvation."

I felt like there was a warning in there somewhere, but I didn't know where, or about what.

★   ★   ★

Back at the house Molly was busy sorting through the cereal. Each boy had his favorite brand to which he was devoted—until he wasn't. Then there was no power on earth that could make him eat it.

"Don't you think Jack might like Froot Loops again soon?" I asked as she tipped a nearly full box of garishly colored small circles into the trash, took out the paper bag and folded it separately, then dismantled the toucan-bearing cardboard box and put it in the recycling.

"Not soon enough," she said. "And don't imagine for a second that another boy will start to like them, either."

She might have given me a lecture on the fallacy of sunk costs—how useless it is, how ultimately nonutilitarian, to try to see an earlier choice through to its conclusion long after it had proven itself useless.

"It does seem a point of honor for each of them to heartily dislike anything any brother actually likes."

"The cereal I throw out would have fed a large percentage of London after the War," Molly said. She looked mournful about this.

"Were you even born then?"

"I was very young. There is a gastric memory. And my parents used to talk about it. Not with any sense of grievance, mind you. They were a tough lot, those who got through the War. It was the second one for many of them. Sometime, later on, my parents seemed even nostalgic for it—the simplicity of it, the essentialness.

The war, that is—not the starvation afterward."

"Interesting," I said. I saw an opening to discuss my research and I took it before Molly could get distracted. "Sheena Iyengar at Columbia did this really interesting research on choice—it's behavioral economics at its best, explaining larger forces in the human psyche by examining buying behavior. When she offered people a lot of jars of jam, they liked all the choices, but they didn't buy. When she whittled it down to three choices—then people bought. And even Richard Thaler sort of backs into a form of benign paternalism, where the ability to make really disastrous choices are eliminated and the good directions actively encouraged."

Molly was staring at me, pausing in her pantry purge.

"Interesting," she said.

"The research?"

"The connection to the War—the fact that there were few choices was actually liberating," she said.

"Do you think there is any part of that that could explain dictatorships or fascism?"

"That seems more a form of sado-masochism," Molly said.

"I'm not sure I'd go that far," I said. "But I do see that there could be a pleasure in forcing a choice on people, but I can't get my head around people *wanting* to be forced into one choice."

"I'm not sure how else you explain the rapidity with which Russia reverted to dictatorship," Molly said.

Was I the one always leading the conversation to Russia or was it this city?

"Maybe it was better than starvation," I said.

"People could have left," Molly said, "after the wall came down."

"And lots of them did," I agreed.

"Not all of them best friend material," Molly said.

I hadn't told her I was spending time with Ana.

"That might not be fair," I said.

"And it might," she said.

It didn't make much difference which way was right as one boy after another came down with strep and then I finally got it. I gave into the drinking gallons of ginger ale, or "green coke," as Isaac called it, and *Beauty and the Beast* was on endless repeat.

Clint appeared on my side of the bed one evening with the cutest puppy in his hands. I thought at first I was having a fever dream.

Clint didn't say anything—he just put her in the bed with me. She gave me a few licks with puppy breath and then settled against my back contentedly as if I were just an exceptionally large and perhaps extra-warm member of the litter she had been longing for.

Clint vanished, possibly to take up position in the bucket brigade of green coke to the boys. He took the puppy out several times and fed her and played with her enough so that she simply lay down next to me spine to spine when he brought her back, delivering unimaginable comfort.

One of those visits, he was calling her "Queenie."

By the evening of the second day of puppy my fever started to break and my mostly strep-drained boys started to show up singly or in pairs to climb into bed with me and Queenie to watch Miss Marple on endless repeat on my iPad. They didn't object to the mystery they didn't understand—my kids weren't much whiners. Queenie accepted them as full-fledged members of the litter. I was surrounded on all sides when Clint came to bed.

"Where did she come from?" I asked as he undressed and cleared the way of sleeping boys and puppy to get to me.

"I know you always wanted a dog," he said.

"We moved too much when I was a kid. Most countries wouldn't let us bring one."

"I thought maybe you were lonely." He pulled me into his arms. The puppy made accommodations and nestled down again.

"I was." I crawled as close as I could get to Clint, my head under his chin, the light weight of the puppy bone and flesh half on and half off him, like the slight tap of a magic wand.

I dropped into the warm, dark sleep of forgetfulness as if dropped into an oubliette.

The next week we watched Clint train the puppy as we recovered. I kept everyone home for the whole week.

Clint had managed to avoid getting sick and Molly had miraculously also escaped, though I suspect she might have gotten a mild from, the kind that just drags you down without knocking you out.

"What on earth did you need a puppy for?" she asked. She was feeding Queenie little bits of hot dog for doing nothing at all the same time she spoke reprovingly.

"We didn't have anyone in the under-one category," I said. "Plus you needed someone to carry about like the Queen carries a Corgi."

She sailed out the kitchen door with Queenie tucked under her arm to let the puppy run in the November sun without comment.

Clint handed me a cup of loose-leaf Irish breakfast tea. I wasn't recovered enough for coffee.

"She isn't a Corgi," he pointed out. "And one of these days she'll be too big to carry."

"How big do Belgians get?" I asked.

The boys were enchanted by PBS that morning, though signs of recovery—and thus chaos—were beginning to emerge like shoots in the spring.

"She'll be around 50 pounds—not too big. I'll show you how to keep training her."

"I don't know much about dogs, but aren't Belgians used in war?"

"They do bomb-detection," Clit said. He seemed a little evasive. I kept my eyes on him. "They are also attack dogs."

"And guard?" I asked.

"And guard," he said.

"Who named her Queenie?" I said.

"Don't you remember?" he asked.

I didn't and I didn't ask.

Whatever had been going on before we all got sick was still going on. And getting worse.

Clint continued working with Queenie long after she had the basic house-training down pat. He drew me in as he went.

We spent hours with her. The boys were allowed to watch but not participate. Clint wanted Queenie to know who the alpha dog was. It was clearly him, but in his absence, me. The idea filled me with dread.

We started with simple commands to sit, lie down, stay. Then things got more complicated—musical carpet squares where she sat on a diminishing number of carpet squares on command. She loved to be told what to do and obeyed with a military crispness that was comical. Molly continued to tote her around when she wasn't training and fed her hot dog bits. The entire household had fallen in love with her long before she got taken away one day and came home with the ability to alert to practically any sound outside the norm.

Granted, there were few, our house being so cacophonous. But I could tell she had a measure of maturity then that came with her new job and she took it seriously. She continued to sleep spine to spine with me as I slept against Clint, but I could feel a tension in her that marked the end of her pure puppyhood.

Clint had been home much more often while we suffered through strep and then entered training. We were cooking dinner together one night when Molly was over at Mother's. The boys were all back in school, but they were still a bit wan and I worried that Dylan might come down with it again. Though Clint was usually a very stern enforcer of school attendance, he let my more loosey-goosey approach to parenting prevail that November. We pulled them out of extracurricular activities and allowed a lot more TV than normal. They were littered around the sunroom, Queenie deep among them, watching the millionth showing of *Lady and the Tramp*.

"What are you singing?" Clint asked me one day.

"Me and Bobbie McGee," I said. He looked blank. I wasn't sure Clint had listened to a lot of country rock in his youth. "'Freedom's just another word for nothing left to lose,'" I sang to him.

"Hm," he said. He used his eyebrow on me.

"I've been thinking about the philosophy behind that. What if it's true? What if freedom isn't what we thought it was. What if we aren't actually free? Of what if freedom isn't really such a good thing?"

"Choice within limits," Clint said. "Choice guided by facts, history, science."

"Good lord," I said, "have you been rummaging around in my head?"

"You'd be surprised where I've been rummaging," he said. He was such a cool customer, so steely, it was that much funnier when he said something sexy.

But the truth was that I had been having some misgivings about my behavior. Maybe the way Clint had taken care of us while we were sick, or the profound understanding of our need for a dog, the soul need Queenie satisfied, had led me to a renewed loyalty. Or maybe the questions Ana asked at Udvar-Hazy about how dangerous too much freedom could be. Or maybe just the fever had burned some rebellion out of me. All I wanted was to be home with my family.

"Have you heard about Connie Edgerton's condition?" Clint asked as he prepped the chicken for the grill.

"No—what is up with her?" Connie Edgerton, the VP's wife from Illinois, was not anyone I had the remotest connection with. "She's always been frail. Didn't some opposition research turn up some health issues in the campaign?"

"Depression," Clint said. "Hospitalized once for it."

"What is going on now?" I was enjoying the rare game of gossip with my husband.

"She seems to be losing her memory. Edgerton is considering making an announcement."

"That would be a first. No one ever admits to anything like that," I said.

"Has Ana said anything about it?"

I stopped tearing lettuce. There was a lifetime of silence.

"Is she a friend of Connie Edgerton's," I finally said.

"Close friends," Clint said. He was brushing marinade very slowly.

"I didn't know that."

"Didn't know they were so close?"

"Didn't know people had friends in DC."

Clint picked up the platter and went into the garden.

CHAPTER THIRTEEN

Adam Loosed

The next day the headlines in the Post read that Christopher Edgerton announced that his wife was ill. In the article he asked for everyone's prayers. The photo was the official inaugural picture. Ana was sitting beside Connie Edgerton, whether by protocol or choice, it would be hard to say.

I thought I'd put my prayers in by going to see Father Bream.

"What do you think about Edgerton?"

We were in his office, the late fall sun shining through the leaded casement windows onto the dust motes our sitting in the upholstered chairs had raised.

"Sad for him—possibly not for her."

"Why not?"

"It might get her out of politics. She never seemed to like the life that much."

"Any more than Ana Trent does."

"That is a very interesting friendship you have."

"I won't even bother asking how you know. No need to be coy. It's a damned strange relationship for me to have. Adam Trent is everything I hate in a politician. Wrong-headed, superficial, self-interested."

"In a nutshell."

"I don't mind real conservatives—they at least have a recognizable agenda. They are among my grandparents' best friends. People who are ideologues, though—those just going for the emotional appeal—"

"While taking home all the jacks for themselves."

"Those I can't abide."

"Adam Trent seems to be among those."

"But not Ana. She seems genuine. Intelligent. She's thought things through. She might have a different point of view—but she has a difficult history. She even seems sort of noble."

"It is a great mistake of liberal politics to believe that every point of view has equal validity."

"Do you mean Ana?"

Father Bream seemed, once again, to be reading my mind. My rebellion against Clint or whatever of the earlier fall seemed to have been burned out of me with the strep fever. I was sorry I'd gone against his implied wishes that I not consort with someone who might not be trustworthy.

"Why did you get close?"

"It seemed like she needed me. Then it was just interesting. And I felt bizarrely lonely. I know how improbable that sounds with a houseful of boys. And Molly and Mother."

"And Clint."

"Clint hasn't been around a lot this fall until we all got sick. Something seems to be cooking."

"It may have to do with the VP."

"What do you know about it?"

"Nothing—nothing at all." Father Bream put up his hands. "I can't imagine he thinks much of your friendship with Ana."

"Who is either of you to decide my friends?" I said. Guilt no doubt fueled the heat that flooded my face and neck again.

"We wouldn't dare," Bream laughed. "It would be worth our lives!"

I cooled down just as quickly.

"He doesn't know. I felt guilty enough about it not to tell him."

"Says a lot."

"I don't think it will continue. I feel like someone was spying on us. Could have been Clint."

"What could you expect?"

"Indeed," I said. Because what could you?

"Coffee?" the text said.

I ignored it.

Another ping.

"Arlington. Movie Tavern. Melissa McCarthy?"

I told myself it was a choice. I didn't tell myself it was a good one.

Ana and I sat side by side in the movie house, tables up in front of us with greasy burgers and fries on them. We were enjoying them as only women who habitually watch their figures would. Melissa McCarthy's hilarious spy movies—several years old by then—was playing. The irony of the least probable spy being pressed into service wasn't lost on me. Not only was I least probable, I would be a complete failure. I wasn't spying on anyone—really—and didn't notice when someone was spying on me. At that point, whoever was watching me could go tell Clint—and Molly and Father Bream, for that matter—I was consuming the whole week's calories in one meal. Not that Clint would care. The strict diet dictates came from my class, not his. There was no one in the theatre but us.

"The boys are all back at school?" Ana said.

"Finally. Has Wolf resisted getting sick so far?"

"He has—how do you say it—rude good health." Ana's face looked rueful in the movie screen light. "He never gets sick so I can keep him home. I miss taking care of him like when he was a baby."

"I know what you mean. You could try a dog. Clint got me one. A puppy. But don't just try one. You are theirs for life."

I could tell I'd lost her. Maybe they ate dogs in Montenegro.

"I hear Connie Edgerton is going to need some care."

"That was what I wanted to explain," Ana whispered fiercely. We could easily have been talking out loud, but we were both constrained by the rule of place.

"You don't need to explain anything," I said, quite insincerely.

"I do, though. I don't want you to think I agree with the Edgerton's politics."

I let that one alone. Why wouldn't she agree with Edgerton and his wife? They were all in the same party. And why would she think I was judging her on that if I hadn't judged her for her husband, who was much worse?

"Connie Edgerton was kind to me when I came here."

"She seems like a pretty cold fish."

The French fries were salty and just the right greasy. Ana was savoring one of hers too.

"She wasn't always so." Ana turned up that elegant palm again. "She used to be human."

"I'd think your politics and hers would be in line with each other. You're all in the same party."

"As if that made us any more alike than in yours," Ana admonished.

It had been a pretty remarkably stupid statement on my part.

"I don't know why you felt like you had to explain. Did you think your friendship with Connie Edgerton would bother me?"

"I thought you might feel betrayed," she said.

"I'm not sure over what." That at least was sincere. "I was feeling bad over suddenly not seeing you."

"You were sick. And the children."

"It turns out my husband knew all along we were hanging out. Whether by spying on us or intuition."

"He has you spied on." It was a statement.

"You make it sound like that's normal."

"He just wants you safe," she said.

I looked at her beauty. What did she know about my husband?

"If Adam wanted me safe, he'd have me spied on," she added.

"You make it sound like a good thing."

"Where I come from anything that makes you safe—that is a good thing."

"Adam doesn't have spied on, does he?"

Ana laughed. "Adam might not care that much. Or he might not be that smart."

I wasn't sure why I thought it—Ana certainly appeared to be subservient—but I had the sense he might not dare.

My phone buzzed in my bag. It was Sidwell.

"Sorry—the boys' school is calling." I went into the hall to return it.

"Jack needs to come home. I guess he wasn't recovered enough," I said when I went back in.

"Of course," Ana said. She helped me get my coat on. "We will visit again, I hope."

"Of course, we will," I said. "I wouldn't leave now except you know how it is."

"Even with the very best of housekeepers, you are going to worry about your baby."

"Take care," I said.

I hurried into town and arrived at the office in record time. It helped that there was no traffic. Why anyone thought it would be a good idea to design a major city like a wheel, with spokes radiating from a center, was beyond me. It meant there was no direct way anywhere.

I got Jack from the nurse's office—she reported that he had come from class saying his throat hurt and he was really tired.

I felt his head as I strapped him into his seat.

"You don't feel too hot," I said. "I think I'll save the doctor for later."

"Ice cream," he said.

"Okay, that would probably help your throat."

"And a hamburger," he said matter of factly.

"You can't be all that sick," I said.

I got him a Happy Meal and ice cream cone. We went home.

He had eaten his meal in the sunroom and was lying fully stretched out, his hands folded on his chest, and his head on Queenie.

"I think maybe you just wanted to come home," I said.

"I thought you might be lonely," he said.

He got up and came over. Queenie shepherded him. He climbed onto my lap.

"With Queenie and Molly home? How could I be lonely?"

"I thought you might be lonely for me," he said. He curled into my body, his slightly sticky Lands End shirt adhering to my leather jacket.

I put my nose in his curly blonde hair and breathed deeply.

"You were right," I said.

But he had already fallen asleep.

★　　★　　★

It didn't take long for Adam Trent to cause controversy over the Edgerton rumors. As Speaker, his job was theoretically to bring the factions of his own party together. But he had a genuine talent for finding the most divisive pressure point and then to press and hold on it. Though Edgerton was a member of his own party and indeed the vote tie-breaker in the Senate and the person who presided over joint sessions of the houses, none of those facts entered Trent's calculations.

When he came into the role of Speaker he very quickly made it clear that he was a sort of mad sheep dog. Where a sane one's job would be to round the wandering sheep up and keep them safe from the wolf, Adam seemed to delight in driving them in different directions. The fact that they were his own seemed to delight him even more.

The question became, then, was he, like Gabriel Oak's mad young sheep dog, going to drive them *en masse* over a cliff to die on the rocks below?

Washington had long been engaged in a battle whose terms of engagement were who could most effectively stalemate whom. If that was not a very productive approach, it was also not usually very harmful. As long as action that was taken was done by executive order by the mild and centrist president, things seemed to go along.

I hadn't realized how much the vice president had applied an extra layer of balm until he, in effect, took a leave of absence to spend time with his rapidly failing wife. Slowly it dawned on people inside the Beltway if not outside that Adam Trent was having more influence with the President and that things were getting more manic—more legislation came through directed by the White House, more executive orders issued—and they seemed to be bending toward more and more havoc.

If Congress could be said to be the most volatile arm of government because there were so many members and, in the House, each served only two years, and the executive branch the one where things could happen quickly, with Adam at the helm of half of one branch and heavily influencing another, the Supreme Court became the last bastion of sanity—and a distant and slow moving one at that.

Immigration, health care, taxes, civil rights, infrastructure, wars around the world, rapid response to natural disasters, and climate change—everything intensified all of a sudden that late fall. And everywhere that mad dog Adam Trent seemed to be at the center—causing problems even in international bodies of order.

My father's usually serene face started to crease with worry and Mother—whose family had so often been in seats of power as the world shifted and changed—had just a trace of fear around her mouth which she tried to convince me was anxiety that the Thanksgiving feast was going to devolve into chaos. She did have performance-anxiety—it always made each event more gorgeous than the one before. I went back to Father Bream's.

"Mother is worried," I told Father Bream. "Father is reading Huxley. Clint is gone again all the time. And I'm not feeling that great."

"I might not be much of a calming influence," Father Bream said. "I'd probably have more grey hairs—if I had any hairs at all."

"You Jesuits are too much of this world," I said.

"It's hard not to be when you live in the middle of it."

"That must make us political snobs—thinking DC is the center of the world."

"It has been for a while, albeit often a wobbly one," he said. He looked out at the dark rain pouring down the leaded window. "Have you asked your new best friend?"

"Ana doesn't know anything. I don't think she and Adam talk. She's more of a decoration for him."

"No smart woman from eastern Europe is politically naïve."

"You'd probably also say no woman has no influence on her husband. But I don't think that's always true. I neither know about nor have any real influence on Clint's behavior."

"Sometimes you have to choose faith."

"I do believe that," I said. "But I don't know what else I believe. Adam Trent seems to be driving the house and now the President to do what they said in their campaigns, although everyone knows campaign rhetoric and what you are actually going to do are two different things."

"Like Macbeth, he is being driven not even by what he

thinks he wants or thinks is right anymore, but by what he *said* he was going to do," Bream said, reminding me of my dissertation.

"Most campaign promises are pretty outlandish. And wasn't it Lady Macbeth who goaded her husband into keeping his word?" I had just lost the influence argument, by my own hand.

I paused only to get a meaningful stare from the priest.

"At least Clint doesn't make promises he doesn't have any intention of keeping. He just doesn't make very many promises," I said.

"He is a man of action—what he does tells you what he believes."

"He got me a guard dog."

"There you go," Father Bream said.

Then he looked worried.

The weird thing is," I told Clint, "he said he was making mischief on purpose."

We were in bed and had managed a child-free moment. Even dog-free. Queenie had abandoned us for the other baby in the house. Dylan had recently graduated to a low child bed, which mean he could wander and also that the puppy could easily climb in with him. For reasons I couldn't remember, I had chosen that moment to talk to Clint about Adam Trent.

"When did Trent say that?" Clint asked.

"At the Halloween party," I said. "Not long before you came over the wall."

"Surprised you, didn't I?" He ran his hand along my hip and grinned.

"You did that," I said. "I was going to be in a right rage with you for not showing up—as soon as I took off my hostess personality. And then there you were."

"You aren't much good at covering up," he said. He was slowly uncovering me. "And I've always sort of liked your temper."

"That would have been something—to see a well-connected hostess at a smart DC party go off like a firecracker at her own event."

"Tagine would have been flying," Clint said. He was getting down to business.

"Vodka mint tea flung," I said. "Mother would have been appalled."

"Molly would have just gotten the mop."

"There were some wild moments in our earlier fights," I said. Was his bicep even more pronounced?

"There were some strange things thrown," he agreed. We laughed.

"Damned up hormones were set loose," I said. "Later on, they were corralled by multiple births." I paused for a slight shiver from Clint's touch at my waist. "Is it possible they are going away? I've been having hot flashes. I have mixed feelings about that. It might not be so bad—if it didn't also mean I was getting older and marching toward death." Early foreplay sometimes made me loquacious.

"What exactly did Adam Trent say?" Clint asked. He had paused in his body work.

"He said he was disruptive on purpose—he knew things needed to be shaken up because they had gotten stuck."

"He sees himself as some sort of joker?"

"He made the more dignified reference to the Norse god Loki."

"The trickster god."

"The weird thing was that it sounded very plausible. What if that was the only way out of gridlock? Even my father had had to admit that the stalemate was starting to look baked in, with the extremes just getting more powerful and the middle eroding."

"And I know how much your father hates change."

"But you don't seem persuaded. Is there any chance that Adam is making deliberate choices?"

"I think his choices are deliberate all right," Clint said. "The chance that they are going to be constructive in the long run—that I seriously doubt. And I think there is more at play than that."

"Do you think there is any chance he could be working for someone else? Like Russia? I know people have thought that," I said.

"Russia seems to have lost its hold over the West, particularly America, since we began fracking and didn't need the oil and gas from them we had before," Clint said. "I wouldn't put it past them to look for someone they could use."

"But how?" I said.

"Oh, they know our Achilles heel—the deep division that can be exacerbated, widened. They have read history. And they know mischief better than anyone."

"But how could Adam have gotten involved? He has no Russian connections."

"He has plenty—most of his money comes from there."

"But surely he is being watched for any surreptitious connections."

"Yes, he is that," Clint said.

He forgot what he was doing for a moment when Trent's name came up. I was pretty sure he wasn't going to tell me more than that, but he'd already told me more than he'd told me before. I kept quiet.

"As long as he isn't disruptor-in-chief," Clint said more to himself than to me. His hand had begun to move again at my waist. He slipped it up under my nightgown and began to stroke my breast. My back arched toward him and he gave my nipple a slight pinch.

"How about some mischief of our own?" I said.

CHAPTER FOURTEEN
Thanksgiving Party Plan

"What's fracking got to do with it?" I asked Clint the next morning. It was Saturday. We had managed to get the boys through breakfast and into the car for Molly to take them to the soccer fields. Clint and I would go later, but we were taking a rare moment to be together alone on a weekend day. The first hour of soccer Saturday was mostly the kids milling around anyway. We were having a second or possibly tenth cup of coffee in Clint's study. It had been a long time since we'd had a lazy political talk—the tension between us earlier in the fall had completely broken through and I was sitting on his lap while he clicked easily through some screens on his double-monitored computer system. The sites all had to do with the success of the fracking industry.

"I'm not sure," Clint said. "But the fact that our old friend Russia seems to have become very environmentally conscious is odd."

"They are anti-fracking? It seems pretty obvious—doesn't that make us less dependent on them and some of their best buddies in the Middle East?"

"Iran and Syria. Clearly that's what's behind their

newfound environmental awareness. What concerns me the most is what way they will find to try to get control over us back."

"Without oil to hold over our heads."

"Fracking has made us less dependent on them."

"And that would be intolerable, I suppose? What will they resort to?"

"The obvious one is debt. The extent that we owe other countries money is the extent to which we are vulnerable. But Russia is broke itself."

"They'll look for cracks they can widen, any way to weaken us?"

"And all of the West. The nostalgia for the Soviet Union is strong. When oil fails, they'll turn to anything. Stalin was certainly a terrible person and god-awful dictator. But the shambles that Russia became after the Soviet Union fell was ripe for criminal corruption. The oligarchs seized the wealth there was in oil and put in power the one person who had the smarts to find the West's Achilles heel."

"Who would and could resort to anything. Including language and misinformation, my favorites."

"And emotion, especially doubt and division. These are the weapons of the torturer. But they are also the hallmarks of a free society."

"Where doubt and division are most easily activated."

"In the post-truth age—when everything is relative—it's readily done."

"He who rules the emotions rules the world."

"It wasn't always that way."

"It wasn't always that way."

"In America."

"It was always that way in behavioral economics."

"Now that you mention it, maybe it *was* always that way—especially in America."

It was only two weeks until the extravaganza at Evermay, which meant that Mother turned into the Vietnamese general at Dien Bien Phu who defeated the much better armored French troops, with the whole idea of a holiday dinner as the enemy and her intelligence, will, and determination the only defenses between her and annihilation by social failure.

Of course, she had never failed before—but that didn't stop her from full scale military planning. She was one of DC's finest hostesses and recognized in several European capitals as hostess extraordinaire—yet still she imagined defeat every time. Flying in the face of the laws of positive thinking, her disaster preparedness resulted always in stunning success. She mustered her troops and executed a brilliant strategy whose secret weapon was Mother herself.

I had been one of her lieutenants for years, up through Boys Three and Four. Then I'd fallen away and let Molly and Jane take over the front line offensive. Now that the boys had gotten a little older and I didn't seem inclined to more, Mother assumed I would return to duty.

And thus it was.

She had held off calling me in till she really needed me that year—her only concession to my large family (never mind my academic work—what academic work?)—now it was time.

I was ready.

We were all apparently well, Clint and I had been restored to sanity, and behavioral economics were feeling a little too real to me as we went into the holiday season. I preferred a little light menu-planning over my latest research on politics and choice at that moment.

Mother and I met at the Peacock Café to war game.

When Antoine has us set up with our still water and lemons (someone had told Mother that Perrier eroded tooth enamel, so that was the end of that), she opened up her impressively small Chanel diary with the minuscule pen to review the plans she, Molly, and Jane had already strategized.

"I think we have room in the dining room for everyone without resorting to the reception room," Mother was saying as she took a tiny bite of sole.

We both looked at my hamburger.

"It's never too early to start banking calories," Mother's look said, though she was far too well-bred to criticize her daughter out loud in public.

I ate a French fry out of daughterly defiance.

"Hopeless," the small shake of her head said. "If I tell her one thing she is guaranteed to do the opposite."

This was such a tired old war between us and we'd been at it so long that in our hearts we had come to see the other's point of view if not embrace it. There was no need for any of it to be spoken.

At only two weeks out from the event—which happened on the actual Thanksgiving Day—we were in full battle mode.

Many people stayed in DC that weekend. Some were international, so there was no event to go home for. The politicians who had jets of their own often stayed in town, not because they had to but because to them "home" was where their votes were, not their voters. And many people would actually fly in from around the world to be at Mother's Thanksgiving. All of them desperately hoped for an invitation to Evermay's Thanksgiving, the hottest ticket in town, priced well beyond any amount of money, requiring class, not cash.

Mother had started the tradition just after Father retired from his last posting.

"How go the RSVPs?" I asked Mother.

At two weeks out Mother had the guest list emblazoned on her mind. She whipped out her iPad and stylus anyway because she liked to. I didn't know where she'd found the Chanel cover for it.

"Let's see," she said, pretending to eat some sole "The diplomatic side has filled out well. We have Austria, France, Switzerland, and Belgium all coming. Of course, we were posted to all those countries, so we do expect them—practically have their thrones in place, though you really shouldn't say that about Switzerland—they would be revolted at the idea of royalty."

"Such snobs, those Swiss," I laughed.

"You can laugh," Mother said with her sober face, "but the Swiss *are* terrible snobs."

"And not that humorous either," I said.

"Well, the Italian Swiss can get loose, but those Zurichers—probably not a laugh among them. Anyway, the ambassador now is from Geneva, so you can practice your French on him."

"I'm sure you have him seated next to someone else—someone whose influence he can use or who can use him. I don't think I need Suisse right now for anything and if Clint does I would be both surprised and have no idea."

"I haven't started on the seating charts yet," Mother said. "I saved that for you."

"Jane will know far better than I at this point. Dylan was just an infant at this time last year. I don't think I helped at all."

"Yes, but you have time on your hands this year, don't you? Surely you aren't thinking about gestating again. Five is enough for any woman. And five boys." Mother went off the rails for a minute about my household population. "And now a dog? Surely she doesn't take up that much time."

"Queenie does take some time—the walks and all—but her training is going along at a really fast pace—father than for most Belgians even, the trainer said. And Molly and I have a little competition over who gets to walk her. So, no, Queenie isn't eating up my time."

"And the gestating?" Mother said.

"I might be getting ready to go through menopause," I said.

"Well, talk to your friends, dear. That was too long ago for me to remember."

I knew I could get my mother off delicate topics by bringing up menopause. She was very comfortable with all things feminine as long as that meant clothes, jewelry, hair, international politics, and society. But biology was never her thing.

"Does Ana Trent talk about such things?" Mother said. "She seems to have all that under control."

"What do you mean by that?"

"She only has the one child. And she dresses so austerely, even severely."

"Unlike my clothes, you mean?"

I had on my Cartier rings that day—the ones with rubies, emeralds, sapphires, and diamonds all thrown together. And my dress was coral—an orange that didn't go with my red hair.

Mother refused the bait.

"She seems almost military—her posture so upright. There is something rigid there, even dictatorial. As if she has herself under very tight control."

"She's a good mom and has a sense of humor once you get to know her."

"Which you have done."

Antoine arrived just then to refill our water and make

the required offer of dessert.

"Et tu, Brute," I said. "You too are going to get on my back about Ana?"

"Clint doesn't like your friendship?" she said after a second's processing. She suddenly looked very dismayed.

"No, he doesn't. And I have no idea why not. He isn't in the habit of interfering in my friendships."

"I can't imagine he would," she said. "Though I also can't imagine how you two have so much understanding of each other with him gone so much."

"It isn't just the being gone—it's the secrecy. Like not knowing why he doesn't trust Ana. Is it a personal or a work thing? I don't know and, worse, no amount of time or research will make any difference—I'll never know."

"I don't think Clint has a personal life outside of you and the kids," Mother said. "It must be hard not to share his work."

"It makes me crazy."

"I meant for him, daughter. He must feel very lonely."

I was brought up short. I'd never thought about it that way—the isolation he must feel, how no one really knew what he was doing, maybe not even one single superior.

"Do you know something about Ana I don't?" I said to cover.

"Not a thing," Mother said. "Other than she's eastern European and married to the parvenu Adam Trent. It's just a feeling."

"And she and Adam are having a lot of influence with the President right now."

"How so?"

"With the VP out of the office so much with his wife. Adam seems to have assumed some of the role."

What made me think Mother knew all about that already?

"That isn't so strange," Mother said. "He *is* next in line."

I was gazing with longing at the cheesecake with blueberries Antoine was delivering to the table next to us. But I didn't want to be responsible for my mother's cardiac infraction. I shook my head a little to clear the vision.

"How is Connie Edgerton doing?" I asked.

Her mother, though considerably older than mine, was among the lesser DC hostesses that followed Mother.

"I don't know," Mother said. "But we'll soon find out."

I plunked my demitasse cup down too hard.

"The Edgertons have confirmed for Thanksgiving," Mother said.

Mother set me the task of first pass at the seating arrangements.

I knew from long experience that whatever I did would definitely be just a first draft and she would change it all to suit the vision she already had dreamed. Like boiling water when a baby is being born, the job was more something to give me something to do while the real work was going on in Mother's head.

Part puzzle, part test of my abilities as a hostess, creating the seating arrangements could always give me a sort of pleasurable social headache. The challenge was to get the ranking right, with the most powerful near the front—the podium if there was to be a talk, the windows to the east garden in summer, the tables nearest the cavernous fireplace in winter.

The usual challenge was in discerning what was meant by power—those who had the powerful positions or those who actually wielded the actual power—not always the same thing.

In the olden days, husband and wives would always be at the same table but never next to each other. Now women had their own power—often at a very different level from their husband—so they might be at different tables, but you wanted to avoid a marital spat on the way home, if possible. Shades of distinction called for great discernment.

Then there were the CIA staff whose positions were murky. Although CIA parties were closed to anyone without top security clearance, a few well-trained top spies were allowed to socialize discreetly. The problem was that their rank was a mystery—their bios were nowhere to be found on the internet and it was, naturally, useless to ask Clint. Still, you were expected to place them respectfully, not clump them together at a convenient table in the shadows.

And then there was the issue of the fact that this was a

private dinner and, unlike at state dinners where position and rank not only followed the obvious rules but also you wanted no uproar at all, at Mother's dinners there was always an element of well-calculated spice—a wild "hare" released every few tables.

But this dinner was turning out to have one of the wildest—what Connie Edgerton might do or say at any time. Rumor had it that her depression had an element of Tourette's to it, as if a lifetime of proper political behavior had been one of the first things to slip as she let go of her attachment to the daily. And there was really no way to calculate that.

Clint came up behind me at my command table in the sunroom. He didn't say anything.

"Do you like my seating plan?"

"I'm not sure I like your doing it at all," he said.

He sat, slumped uncharacteristically in his arm chair across from me.

I had taken my mother's words about Clint's loneliness to heart and was determined not to get my back up.

"I'd be insulted—you've never been the kind of husband who thought he could tell me what to do—so something must be up."

"And you've never been the kind of wife who would do it if I did tell her. And, yes, something is up."

"I'd ask what, but you wouldn't tell me. Could you tell me what is wrong with Mother's party specifically?"

"Nothing, usually. Her parties are not only entertaining but they are also great places to understand what is really going on. She has maintained the old ways—she invites such an inclusive guest list most of the time it ends up being quite a catholic assembly."

"That's the common noun, 'catholic,' not the proper," I said unnecessarily. "I've always enjoyed that too—seeing the usually invisible market for us behavioral economists at work—the conversations of desire and satisfaction of desire that takes place in the cocktail hour when people mingle is a particularly rich field for research."

"And the repudiation of desire—that can be the most telling. But I'm always interested in the dinner arrangements. Your mother has an uncanny ability to mix and match people at dinner so that those sustained conversations—who is animated, who is bored, who turns away from the person on the left too soon, who tries to talk around the person on the right—tell a whole collection of short stories."

I emailed my seating chart draft to Mother. The boys were spending the night there, celebrating wellness, and Molly was out for the evening.

"Some years, those stories were set in motion by yours truly," I said. I indicated the spread of sheets in front of me showing sketches of tables and various penciled attempts at drawing a human design.

"I might have guessed you were the puppeteer—or the Scheherazade," he said.

He and I had been carrying on the discussion about choice that Father Bream—and Molly and Ana—and I had going. We had been focused mostly on political choice and the ways in which poverty and instability opened the door to fascism, but we had also spent some time on the ways in which extreme libertarianism could also allow for grossly mistaken ideas to take hold. Clint had read my dissertation back when I'd been writing it and he became intrigued by the use of language and story to both deceive and to convey the truth. We had temporarily exhausted the subject at the moment.

One thing led to another and, not for the first time, we ended up entangled on the thick oriental in the sunroom. I never could resist Cint's compliments. There was a gas log fireplace we turned on so that we could lie there without cover, the moment of spontaneous, uninterrupted passion so rare.

His body had remained lean and muscular—he owed that to his job and the gym there—while mine had softened and become even more voluptuous than when I was young. His big hand rested on my hip as we lay there and occasionally strayed upward to the full round breast that had bloomed over five pregnancies and nursing five hungry boys. He stroked and cupped it so that, even sated, my nipple stood up.

"You never said why you were worried about this dinner," I said.

"Because there is too much instability," he said. "There is really no way of knowing how it will end."

I don't think Clint had any idea what would happen, but I should have paid more attention. That was for sure.

★　　★　　★

Mother was frantic when I got there the next morning. Dressed in casual Ralph Lauren, she was, to begin with, at less than her most chic. Her hair had come down from the politically incorrect antique ivory chopsticks apparently holding it up. Delaney had seen that the boys got breakfast and then walked them home to a waiting Molly.

"There are just too many people coming," she said. We were in her morning room, the cool November sun barely making an impression the lady-like Empire desk Josephine Bonaparte might have sat at. She was looking at my draft seating charts.

"I think we might spill into the reception room. And that would *not* do. What tables would we put there? The Party Place would have nothing suitable. I've been through their warehouse a thousand times. I see *no* way to decide who sits where. The Congressional interns? Do we stick them at the bottom of the room? That would be just plain *rude*."

"Plus some of them are the most interesting—if they haven't become terminal ass-kissers already, then they might have some idealism left," I said. "I've already put a few of them with ambassadors."

"Of course, dear, but what if there are too many?"

I knew I was taking my life in my hands with the next suggestion.

"You could always go to ten-tops."

Mother looked at me over her half-glasses with her "surely you jest" look. Tables that seated more than eight were taboo—there was no way a general conversation could be had across that distance.

"Don't worry, Mother," I said. She had permitted my comment to pass without comment. "You always worry about overpopulation, but it never actually happens."

"What about the *unbelievable* people who show up without RSVPing?"

"They are always balanced by the people who accepted but didn't show up," I said.

"Yes, of course. Thank you for reminding me. But Jane will have a nervous breakdown if we don't have close to the right numbers. She will not tolerate a crowded table."

"I'll call every single person to confirm—"

"Would you, darling? All the one who accepted and all the non-responses? That would be so lovely." She gazed abstractedly out the window, allowing her nerves to recover for a second. "You won't let Molly do that? It must matter so much that it's you."

We were back to nerves.

"Let's go look at the dining room," I said.

At a certain point in the party planning, thinking became dangerous. There was no way I was going to call 40 people personally. Molly and Jane would take their share. I wondered if Jules was at an age where he could take on a short list.

Mother stood next to her chair at the far end of the dining room, near the windows. Her petite figure was outlined against the early northern light. She looked like a lovely, social sprite.

I walked across the highly polished oak floor, hearing its comforting, untrod early morning crack and creak, as if all the generations walked lightly with me. The china in the huge bow front cabinet chimed together as good china and crystal will. The sound in the room echoed and reverberated as only big, old rooms can. Even the slant to the floor that would send my children in unexpected directions in their roller chairs and caused every one of them to be momentarily terrified before they were delighted—even that reassured me.

I wasn't sure how my mother had gotten across the room without waking it up as I was, but I knew from long ago that it wasn't always wise to question things that happened around Mother. This was her family's home and the ancestors might just have picked her up and carried her across.

However it happened, she was across it. She was stepping out imaginary table tops, looking at my draft chart, and counting seats.

We went over it and over it, moving our phantom guests again, adjusting the draft chart again, moving others until the chemistry began to seem right to her.

"I hope you don't mind—it looks like we completely changed your plan," Mother said. I couldn't tell if it was a specious apology.

"Not at all, Mother," I said, laughing. "If I was going to be wounded by your changing my seating charts, I'd have died long ago. I always learn a lot."

"So does your husband," she said. "I think he uses my parties for research."

"I wouldn't say you're wrong," I said. "I think he might use everything for research."

We sat down in the Polish and English ambassadors' seats at the head table that was always there. Marie brought us coffee on a pewter tray. I doctored mine. Mother stirred hers to keep me company.

Mother's eyebrow was up.

"Normally, you know, agents' families wouldn't have so much social life. Our kids aren't even supposed to go on sleepovers."

"I can see that," Mother said. "Too much vulnerability either going to someone's house or having other kids in. Who knows, generally, what kids will get into or say."

"So the fact that Clint married into DC society caused some consternation at first."

"I remember," Mother said.

"Our parties seemed like something we could control—and lord knows how many agents were actually there. I suppose Clint knows. But your parties—they were so well-established and so big and everyone important comes to them. I think they still worry him. And this year seems worse than usual, with the instability at the top."

"The vice president and poor Connie," Mother said. She looked out the windows at the end of the long room. A faint worry line appeared between her brows. "You put Clint right next to me, didn't you, dear?"

"Of course. Where he always is."

"Let's be sure to keep him there," she said. "I always enjoy his company."

"You enjoy flirting with him."

"Yes. Yes, I do," she said.

But there was no flirtatiousness in Mother's face as she said it.

★   ★   ★

"I want to understand the irrationality of choice," I said. I meant what I said. But Father Bream and I both started laughing.

"The curse of the intellectual: let's be rational about irrationality," he said.

We were perched at the island in my kitchen as Molly cooked behind us and the boys wheeled in and out of the kitchen and in circles all around us. For someone used to the quiet life of the priest, Father Bream's equanimity in my house's chaos always surprised me. It was one of the many contradictions his Jesuitical mind seemed to hold lightly—the deep love of the spiritual and the hearty embrace of the worldly.

"Well, you've got me there, but I'm pretty sure the whole field of behavioral economics was born of that impulse," I said.

"You're right," he agreed.

"She does often have quite a good grasp on the obvious," Molly announced from the stove.

"Thank you for saying so," I said, fake huffy. "What I want to know now is do the same principles we study in behavioral economics apply to politics?"

"Generally speaking, it doesn't do to cross discipline boundaries without an abundance of caution," Bream said. "But I'm intrigued."

"We know from Alan Lichtman's work that elections that seem irrational, as in not based in logic, also follow a pattern. And from studies on authoritarians and the intolerance and injustice they bring—the personal—come out of people's fear that they will be treated unjustly if they don't inflict it on someone else first and are thus also predictable."

"Lichtman identified several keys, I believe, that predict election outcomes. One was—as I recall—the force of personality."

There was a great crash in the living room that set Queenie into a barking frenzy. In the kitchen three adults paused until five individual boy voices could be identified as alive and well. Then we all went back to our tasks.

"So, a completely controlling—even a dictatorial or totalitarian source—could create a sense of choice that was fake," Molly said.

"And American 'individualism' and 'choice' that is based in not being told what to do could be in someone else's control," Father Bream said.

We all stopped talking. The stew bubbled.

Clint came through the back door.

"Who died?" he said, looking from one appalled face to another.

"Democracy did," Father Bream said, quite cheerfully, I felt, in the circumstances.

"The calls for Laphroaig," Clint said.

"The only option for a wake," Molly agreed.

"Wait, this is serious," I said as the men headed for the butler party bar and heavy glasses.

"I know it is," Clint said. He poured a couple of fingers all around. Father Bream and Molly took hearty swigs. Mine didn't look that good, though I ordinarily loved the warmth of Laphraoig on a cold night.

"What if it actually *is* possible to un-do this experiment?" I said. "What if the greatest experiment in freedom and self-governance can be undone so easily, so quietly?"

The older people—Molly and Father Bream had sympathy for me, I could tell, but they were closer to the time when the whole idea of freedom had been under threat from what seemed like a small and improbable source. It had survived. That was the consolation they had to offer me.

Clint stepped forward and wrapped me in his arms.

"It's important not to go too far down that dark road," he said. "It's important to remember that the other side is operating out of fear and is thus vulnerable."

"I can see that," I said, though I still felt the hysteria right below my breastbone, a terrible heartburn. "But what is everyone so afraid of?'

"Of annihilation," Clint said. "And if one side can be made to feel the fear of the other, then it can be brought down."

I was holding on to him more desperately than the first-class kitchen, bubbling beef stew, beloved friends, and teeming family seemed to warrant.

"So, you're telling me to have faith?" I said. My fingers dug into his tweed jacket sleeves. It might have sounded like a typical question—the cry of a despairing intellectual. But Clint knew it for the sincere question it was.

"Yes, Agatha, that is exactly what I'm saying," he said. He was looking straight at me. Both of us were deadly serious.

"But isn't that like having faith that the lunatic asylum would be well-run if the inmates took over? Or the kindergarten would fare well under the self-selected most powerful, even if he were a bully?"

"Think about your own parenting, Agatha," he said. "You are a good mother. How do you balance power with permissiveness?"

I wasn't going to take my eyes from his because there was something that was flowing there—some transmission that was crucial and something I was going to need perhaps for a very long time.

I could feel without looking that Father Bream and Molly were saying the same thing from their survivors' experience.

This way was the only way that had life in it.

CHAPTER FIFTEEN
Heating Up

It'd been up to my eyeballs in Thanksgiving for a week. Mother had completely taken over the seating charts and wasn't trusting anyone—even Jane—with final placement.

That left final menu tweaks, linens, and follow up calls to lists Mother handed out to Molly, Jane, and me. After a while I got through my list, none of the boys was sick, and Clint seemed to have normal working hours, more or less.

His worry level was not lower—and might even have been higher, if that were possible. But after a few (hundred) tries, I gave up on finding out what he was worried about.

I discovered that if he worked with Queenie an hour or so, he was much calmer. Many dogs couldn't have taken that much human attention, but Queenie ate it up. She loved Clint's commands more than hot dogs themselves and was simply full of herself for learning the most complicated of them. She could detect and discern among all manner of things from suspicious-smelling objects that might be explosives to chicken carcasses to each of the boys' distinctly-scented clothing. She wasn't even out of puppyhood and she could follow the commands of a look on Clint's face, a quirk of his upper lip, and a raised eyebrow might as well have been a gunshot to her for her ease in noticing and responding.

I hadn't been home much, but Clint was teaching me how to give the commands when I was. It was clear he meant to transfer the authority to me before the end of year. Molly watched, fascinated, when she wasn't making calls for Mother. Jules had become his father's top lieutenant, glued as he was to Clint's side most times he was home.

As it grew darker earlier and colder, Clint took over masterminding activities from the time he finished dinner to the time the boys were out.

There was an intensity to his organization—or more of one, as Cint was always intense. We did all the things we usually did—full team kitchen cleanup with Molly, each boy having a responsibility down to Dylan pouring carefully measured dish soap and water on his high chair tray and slopping it around with a cloth until the worst of the dinner detritus was at least moved around.

Then there was the compact homework period for the ones who had it, a rapid-fire TV time, a quick bath—two at a time in two tubs with Dylan thrown in whichever tub Jules was in because he would never let the baby drown—pajamas that had been laid out donned, a group bedtime story, then an uncompromising goodnight to all with times set for the older ones to finish reading before their lights too were out, a friendly, firm good night to Molly and then an unquestionable hustling of me into bed.

We never went to bed that early. Clint was in his study and I was at my desk or having a nightcap and a gossip with Molly as we wound the day.

But in that time between Halloween and Thanksgiving, all the unwinding for me went on being with my husband in our bed both of us stark naked or our huge bathtub.

The intensity of Clint's desire for me called out a tenderness in my body—a tingling, a swelling, a sense of both expectancy and fulfillment. Not since the early days had our desire for each other been this strong or impossible to slake. More sex, more ways, more times only made us want more and there were days I found it harder to walk than usual. To be fair, Clint did too.

It was a Renaissance—a rebirth—of our desire for each other. It had never gone through a Dark Age—in that there was never a time we had no sex for ages—but it had dimmed just a little with each birth and then all those babies.

There was no sense of fulfillment like that sense of fulfillment. Both slaked and still thirsty, I felt more alive than I had in years—or maybe ever had. I never enjoyed being pregnant, so the state I was in didn't compare to that state of itchy get-this-over-with anxiety. Neither did it compare to nursing, which I always did and mostly enjoyed—the bounty of my full bust put to its most natural use—but difficulties with latching early, cracked nipples, and worrying about supply always made one wonder if there weren't some design flaw in the whole business that a nice bottle of formula wouldn't magically solve.

Ana and I met at the movies again.

I wasn't sure why it felt different this time, but it did. It was a bit of a surprise to me that I had the bandwidth to respond to Ana's call—and that I would go against Clint's wishes at the moment when I felt most deeply entwined with him. I had no excuse—I went anyway.

This time it was a classic—The Maltese Falcon—and there were some young people there. We ordered lunch, splitting an order of fries.

"How are the boys?" Ana whispered.

The movie had already started. I knew I'd seen it before, but I didn't remember what happened and found myself more caught up in the plot than I expected. Mary Astor was really something—stylish, smart, cunning.

"They're fine," I said. "Miraculously none is sick." I watched Humphrey and Mary at work. "How's Wolf?"

"He's looking forward to the vacation," she said. "He doesn't really enjoy school. Do yours?"

"Mine cover the waterfront," I said after thinking about it for a second. "Jules loves it—can't get enough of classes, teachers, homework, after school, sports. Dylan would just as soon be homeschooled. The other dudes are in between, with each one liking at least some part of it."

"Wolf just wants to be with me," Ana said. "And I love the American holiday. It is so generous."

"What are you doing for Thanksgiving?" I asked before I had a chance to stop myself. Normally I didn't ask people that because they might not be on Mother's party list so asking was either rubbing it in, or—if they were invited—an open invitation to some serious jockeying for a better seat. There was no way Ana and Adam were invited, though. Mother definitely wasn't that inclusive.

"Oh, didn't you know?" Ana said. "We are coming to Evermay."

Large, black, jewel-encrusted birds flew right out of my head.

"You are?" I said, stupidly.

"Yes," Ana said. I could see in the dark that she looked genuinely concerned at my surprise.

"You are?" I said again. I probably couldn't have looked much more stupid—my jaw completely dropped. "I guess everyone is capable of surprise," I said. "Even my old mother." Especially my old mother, I added to myself.

Mother had her ways and reasons, but these shenanigans were new and different. What was she up to? And why hadn't she told me? Why had she given me the seating chart challenge without also giving me not one but two wild cards she had put in the pack?

"She doesn't tell me everything," I said. Even when she had tasked me with the seating charts. Was she starting to act like Clint?

"I was afraid you might not know," Ana said.

"Mother likes to diversify, but this is beyond her usual mixing it up."

"You mean she generally invites classy people," Ana said without shame or blame. "Adam is able not to behave like a boor for short periods of time."

We paused there in the dark. Then we both started to laugh.

The young couple in the back hushed us and we got a grip on ourselves. We pretty much watched the rest of the movie that was astonishingly complex and well-done, as if the general movie-going public of that time were smarter. It was amazing to me that none of the technological advances in film outstripped a good problem, characterization, place, and plot.

We were getting our coats on and finding our bags when I thought to bring up the Vice President's wife.

"How is Connie?"

Ana paused, then said, "She's better, I think."

"That's good," I said. "How did you two get to be such friends?"

"We have known each other for many years. She was kind to me when I first got here. Like you."

"Be careful you don't cross too many political lines there, my friend. We wouldn't want to be seen as all having too much in common."

I didn't say—but I did think—that the ultra-conservative, conventional midwestern Connie Edgerton could hardly have seemed to have less in common with the exotic Montenegrin.

"I just mean you asked about her like you really cared."

Ana and I were outside, saying our good-byes.

"You are a good person, Agatha," she said. "Though you think you are all head, you are really a heart person, deep inside."

"Don't tell anyone," I said. "You could ruin my reputation."

"You may be one of the only people who don't know this about you."

"Clint may, but I don't usually get close enough for anyone to guess," I said.

There was something sweet in what she said. Is there anything we wish more deeply for than that someone knows us? Later on, I thought it might have been a warning.

When she said good-bye with those long cat eyes, she seemed to be somehow apologizing, like Rapunzel leaving the tower just a little regretfully.

★　　★　　★

"I don't think I know the people I know," I said. I wasn't kidding. I felt fuzzy-headed and slightly unwell ever since I'd seen Ana. Nothing else had helped, so I'd gone to see Father Bream, my port in every storm.

He just raised an eyebrow, which he knew from experience would unleash the confessional flood, a flood so wild and unpredictable this time, so outside of any boundaries that any reputation for rationality was immediately ruined. Bream had heard me in full flood before, but I wasn't sure either of us would find our way back to land after this one.

"First there is my mother," I said. "I know she is her own person and God knows she works in mysterious ways. I'm not saying she has to have my permission to ask people I don't exactly approve of to her party"—a fatherly eyebrow went back up. "Yes, I know I only disapprove of Ana publicly. I actually like the woman, or admire her, or am intrigued by her. I'm not sure which. Her hauteur, her self-containment seems somehow so different, so elusive—I can't help being mesmerized. Maybe it's the messy, out of controlness of my life that makes hers so appealing, even mystical. The so clearly not being in love with her husband. The one, tidy child. I don't know what I like about Ana. She seems the perfect political wife—really the Stepford political wife, if truth be told—but there are clearly depths there. But let me get back to Mother."

A priestly nod of agreement.

"Talk about a wild card. Mother always has been one. But why would she suddenly invite not just the stodgy, boring Edgertons but also the Trents—at least Ana is fashionable, but Adam is truly a boorish carnival barker?"

A priestly inquisitive eyebrow there.

"Except Connie seems to have gone off her nut. Why would Mother want that at Thanksgiving? Let's get back to the Trents. Let's just say hypothetically that she sees what I suspect—that there is some actual purpose to

Adam's insanity, even if he isn't genuinely in control of it? Which, by the way, begs the question, can you be in control of chaos? What if there is some force in the universe that destroys in order to strengthen? A terrible fever used to clear out the old ways, thoughts, blockages out of the path—a flood or fire that destroy, for sure, but also clears?"

Bream had one of those completely enigmatic smiles going—Mona Lisa in a beard with bushy eyebrows.

"Oh, I know that look, damn you. You are on about having faith in truth. Well, you can just take your faith," I said, more forcefully than I meant to. But once I'd started down that road, there was no going back. "Because the worst is my husband. What don't I know about him? I love him more deeply and absolutely than ever now. My love for him doesn't grow stale with time—it just burns deeper in the wood. And yet I don't know what he does on a daily basis, where he is, and I never know what he is thinking. No really. He seems to love us so absolutely, so do or die. I don't question that he would take a bullet for us—or shoot anyone who threatened us, for that matter. But how do I know that for sure, when I know so little?"

My voice had risen at the end, a *cri de coeur*. Bream's sad, compassionate face didn't help at all.

"And what is more, my dear," he said, "is you have no idea if any two are working together—your mother and father, Ana and Adam, you and Clint."

He had his hands over my hands. It was only the

warmth in them that kept me from washing away, that kept me on land.

I looked deep into the old blue eyes and knew there was no dry land left in this world. There was only Atlantis, to be found by taking a very deep breath and diving, diving down into the depth. There was only miracle.

CHAPTER SIXTEEN

Thanksgiving

The question of when to press for power and when to let go was a complicated one. I could speak from firsthand experience that the decision to go for a Caesarean when I had insanely insisted on going on pushing had taught me a lot about not sticking to my way and taking the medial highway when necessary. My fifth son might well not have gotten here without Clint's taking charge.

With Molly it was an entirely different dynamic. She often was in charge—it would also have been insane to micro-manage her excellent management of the gang—but we also knew when a decision was entirely up to me—schools, diets, discipline. We danced well together.

Where I'd really lost control was with the kids. Oh, sure, I was the boss, no question—except when Clint was home and running the show. But it took very little for any one of them to find and press the button that destroyed my ability to say no to him. When it had to with school or health or psychological well-being, I was as tigerish as could be. But anything emotional and I was a kitten. The closest I'd seen to the tender ferocity of it—the willingness to go to any length of love and protectiveness was, strangely enough, in Queenie's eyes. She was already so attached to us that I could tell her love was unbounded—as was her willingness to bite in our defense.

Father, Mother, Delaney, Molly, and I would be at Evermay early for Thanksgiving. Grandfather was at home in Virginia and rarely left anymore. Grandmaman was in London and rarely crossed back. Queenie would spend most of the day in her crate. Jamie was away on assignment.

Clint would bring the boys at the right time—or at least that was what I thought. If he had to leave, he would let Molly know and she would scoot home to take over. Until then she and Delaney and Jane would serve as the generals of the staff army while Mother finalized the appearance and seating and went over any last minute strategies for guest management.

Like most experienced social commanders-in-chief, Mother had war-planned for all contingencies and would probably have a plan in place in case of nuclear attack. She didn't share that with me, but I overheard Jules asking her anxiously one day what would happen if such an attack ever happened.

I couldn't hear her response, but Jules, who could generally not easily leave an anxiety alone, seemed to stop worrying entirely about that one.

Mother met me at the front door. She gave my outfit a good once-over, gave a short, sharp nod of her head to my long black velvet skirt, gold lame shell, and long black silk over jacket with simple gold and diamond necklace, bracelet, and earrings. She didn't overtly check my shoes under my skirt, but I was pretty sure black ankle strap low heels would pass the test. Mother didn't ordinarily go for fashion ostentation and discouraged my use of jewel colors. Her Thanksgiving was the one time I bowed to her fashion dictates.

"Delaney's in the kitchen, dear," Mother said. "Guests will be arriving in an hour, so he is making sure everything there is ship shape. One of the cooks didn't seem to quite have everything under control, so he and Molly have seen to that."

"And Jane—she's here too, right?"

"Yes, of course. She has the parlor maids checking the coatroom is ready and the powder rooms perfect."

"How many coats are you expecting?"

"At least 85 this year," Mother said. She had taken over the seating chart challenge completely toward the end so I had no idea what the final count was. She was moving briskly toward the living room, but I had stopped in the middle of the entrance hall.

"It looks gorgeous, Mother," I said. She had taken Federalist Thanksgiving to a whole new level. Without actually going there, she had managed to insinuate notes of a Victorian Christmas while she was at it.

"Grand" was the word for Evermay on any occasion, but when Mother put on the Ritz it went right over the top.

The entry hall was decked with greenery over the doorways, and every wall had acquired a fixture that looked very much like a gas light, so that the light flickered and created shadows. It might have been early evening in Washington, DC outside, but you lost all sense of it as soon as you entered. The blocks of Carrara marble tile under our feet might as well have been in the Victoria and Albert Museum. The mirrors and crystal of the unlit chandelier caught and tossed around the light from the torches. The dark colors of the rooms—blood red in the hall, marine blue in the living room, and deep pumpkin in the dining room at the other end of the hall were, in that light, old colors that had acquired new power.

I stood in the middle of the drama—it did seem as if it were a stage, set up for a production to begin in moments—and admired Mother's stagecraft. Whether it was going to be a musical, a comedy, or a tragedy, I couldn't have predicted at that moment. Mother had breezed on to the next set and was calling me.

"Delaney will be at the front door to greet guests," she was saying. "But as soon as everyone has arrived he'll come in here to make sure the bar is going smoothly. We have Bruce pouring, so that will be fine and no one drinks the way they used to anyway—such health concerns they all seem to have—such a pity . . ."

"Less to manage," I said.

"That is so, but so much less intensity too. Well, can't be helped. Prohibition was probably more interesting."

"How many people do you think can circulate in here, Mother?"

"I know—it seems cavernous, even with all the furniture still in it. Jane will move people around so there are no clumps. She'll begin to move them after about an hour and start seating them, starting from the back."

I pictured Jane as a particularly talented sheep dog who could cut out just the right sheep and place them right where they belonged.

"The musicians are especially good--but no one will hear them unless there is a lull in the conversation."

"Which there never is," I pointed out.

"But if so, there they'll be—a harpsichord and a violin.

"Mother, why do you go the trouble of having musicians if they aren't going to be heard?"

"Background, dear," she said. "Tasteful background." She gave me a look that clearly said "Tuareg band." "Now if you could just stay in here while Jane moves people into the dining area that would be very helpful. There are going to be a lot of embassy people and so many of them are spies. I think they'll be most comfortable with you."

"What on earth makes you think the embassy staff are spies, Mother?

"Because our embassy staff was so often sprinkled with spies, so I'm presuming this is true of other countries," she said.

"I'm not a spy, so I don't see why they would be more comfortable with me, even if they are all spies."

"Because you sleep with one," Mother said. She looked about her distractedly, as if counting invisible bodies, then she moved purposefully toward the dining room.

"And why don't you want me in the dining room, Mother? That's where you usually have me stationed." I was trailing in her wake, but she stopped abruptly before we went through the dining room door, pulling me up short. "What do you not want me to know?"

"What on earth do you mean?' she said. She looked a little guilty, under her haughtiness.

I could see her sorting through her possible roles, deciding which one to play—hurt mother, harried hostess, dumb blonde?

"It's complicated, dear," she said. "Can we talk about it another time?'

That card, I felt, she played with relative sincerity.

Jane, Molly, and Delaney were waiting in the dark doorway of the dining room for us to get finished with what they could tell was an awkward conversation. I knew I needed to release her.

"You and Clint," I grumbled.

"What's that?" she said.

"Nothing," I said.

"Later on, dear," Mother said, breezing into the dining room, her silver glitter scarf trailing. "I'll explain everything." As if she were going to fill me in on the facts when I was a bit older. She disappeared behind the solid dining room door into the distant, darkly glittering dining room.

When party guests started to arrive, they came in waves. Delaney opened the door to ten or so at a time and I barely had time to greet them and direct them toward the bar before the next wave came. With Jamie away on assignment, I wouldn't have sibling help with this task. One of Jane's assistants took their coats and off they went. No one dared to be late to a dinner of Mother's. Some of her guests I knew personally and some I knew from the news. Sometimes the outfit was understated DC, or plain Midwest, or exotic Middle East. Men came in robes and kilts and black tie. Ladies came in silks and saris. The scents ranged from Parisian to spicy—from the cutting edge of high class to the warm earthiness of the desert. Skin tones ranged from the deepest black to palest Scandinavian. If there were spies in the crowd, they didn't stand out And, if any of them were nervous or felt out of place, they covered it well. They might have bit parts as lobbyists. They might be stars—ambassadors or kings or senators. Or they might be staff. Tonight, they were all on stage.

Even the Trents.

Or should I say especially the Trents?

Adam Trent always stood out. Tall and big, he had the presence of a showman and paused wherever he went, posing for attention and applause, even when no one was looking he seemed to hear the applause anyway, as if an applause track ran in his own head.

He was striking even if he was a buffoon. You had to give him that.

And Ana played her part exquisitely. While never showing a disdain for the carnival barker beside her, never giving her contempt away, she nevertheless kept an absolute distance from him. More than that, even—she had a self-containment that seemed inviolable—a way of holding apart from him, from all of us.

Except for Wolf, who held her heart.

My kids happened to swarm up behind the Trents as they arrived and the tidal wave of them promptly separated from Clint, engulfed Wolf, and carried him off to the children's dining room where Betsy had a team of nannies in charge of food and entertainment for the duration.

Clint greeted the Trents, gave me a kiss with only a tiny suspicious tilt to a frown in their direction, and went into the living room.

Out of the corner of my eye I saw Ana clip-clopping on her tall heels, disappearing into the deep sea of the living room right behind Clint.

When I looked back at Adam, looming still inside the front door in his formal black wool coat that didn't change in any way the essential cheapness of his demeanor, I was surprised to see his gaze on his disappearing wife. I was surprised by the fear there and, I thought, a sadness. Could he actually have feelings for another human being? Did he love his wife?

"There she goes," he was saying, mostly to himself. "The huntress."

So, no. Not love. Something else. I wasn't sure what. But not a love I understood.

"So, here you are, Agatha," Adam boomed out, "doing service for your illustrious mother. I notice she doesn't have a bunch of Moroccans to lower the tone."

I was too appalled to speak. How could he have insulted in so many ways—or shown his complete lack of class—in one brief meeting? But then I remembered it is the job of the huckster—or Loki—to throw you off balance. I struggled back to solid ground.

"Good one, Adam," I said. "Or ones. Mother's taste is notably better than mine—in most instances."

"Yeah—I don't know why she invited me either," he said. "I thought maybe you'd asked her to."

"That wouldn't have been a good idea," I said.

"I'm guessing your husband disapproves."

I didn't bother to reply.

"Then you two better stop seeing each other," he said.

I raised my eyebrows at the implied threat.

"Ana has a bad habit of making people fall for her," he said.

"I think more people feel sorry for her."

"That's how she gets in," he said. "With some people."

"Not you, though, I don't imagine."

"Nah—not me. I married her because she's so hot," he said. He winked and leered, a caricature of sexual predation.

"Good lord," I said, giving up on maintaining my balance.

His goal achieved, Adam Trent sailed into the living room.

I thought for a moment about how wrong people could be about people, even those as close as you could get. What was there about Ana that was a huntress? I reviewed my knowledge of her—the indisputable intelligence and independence—but nothing I could think of said "hunter." More hunted, I would have thought, if anything. How complicated that issue would get, I could not begin to guess.

I was trailing behind Adam, my greeting duties seeming to be over, and Jane was beginning to move the early arrivals into the dining room. Plus, I was beginning to feel a bit like Mother's servant.

But the front door opened again. Delaney had left his post by then so I was alone in the hall when the Vice President and Mrs. Edgerton came in. Phil came first and seemed to be shielding his wife. She was much smaller, a sort of bird-like woman, and moved hesitantly, like someone physically ill.

Of course, the Secret Service had already been there— had come the day before, in fact, to sweep for devices and check for safety. I might have noticed that the whole Vice Presidential motorcade including an ambulance had swept down the street, but I had been distracted by Adam Trent. When the Vice President and Second Lady came in, it was unusually understated—almost secretive, as if her fragility and the desire for discretion had overcome protocol.

I held the door for them and welcomed them to Evermay.

Phil handed me his coat not realizing who I was at first and preoccupied with his wife.

"Oh, so sorry," he said when he recognized me. By then I also had possession of his wife's mink wrap.

"Not at all," I said. "So glad you could come."

"Lovely of your mother to invite us," Phil Edgerton

said. His midwestern manners forebad any sort of insulting confrontation over why he and Connie were there.

"I don't believe I've met your wife," I said. The coat over my left arm, I prepared to shake her hand or not as she so inclined. But when she raised her head to look at me, I saw that such a nicety was out of the realm of her possibility. Because you could see quite clearly in Connie Edgerton's eyes that she was no longer a player in this real world. She looked like she'd gone off either with Jean Cocteau or otherwise to play with fairies.

I looked at Phil Edgerton for a moment, wondering why he would bring his fragile wife to this free-for-all. What could be more full of undercurrents—even riptides—than a Washington power party? Anyone who was able to survive in DC had to know, understand, and even enjoy the fact that he who rode the wave today would be first to drown tomorrow.

But Phil Edgerton just looked stoic—handsome, chisel-faced, he looked about as sensitive as granite. Connie's condition might be bad, but being invisible in Washington was fatal. Even lying low as long as he had had exposed him to rumors that he was done. And in DC perception was reality. So he probably made that calculation—hide and go down for sure or appear and take a chance—and decided to risk it.

If he'd asked me, I'd have said don't. In fact, I almost put my hand on his arm then in the Evermay hallway to say stop this madness. But he hadn't asked, nor was he likely to listen. I disposed of their coats and followed them into the sea of humanity, languages, colors, and scents that was my parent's living room.

By then, my parents swept in to greet the VP and wife, taking them off to meet other grand guests.

I stood next to the appetizers table, bemused. Bruce, Mother's longtime bartender, looked over from the bar.

"Other people have crackers and cheese balls," I said.

"While your mother has raw vegetables in their original state," Bruce said.

There were raw carrots with their green tops tied together in the center of the table, artichokes cracked open, fennel and radishes tossed among berries, and pomegranates split and spilling—all the creamy dips nestled around a tureen almost hidden so that the carrot tarragon soup looked more like a hidden forest pool than an appetizer.

"I'm pretty sure some of this is cooked," I said.

"I'm sure it's all vegetarian," Bruce said. "And you know what that means."

"There will be something wildly improbable in the dining room."

"Take heed."

I stood at the end of the bar, ready to catch anyone uncertain where to turn. Someone from the Polish embassy stepped between me and Bruce and began to tell me stories of how he remembered me as a child. I didn't remember him at all but that didn't stop me from agreeing enthusiastically with him about his memories.

He remembered me as wilder than I remembered me—perhaps I had edited my memories to make me more my mother's daughter. Sometimes I thought the boys had wiped out my memory bank—and maybe even my personality bank.

Another woman came to talk to me—someone who had known us during a brief stint in Cairo. She had the nobility of so many Egyptians, the tall elegance, and the knowledge that, compared to her family, we were all nouveau. She asked about my children, whose names she knew, and I felt as if I'd been talking to an old and distinguished family member by the time she moved on. Molly popped up just about then to tell me it was time for everyone to move toward dinner with a conversational bark here and a nip of an elbow there until the whole mass was moving. But they weren't moving toward the dining room. They were moving toward the ballromm. Mother stood at the door to the dark ball room, directing the flow with the exact right speed, typical of the social field marshal she was.

I had been in the Evermay ball room hundreds of nights—it completely stunned every time—but this time it almost knocked me down.

We had arranged the seating charts the way we usual did—with eight to a table, 11 tables fitting easily into the Evermay dining room. But Mother had changed all that sometime after she took over. She had changed it from a state dinner to a royal one. She had moved the whole affair from the dining room to the ballroom, leaving the dining room for plating. In the ballroom, the tables were arranged in long lines parallel to the walls with a shorter table across the top. Once I began to get over my shock, I wondered who would be seated there alongside my parents.

It was bad enough to arrange 11 eight-tops—with the social Rubik's cube of not only who gets seated where at each table but also how close or far from the prestigious front of the room. But at least there you had some scope, some slippage, some table arrangements that might be open to interpretation.

Not so with the royal dining arrangement.

Here you needed centuries of experience of perfect seating because one little move below the salt and you were relegated to the less noble if not the negligible.

If the head of the table was Georgetown and the top of each side table was Kalorama, Adams Morgan, and assorted Embassy dwellers, by the time you got to the ends you were in the burbs.

Not that I doubted Mother's ability at arranging this properly. And, if truth be known, I was relieved that I hadn't known. Now I could witness her artwork with curiosity and a bit of amusement. Because she was known to add in a little spice, her own little joke in the social arrangements if you knew where to look.

I turned at the sense of warmth behind me, almost a scent, though nothing overt. Clint was standing there.

"Mother's gone royal on us," I said.

"The table arrangements, you mean?" he said. "Have you seen what's on them?"

I looked more closely at the tables themselves and saw game birds—pheasant, grouse, and partridge—on display, their feathers intact, their corpses quite dead.

"So she has gone beyond royal," I said, "into the wild. Good thing the appetizers were all vegetarian because dinner decidedly isn't."

"Oh, I wouldn't say it isn't royal—just more like Queen Victoria royal."

"Calling Prince Albert," I said.

Just then Adam Trent came in, ushered by my father to the top of the right hand long table, perpendicular to Connie Edgerton who sat, rearing back slightly from the pheasant nearest her, at the high table.

Clint and Father exchanged a nod across the room. I looked at my husband, then at Father.

Was there anyone *not* in this, except me?

I was seated at the top of the left hand long table, well above the salt but not at the head table, a liberty Mother could afford with her own daughter. I hadn't quite identified where my husband was—somewhere not far from Mother.

Except just then I could have stood to be closer to Clint. He was always reassuring to me—his body the familiar temperature, his scent so deeply known. Though his profession was the most dangerous, I always felt deeply comforted around him.

Though that didn't make much sense—what was more dangerous than entrusting your whole heart—more than that, your whole being and that of your children—to one secretive man?

I pulled myself back from that dizzy precipice. I looked around the room.

People were still involved in the ordinary chaos of finding their places at the tables, peering at place cards while Molly, Jane, and Delaney took over for Mother in that task as she took her place at the center of the high table. I saw she had slipped on a long fox-trimmed over-jacket. She sat in her high-backed chair, regnant.

She was watching shrewdly as people sat and then gasped at the dead game on the tables—gorgeous and grisly—and then tried to hide their surprise, as if everyone shot fowl and then draped them across the formal linens.

I knew the army of wait staff would deliver far more reasonable dishes as soon as everyone was seated— probably a turtle soup, as if that too weren't primitive, on reflection. But Mother had wanted to shock—to unsettle this normally consummately controlled crowd.

For many of the diplomats armed insurrection was commonplace enough, or ongoing combat between rival sects, or terrorism on their streets or in the seas. But they had thought Washington was a port in the storm, if only on the surface. But Mother had, by a design I couldn't begin to guess at, brought the shadow to the surface at her table.

One effect was that people had less time to react to the rest of the seating order. They would talk about that much more later. Because Ana and Adam Trent were, each, at the opposite ends of the high table.

That put Adam Trent, leeringly, practically in my lap.

In a very unusual disruption of the boy-girl order, all of the men were on one side of the high table, so Adam sat next to Phil Edgerton who sat next to Father. Mother was beside him, with Connie Edgerton on her left and Ana on Connie's.

I gasped as I continued to survey.

Adam Trent, whose hand I could feel making its way toward my knee, stopped abruptly and leaned forward to see where I was looking.

"What?" he said. Then, "What the hell?"

Right next to Ana, at the top of the right hand table, so directly across the dead birds from me, was the Russian ambassador. I didn't know he was even in Washington, never mind on Mother's guest list. How had he snuck into the dining room? Who had seated him directly across from me?

Ana either knew already or nevertheless welcomed him.

She leaned toward the small, upright, tightly controlled man with the familiarity of a lover. Her lovely long neck was bent toward him as he spoke in her ear and she nodded. Of course, she understood his language if not he hers.

Neither of them was looking at the other guests— neither was aware of anyone else. Theirs was a private conversation—intense and intimate.

I looked at Mother who was gazing at them, then she leaned back in her chair, gratified.

The fire in the enormous fireplace behind her flared up.

Just then Adam choked on the sip of wine he'd taken and began to cough. The Vice President stood up and pounded him on the back.

It wasn't that it was strange that Mother had seated Ana and the Ambassador together—they were, after all, two of the only people who share a language. It was the lack of strangeness, really, that was so striking. The way they leaned into each other not so much like lovers as like family. The Ambassador, whose name wasn't Rasputin, was always called that out of his hearing because he was so clearly the person who actually wielded the power in Russia, even from his ambassadorial position in Washington.

The sound suddenly seemed cacophonous, the heat of the room unbearable. I would have stood up to leave the room except I didn't think I could.

My father was suddenly behind me, gently pulling my chair out and offering an arm.

The wait staff was serving the first course and everyone was talking full tilt. As far as I could tell no one else beside me and Adam Trent was shocked by Ana's apparent close tie with Ambassador Rasputin. I wasn't even sure that Adam was surprised as much as caught off guard by the openness of the familiarity.

I let Father guide me up and out. When I came out of the powder room he was there, studying an ancestor's portrait as if he'd never seen it before. One of Mother's, of course, as the blues, golds, and reds of their outfits made for much better portraiture that his good, grey forebears.

"A momentary thing," I said. "I didn't feel at all well."

"I could see," he said. No need for either of us to point out that Mother wasn't the one to notice. She had bigger game to watch.

"What in the world?" I said.

I didn't need to explain that to Father either.

"For those of us who were steeped in the Cold War, as I was," he said, "an American Congressman's wife on the friendliest terms with America's once-sworn enemies seems—odd."

"To say the least," I said. "It isn't as if Russia isn't still taking active measures against us. Their involvement in dividing the country via social media is at the very least proven and known. Even if Ana and Rasputin know each other, shouldn't they at least act more distant in public?"

"I'm not sure I can explain much," Father said. "I'm not part of this administration, so I don't know if there are any initiatives afoot."

"Let me go backwards then," I said. "Ana is Montenegrin. Montenegro was part of the former Yugoslavia, right?"

"Yes, it was one of the six countries that formed Yugoslavia after World War I, seven after Serbia and Croatia split."

"And it wasn't Muslim?"

"Only Bosnia was declared Muslim, though all of the six had once been part of the Ottoman Empire. The Montenegrin language is only slightly different from Serbian and has a Cyrillic alphabet, thus closer to Russian than to German or Arabic."

"But Montenegro, like many of the smaller countries in eastern Europe, had no love for the Soviet Union," I said.

"In fact, it was Communist without being part of the USSR. It was behind the Iron Curtain, of course, by Churchill's definition, but it didn't have any real allegiance to Russia. In fact, the countries that made up Yugoslavia banded together in order to resist Stalin. It has always had a fierce independent streak."

"But they were not only communist but also run by a dictator?"

"As were all Communist countries. Marshal Tito was indeed a strong man, but many former Yugoslavians have a sort of nostalgia for what seemed like a benign dictatorship. Tito was in favor of levelling classes through education and he also was relatively tolerant of religion. Sometimes the conditions for freedom don't exist in a particular place or time," Father said.

"'Freedom's just another word for nothing left to lose'?" I mumbled.

"Lenin saw capitalism and democracy as less developed states than communism and socialism," Father said, ignoring my mumble.

"And yet they were necessary before reaching a stable socialist society."

"The leaders of the Russian revolution did not think the society could stand to take that long to evolve," Father said.

"Mostly communism came from the top down."

"Not choice," Father said.

"Poverty, war, instability, death, and fear—these can be very powerful motives," I said. I had at least heard what Ana said. "But Ana isn't suffering. Why would she be so overt about her connection with Rasputin?"

"That seems to be what your mother was after—how much they would own up to in public."

"Did my husband have anything to do with it?"

"Your husband is a mystery to most of us," Father said.

We went back to the dining room and I looked for Clint. He was nowhere to be seen. Father steered me back to my place. Delaney himself appeared with a Cornish game hen for me and served it as I sat. I began a delicate dissection, surprisingly hungry.

But I felt an absence nearby and looked up to see that Adam's place was empty.

I looked across the table again and there was Ana, her head inclined familiarly toward Ambassador Rasputin. Adam Trent was behind him on his other side, blustering and gesturing, trying to distract his attention away from Ana. Or Ana from him.

I was much too far away to hear what Adam was saying, but I wasn't too far away to feel the heat of the Ambassador's gaze.

He stared straight ahead with a beam of power that didn't burn so much as sear. I knew that they hadn't succeeded yet in reliably generating it, but if scientists needed a model for cold fusion then here he was.

At first, I thought he was just gazing straight ahead, at

nothing, letting both Ana and Adam feel the power of his neglect.

But, then, when I moved to one side to avoid the beam, it went with me. Rasputin was staring at me.

Rasputin held the reins in that part of the world without question. As secretive as Ana, power-driven, as self-involved and self-aggrandizing as anyone could be, he had had acted as prime minister once. He understood the need in Russia for reassurance, for the restoration of untrammeled power, for someone in charge. If the need hadn't already been there, he would have created it. He had that much power—or seemed to.

It didn't seem to matter that the people suffered as much, were as poor and oppressed, or that wealth was concentrated in a small group of oligarchs as much as it ever had been in czarist Russia.

With him had come a restored respect for the country, or a fear of it. His dream was to reinstate the USSR, if not in fact than de facto.

Like Tito, Rasputin picked his battles strategically. He was tolerant of religion and then some. He used it to con people to be loyal to him. What he was intolerant of was anything that didn't have to do with him. He prized loyalty above all else. And he knew how to use people's desire for a leader, for a reason to believe, to consolidate power not in the old ideals of socialism but in him personally, as he built power and wealth like the czars had, beyond most people's wildest imaginings.

There were even rumors he had breached America's

political infrastructure, using its very openness as a weapon against it, using the decentralized leadership, the primacy of choice, as ways in, to sow discord and disharmony so that he could use the wedge of focus, self-interest, and pure power to divide and conquer. He had almost certainly been the mastermind behind the abuse of social media platforms.

There had been rumors that Rasputin had been behind Adam Trent's rise—that they were two of kind except that Rasputin had a wiliness that Trent lacked, a cunning intelligence the American had none of. They said that Rasputin had something on Trent, but no one knew for sure what.

How would the puppet master manipulate the puppet then? Where were the strings?

I looked at Adam. He surely didn't have the intelligence to partner with this wily politician. What kind of trickster would he be then? Rasputin was the master trickster, but there was no evidence that they even communicated. What drove the loyalty when self-aggrandizement was the only goal? There was nothing to heal the world in that, only to destroy all the connections, all the beneficence, that, despite all, seemed to outweigh it in such a delicate balance?

What if the time had come for the final trick, for the wave of darkness that absolute self-interest and all its servants—choice without moral compass, fearful sycophancy, the willingness to believe the wrong things because they felt right and the right things were hard, a belief in authority that did not warrant it, that captured attention simply through the bedazzlement of movement, the refusal to look below that surface glitter, to see facts—suppose the wave had come?

Just then Connie Edgerton stood up at her place and began screaming as if she were indeed possessed by the devil.

All hell broke loose. Phil Edgerton leapt up and threw his arms around his wife, looking around with the perfectly pressed face to see if anyone had noticed.

But Connie was having none of it.

Years of behaving well were having an equal and opposite reaction. She was shrieking and flailing. The vice president didn't have enough hands to hold her arms and mouth at the same time. When he got her from behind well enough to pin her arms down, her feet shot out from under her tight velvet skirt and hit the high table with such force and intent that she heaved it straight over. Mother's place settings, flowers, and the dead pheasants went sailing through the air to crash between the long lines of table on either side.

In case anyone had missed the mayhem at the far end of the room before the crash got their attention, china, silver, and crystal exploded with the high, clear sound only the best dinnerware has. The boules of bread rolled clear down the room to hit the far wall and, one, to roll through the door and down the front hall, making a bid for freedom.

There was an astonished hush that fell among the

hundreds of people that I didn't think was possible. It lasted a nanosecond, then Father and a couple of secret service men came to Edgerton's aid and helped him get a grip on Connie.

She seemed to have gotten enough out of her system to let my father's calm politeness work its magic on her better than any force and she leaned against him.

I was standing by then, the staff had entered *en masse* to begin clearing up the mess, and Mother was having a word with Delaney. I saw Molly leave for the kitchen on a mission. I looked back at Mother.

She stood at her place, in front of her high-backed chair, not a hair out of place, elegant and shrewd as ever. She was surveying the scene.

With a different hostess, I would have expected upset, hysteria even.

Not Mother. She looked over the ruin of her event with calculation, assessing the material damage, first, dispensing with the social—the disorderliness of the event: that too was covered in whatever she, Molly, and Delaney had decided. Now she was on to the political— the economy of the people what had been set in motion. I looked more closely at her, searching for concern.

No, she wasn't. She knew there were costs, for sure. But they had long since been calculated. There were risks in the game she had played.

But there were also benefits.

I looked around the room.

Clint was nowhere to be seen.

Father and the vice president had Connie wrapped in her mink as if it were a straightjacket and rushed her out the door before anyone could take note. The Secret Service swept in behind them, ushering people quickly and efficiently toward the door. Although many guests tried to stay in place and collect as many details as possible, the Service gave them the bum's rush toward the door. Delaney and Molly had coats ready for everyone else and the entire group was marshalled toward the front hall and out to the waiting line of chauffeured cars with the same grave order as if nothing had happened.

The only difference was that each guest was given a linen gift bag with a covered sterling silver dish of dessert, a pavlova covered in delicate berries. There is no way Mother's party plan was going to fall apart at the end.

After I'd done my part to assure the orderliness of the going, I went back to the dining room. Mother was in motion, commanding the troops in the clean-up operation, including Father.

She had corralled the reporters into the living room where Bruce made sure their cups overflowed until Mother could get there.

I watched her disarrange her hair artfully and create an aura of harried hostess in her clothes—just enough for the camera to catch but not enough to disturb her overall elegance—and march into the living room, pausing at the door to acquire the gait of a middle-aged hostess, and a sort of vicar's wife demeanor of capability in the face of uproar.

"A positive disaster," she was saying to the group as a whole. "I can't imagine what happened. The party was so lovely—as you know—" her she paused to review the Washington luminaries who attended—"and then suddenly the Vice President's wife was taken ill."

Taken ill? Was that going to be the story? I looked around the room of faces. Of seasoned reporters, who forgot just in that moment that they had meant to ask questions about the high table, about Rasputin, about the Trents.

There was a babble of questions—these weren't the society page reporters but the A-list of political reporters and the questions wouldn't normally be softballs. But they had somehow been put under the spell Mother cast and suddenly as smart and hard-hitting a reporter as could be found anywhere was asking Mother who designed her fox trimmed jacket.

Mother answered graciously—a designer I'd never known her to use before. And then she went on.

"I'm sure you understand the need to respect the Vice President's privacy during this difficult time. If I learn anything more that I'm able to share, you can be sure that I will. We in America enjoy a less adversarial relationship with our press than, say, the English. Please continue to enjoy the bar," she said, nodding to Bruce to let the liquor flow.

Robert Erghart walked with her to the door where I could hear him say, "Nice job, Madame Ambassador, steering everyone away from Rasputin and Trent."

"Oh, do you think so?" she said, feigning innocence. She promptly dropped it. "Not a one of you was fooled."

The reporter, flattered, exited.

"So, Mother, what were you up to?"

"Not now, darling, and not here," she said. "Coffee at the Peacock in the morning."

CHAPTER SEVENTEEN
Aftermath

Clint didn't come home.

That wasn't unusual, though, so I didn't think much about it. With the level of fallout from the party—his own mother-in-law's—there would be business at the agency to attend to. There was the domestic political—the fragility at the top of the executive branch—and the international political with Rasputin and Trent's palliness. I wished I could talk with my husband, though, because what interested me was Ana Trent's closeness with Rasputin.

On second thought, though, I wouldn't be able to ask him even if he were home. I was supposed to have lost interest in Ana. The question itself would betray my ongoing passionate curiosity about her—the secretive, contained elegance, how trapped she was, how impossible the rescue—and also how much I knew her not at all.

The kids all, one by one, ended up in my bed, the ordinary eclipsing the extraordinary every time. It would have been very crowded with my hunky husband in it too, as Queenie added her half-grown body to the top of the pile.

She got on top of us all and slept hard, as puppies do, but I could feel the tautness of her muscles, even from under the duvet. Though she slept, she was ready to spring at any moment.

Clint was still not home in the morning, but it was hard to miss him in the rush of boys. It was, of course, a day off from school, which meant a day on for Molly and me. I would have asked her what she and Mother had been up to, but their league was deep and exclusive.

Nothing was going to interfere with my meeting with Mother, though, at the Peacock Café. Molly and I got the boys through breakfast, dressed, and Jules and I ran Queenie around the block. Then Jules organized the others for a backyard soccer game. I dressed and came downstairs just in time to watch a kick send the ball off the back wall and straight toward the French doors. It would have gone through except Molly was stationed in front of them as goalie.

The boys no doubt would have considered it satisfying to have smashed it through, at least for the moment, until their more civilized selves took over and realized it was going to lead to some consequences. Still, sometimes it was worth smashing things to smithereens.

Maybe that was what Mother had been thinking. I certainly hoped so. I hoped there was a plan of some kind. Because I could tell without turning on the TV that the town was alive with anxiety. There was something palpable about the air in DC, something that emanated from the bog beneath the city—or was carried by it.

There was a miasma. If DC didn't have London's fog, it had something equally atmospheric if less visible.

The air of late November had a snap to it and a smell of old, decaying leaves, a smell that reminded me of both sex and death.

Molly had the boys' snacks set up and *101 Dalmatians* cued up on the DVD player when I snuck out the side door to go to the Peacock. The boys had their first fever of the day run out of them and would be quiet, more or less, until some rest restored them for round two. The problem, was, I felt again, that I was probably done for the day. Note to self: next lifetime, have children when you are yourself a child and haven't already flamed out.

Mother was already there, coffee neatly in front of her, at our table overlooking the back garden. Antoine appeared from nowhere with my cup.

"Darling," Mother said, "you look tired. Let's have some biscotti."

"A full English breakfast wouldn't restore me, Mother," I said. "I've already had several lifetimes with the boys, just today. Plus, I don't know if you've heard, there was a big party at Evermay last night."

"Yes, I know," Mother said. She signaled Antoine. "An omelet, please, for my daughter."

"If there is kale anywhere near it, I'll know it," I said to Mother.

"Hold the kale, please, Antoine," Mother said. "My daughter has an allergy to anything that might go in a green smoothie."

Antoine smiled, as close as he would get to joshing with a customer.

"I also heard there was some sort of uproar at the party," I said.

There was a buzz all around us. The Peacock was usually quietly busy all day—the Georgetown residents took it as their private restaurant—but today it was packed. I was pretty sure that was not only because it was a federal holiday but also because it was a well-known fact that my mother frequented it. No doubt there was a lot of curiosity about how she was going to look that day, with her elegant party gone to shit.

If they thought she was going to look undone, they did not know my mother.

She wouldn't have shown any disturbance under any circumstance, anymore that the Queen of Denmark would have. But if you knew her at all well, you could see that she was not only undisturbed but deeply satisfied, a cat licking her whiskers after a particularly tasty meal of mouse.

"Eat, darling," she said as Antoine laid a scrumptious, un-kaled omelet in front of me. "You're looking a little off-kilter."

"Mother," I no doubt spluttered, "what on earth do you take that makes you so cool? The whole town is in an uproar because your party ended in one. There might, for all I know, be a constitutional crisis in the making and you tell me to eat my breakfast because *I'm* looking off-kilter. Why aren't *you* off-kilter?"

"Why on earth would there be a constitutional crisis? My table was what was up ended—not the orderly conduct of government."

"But it was up-ended by the Vice President's wife—that's why. And he was already taking a leave because of her. What if he has to step down?"

"Well, that would be a shame," she said. "But there is a system for that."

"Yes—and it involves Adam Trent moving up. The President could appoint him. And that would be a real disaster."

"Really, dear, the omelet is getting cold. You should eat," she said. I swear I could see her in the forties in all her glamourous elegance, knocking the ash off her cigarette in a long ivory holder.

"What do you mean? Everyone hates Adam. He would be awful as a vice president—and scary that much closer to the presidency. Didn't you see Adam talking to Rasputin?"

"Was he?" Mother said, taking another imaginary drag. "What I saw was him talking to Connie Edgerton, right before the table went over."

"What?" I said. "Adam Trent said something to her that could cause a complete meltdown. What in the world could that have been?"

"Something involving her buttoned-down husband, I would imagine," Mother said. "Antoine, could you bring another omelet? My daughter has let that one get cold."

* * *

"I don't understand," I said to Father Bream.

He just lifted a brow. He could see I was in no condition to be asked questions of—and I needed no encouragement to let the torrent of confusion flow. He wasn't likely to try to stop the flow with an omelet, the second of which I didn't eat either.

"I don't understand why people make stupid, self-defeating choices. I assume Edgerton had done something stupid—or lots of stupid things—what man in power hasn't? Maybe he'd had an affair—or a love child—or he'd done weird things with prostitutes. Lord knows, there is a range of options there. Why would anyone in power—who wants more power and portrays himself as super-strait-laced make stupid decisions like that?

"Because I don't doubt that he did," I ranted on. "Or that Connie Edgerton knew on some level. So what makes people *not* know what they know? Why would she tell herself that Mr. Squeaky Clean probably wasn't, given the power he had, and the odds against anyone being so perfect?"

Father Bream opened his mouth, but the river rushed on. I was up on my feet, pacing from one end of the dusty, book-stacked study to the other, hoping that motion would help my rising panic and nausea.

"And why would Mother foster that sort of chaos? She, who is all about elegance and order—why would she create the circumstances?"

"Well, as I understand it, she didn't originally seat Ana next to Rasputin," Father Bream managed to squeeze in. "He moved over there."

"What do my mother and Clint have going? Why do I have the strong impression they were working together— and that neither was surprised at what happened?

"I'm not done," I said, stopping Bream's attempt to address those questions. "Why was Ana so chummy with Rasputin when she has all the choices in the world, when she has money and intelligence and power, why would she associate with someone who is all about repression, authoritarianism, loss of freedom, control?"

Father Bream grabbed my hand as I passed him and guided me into the chair across from him. He took both my hands.

"If there is anything we know from our discipline," he said, "it is that people make choices for reasons that aren't necessarily rational. If they did, the world would be very different."

"Yes," I said, calming as always under the influence of Bream's voice and the predictability of unpredictability. "People are strange."

"I believe it was the great behavioral economist Jim Morrison who said that."

My panic and nausea lessened.

"And one thing we know for a fact is that people like what is familiar."

"Confirmation bias. Combined with time myopia."

"And loss aversion. People don't like too many choices,"

Bream said. "Which might or might not explain today's headline."

I had been too off-kilter to read it. "Which was?" I said. The dread and foreboding came rushing back.

"Edgerton stepped down," Bream said.

Good thing he was holding my hands because everything else swirled.

"Where is Clint?" I heard myself say before the dark tide washed over me.

Clint came to get me. I didn't quite pass out completely, but Father Bream put my feet up on a stack of books, made a particularly strong cup of Builder's tea, and speed-dialed Clint. He was at home.

"Yes, she's fine," I heard Father Bream say. "But I don't think she should walk home. She was a little shocked by the news about Edgerton." Pause while Clint spoke. "Yes, I thought she should hear it from me and somewhere not at home." Pause. "Agreed. I think this is what has been in the works all along. I'm not sure where it will end. Agatha doesn't know." What I didn't know would fill volumes, so I wasn't sure what he meant specifically. "Yes, just come up. The porter will let you through. Oh, and, Clint, I think Agatha has some news for you."

"What don't I know?" I said when he had hung up.

"You don't know what will happen either," he said lamely.

"I didn't know you had Clint on speed-dial. Since when did you two have hotlines to each other?"

"He's your husband," Bream said soothingly if also lamely.

"And a spy," I said. "Are you in cahoots with him like Mother is? Did the three of you engineer the Thanksgiving debacle?"

"I wouldn't underestimate your mother," Father Bream said. "Or your husband."

"Or you, for that matter," I said.

"Or you," Father Bream said and toasted me with a steaming hot cup of Builder's tea.

When Clint came in Father Bream poured him a mug of tea and Clint took it after giving me a once-over.

"I'd ask where you've been, but I know you won't tell me, so I'll save my breath."

"You just used it," Clint said. "I was taking care of business. And what about you? How are you?"

"I'm fine except my mother's annual huge, society event seems to have caused the Vice President to resign while a snake in the grass if there ever was one rose to be the second most powerful person in the country and his wife seems not to have given up her past all that much and, oh yes, my husband and mother—possibly both parents and longtime academic and spiritual advisor—are all involved. Wouldn't be surprised if my nanny and Mother's butler had a hand in."

"What about you?" Clint said. "Father Bream says you're holding some cards close to your chest yourself."

"Well, I don't know how he knows," I said huffily.

Father Bream looked toward the ceiling and we all laughed.

Clint shook my hands he was holding in his.

"Well, I am," I said.

"Hooray," Clint said and gathered me into his arms.

"I'd say 'we' were pregnant," Clint said, perching on another stack of books. "But 'we' aren't—you are. I know it's not easy. It's hazardous. But I'm so glad. I think it will be a girl this time. But, mind you, I'm perfectly happy with a sixth boy."

"That was one of the longest speeches I've heard Clint make," Father Bream said. "Make it an even half dozen."

Father Bream beamed at us both and then looked again toward the ceiling, such happiness radiating from him and from Clint that it filled the room with a brightness that didn't come from the desk lamp, on because of the falling darkness.

I felt it too—the irrational, overwhelming sense of hope the promise of a child carried, even when, as Clint and I already knew well, the actuality was complicated and often just plain hard. And then there was the state of the world—always precarious but now seeming to take a quantum leap in the direction of chaos.

And yet there we were, filled with a tremendous sense of optimism, as if the darkness were held in enormous, warm hands of light.

Clint was always more solicitous of me in early pregnancy—which was to say he informed me slightly more often of his whereabouts. He was busy those first weeks after the resignation. I was tempted to call it a coup, but, really, it was an orderly change in the administration, planned for by the framers, if one of the top members of the executive branch became incapacitated. In this case the President simply appointed a new second-in-command. It didn't seem too illogical that he chose the Speaker, Adam Trent.

At least it wasn't like when Woodrow Wilson had a stroke and his wife and doctor kept it secret while the wife *de facto* ran the country.

Connie Edgerton's meltdown was of such enormous proportions and children so young and confused, it was clear that Edgerton wouldn't be able to go on as a functioning vice president.

"Why do so many people view the changeover as catastrophic?" I asked Molly one night as the two of us got dinner ready. "Because it doesn't really have to be. It's not as if the President isn't still in charge."

Molly looked at me as if I'd completely lost my wits.

"Really?" she said. "Doesn't Adam Trent's nearness to the top worry you? He has his own agenda—and It's clearly not the same as the president's. They aren't anything alike."

"They *are* in the same party," I pointed out.

"And there the similarities end," she said. "The President is recognizable."

"And Adam a lunatic," I agreed. I wondered if I proceeded naively enough if Molly would be irritated into spilling the beans about what Mother was up to, possibly with Clint, Molly, and Delaney's collusion.

"Adam doesn't so much want new policies as to destroy any idea of policy or system itself," I went on.

"I understand there is a certain type of psychopathic personality that not only has chaos at its very core but sees engendering the same sense of chaos in everyone around him as imperative—a matter of survival."

I thought about the sense of dis-ease, of agitation I always felt around Adam—a kind of excitement that also demanded rescue, a call to fight or flight, like an overdose of adrenalin.

"So those people had an experience of growing up that, instead of slowly creating structure, a framework for the chaos of unregulated desire, instead lean toward disintegration."

"Yes," Molly said. "And, worse, the need to project that chaos, to sow the same sense of shambles in others."

"A way of normalizing the chaos they feel."

"Anyone who has a stable ego—a real one—is an affront," Molly said.

"A threat," I said. "But what would attract people to such a person? Why would he have a following? In a politician's case who would vote for him?"

"People who can be made to feel fear," Molly said. She finished dishing out the beef stew and began to butter the homemade sourdough bread on each of eight plates.

"But, Molly, why would Mother and Clint be involved in encouraging that?" It was my most desperate question yet and I took a chance on Molly hearing it and understanding my need for an answer.

She paused and reflected a moment.

"A boil has to be seen to be lanced," she said.

And with that unappetizing metaphor she handed me two plates to put on the table.

CHAPTER EIGHTEEN
Baby

Clint was home for dinner and, over the babble, communicated in French that he thought we should tell the boys.

"Tell them about the vice president?" I bellowed back in French. Not knowing how to say vice president in French, I'd had to resort to prime minister. "I don't think they need to know that."

Clint inclined his head toward Jules who was listening intently to us. I'll be damned if it didn't look like he understood everything we said—the French *and* the implications. Was that possible? I looked at my oldest son's serious, concerned face. Clint was watching him too. Our son didn't stop looking concerned, but he forked up a mouthful of mac and cheese to make us feel better. Some souls arrived here very old and kind.

"*Non,*" Clint said. "*Que tu es enceinte.*"

"Oh," I said. "It's early days yet."

"No time like the present," he said. I would understand only later what he meant by that.

"Okay, I said.

"Boys, boys!" It took some banging of his fork on a

plate to collect all their attention. "Your mother and I have an announcement!"

"We're getting a pony!" Theo said.

"No," Clint said. "Queenie is plenty in the pet department for now. Guess again."

"Mother is pregnant—again," Jules said. He said it was such gravity and finality the whole table settled into a state of seriousness.

"Yay!" Dylan burst out. "Baby!"

"Another brother," Isaac yelled.

"Well, we don't know. We're hoping to finally get a girl in here," I said. "Molly and I need some reinforcements."

"Queenie," Dylan said.

"She's a girl," Theo pointed out.

"It *could* be a girl," Jules said. This seemed to cheer him up some.

"Let's hear it for Mom!" Clint said. "She's got most of the work to do for now so try not to drive her crazy. Then later on we'll all pitch in and help."

"Yay!" most of them yelled. Jules still looked skeptical.

"Actually, Molly will do most of the helping," he pointed out, pedantically.

Molly and I were putting the finishing touches on the kitchen cleanup after Clint and the boys had done their part and gone to the tower for final playtime.

"Jules is right," I said. "Are you surprised about another one?"

"Oh, no," she said. "I always love babies." She wiped the counter. "And I already knew."

She untied her apron and went off to her quarters.

Was Molly some sort of witch or seer? I didn't know—but I didn't doubt she knew I was pregnant even before I did. And if I had any qualms about it—which I would be crazy not to—well, Molly was even crazier because I could see she had not a single one.

The same couldn't be said for my parents. Well, one of my parents. The other one took a completely different approach.

Father was, naturally, delighted. He also had some second thoughts.

"Are you sure?" he said.

"Sure I'm pregnant? Yes, I'm sure of that."

"Sure this is the right time."

"Because of the upheaval?"

"Experience tells us that sort of upheaval has little impact beyond the Beltway," he said reassuringly. "It's hard to get the whole world involved in our domestic issues, if you really get down to it. No, I mean you and Clint. Dylan is still a baby and Clint is gone a lot."

"We've made it so far," I said. "And I have a lot of help." I squeezed his square, warm hand. He was a very hands-on grandfather and often took the boys off individually on adventures. He and Jules had a particular affinity and they often spent Sunday afternoons at Udvar-Hazy.

I wasn't going to mention to him that it was too late

to do anything about it easily. I had thought I was menopausal well past the 12-week point—and anyway I wouldn't have. For some reason, though Clint would himself never dictate my choice, his Catholicism had seeped into me in this arena—a life was indeed a life. And we had the means to care for it well. For me, pro-choice meant just that.

"Yes," Father was saying, "Molly is a miracle."

Neither of us was going to make the mistake of saying Mother was the most grandmotherly grandmother around. Her rare interactions with all the boys were well-ordered—they shaped up around her and formed into a crocodile-shaped line behind her like a well-schooled collection of convent girls. They always learned a lot on outings with her and came home quieter and more serious—until one of them farted. Then the natural chaos was restored.

Mother came in then, her coffee cup in hand.

"What is the news?" she said.

"I'm pregnant," I said.

Father's smile broke out spontaneously.

"What, again?" Mother said. She couldn't her slight moue of disapproval any more than Father could his spontaneous smile.

I threw my arms around her.

"Mother, you are one of a kind," I said. "Some grandmothers would be glad—or concerned. Not you."

"I am glad, darling," she said., putting her coffee cup down delicately. "and I'm also concerned. Pregnancy and childbirth aren't always easy for you."

"I know, Mother," I said. "But everything is always a risk."

"Let me know if there is anything I can do," she said. "In the meantime, tell me all you know about Ana Trent. I think you haven't told me all. There is clearly more there than meets the eye and you know her as well as anyone."

"Plus, she's the Second Lady now," I said, "making her even more central to the palace intrigue."

"She seems to be very close to Rasputin," Mother said.

"You were the one who seated them next to each other."

"That was a little test of our theory."

"*Our* theory? Who is this *our*, Mother?"

"Well, your father and I were curious. It seemed like the communist bloc was starting to re-coalesce and we wondered if there was any American involvement."

"You don't mean Ana Trent?"

"No, no—we just wanted to know if Ana and Rasputin were friends. Then Adam Trent made himself part of it. And Connie Edgerton's reaction confirmed a tiny suspicion we had, that there was something going on."

"Maybe she just lost her mind."

"One only loses one's mind over something political in this town, dear."

"Maybe it was poison," I said. No one said anything about this. "Is there any chance my husband had anything to do with this?"

"Well, Clint does always take an interest in our events,"

Mother said. I waited her out. "He did take a peek at the seating arrangement." I waited some more. Like most well-bred people, Mother couldn't leave a good silence unfilled. "And he did have a couple of suggestions."

In exchange for this information, I reviewed with Mother what I knew of Ana Trent, which was precious little.

"The funny thing, when all is said and done, even the scene with Rasputin, I feel like I should either dislike her—she is part of the enemy camp, after all—or feel sorry for her—she is in a whole other category from her husband—smart, canny, worldly in ways he never could be. Yet I don't dislike *or* feel sorry for her. I feel like she is more in control than she looks and, here is the worst part, I just like her, even if she is playing me somehow. As she most certainly is."

Mother got up.

"I got you some salsa, dear. I know how you devour it when you are—like that."

Mother was right about salsa—I liked it okay normally but could drink it from a fire hose when pregnant—the hotter the better.

I wasn't going to look too deeply at the fact that Mother seemed to have known all along I was pregnant—at least long enough ago to lay in a supply of salsa.

I seemed to like milder forms of salsa this time around—which Mother also intuited—and attributed that to the fact that this one was a girl.

I wasn't sure how I knew this and I'd have some

qualms—my mother's and my relationship was so dark and involved I wasn't quite sure why I wanted to recreate a mother-daughter bond of my own. But I knew this was a girl and Clint seemed happy about that too. Only once did I catch him looking longingly at the soccer team he was building as I prattled on about pink things. Of course, she was going to have to look good in blue and red and mud as she was soon to meet a tidal wave of hand-me-downs from her brothers.

One day I found Isaac cleaning out his bottom dresser drawer, placing the clothes neatly into a carryall.

"I'm packing her clothes so she'll have something to come home from the hospital in," he said when I asked him. "And she can sleep right here," he said, indicating the empty drawer.

Indeed, he had lined the drawer with his spare bankie and added a little-used pacifier at one end.

I just nodded and thanked him for his thoughtfulness and generosity. Isaac would have been overwhelmed if I'd grabbed and hugged him as I wanted to do. I went about my business a little choked up, though.

I'd never known how tenderly loving boys were until I'd had my own. Rough and ready for sure—boisterous and physical—I could no longer claim there weren't inborn differences between boys and girls. Any dolls we gave them promptly became train passengers or guerilla fighters—or weapons. Doll houses were for climbing on. And, though we allowed no toy artillery in the house, sticks and carrots were called to duty anyway.

But there was no girl I'd ever met as sweet or genuinely, unquestionably, uncomplicatedly loving as my boys. In entirely different styles, each would go to any length to care for people they loved. Their feelings ran ocean deep. They would be splendid big brothers to a lucky little girl.

Jules would radiate love, shining it on her constantly. Theo's love would be thoughtful, and the twins' would physically engulf her. Dylan's love would be a jewel—a precious gem he gave to few, but those who got it would have a real treasure.

But I didn't have time to ponder any of the mysteries of my children—present or to come. The Christmas crazies were upon us, kicked off by Jules' birthday. He'd had the sense not to arrive right at Christmas, but his birthday early in December kicked off the season of nuttiness. With five kids all wanting different things, all about to be home full time for the holiday, and my house the center of Christmas festivities so that the boys and their presents didn't have to get packed up and moved to Evermay, there was plenty to keep me and Molly on the run. It went without saying that only-sibling James' apartment at the Kennedy Center was no place for us to congregate. He had a bit of a clandestine life anyway, whether thanks to his job or his personal life, and Mother and I tended to grant him his privacy.

We had long since given up having location birthdays. It was way too much of a hassle to create a big birthday party at the local firehouse and the year we'd had one at Udvar-Hazy had gone down as the year we lost five boys—two of them mine—until after the museum closed and we found them piled like exhausted puppies, asleep in the back seat of the Sopwith Camel. Having parties at home where doors could contain them proved a far better idea.

Clint was always in charge of Jules' birthday party in particular. They had a special bond that went way back. I could see in Clint's eyes how much he regretted not being able to spend more time with his eldest—because of his job during normal times but now with so much mayhem.

Though the White House seemed orderly enough then, there was something quite off, and it was a good bet that Adam Trent was at the center of it.

Molly and I regularly looked at each other during the morning news.

"Did he really say that?" she wondered.

"Yes, he did," I said.

"But no decent human being says things like that," she said.

"No one said he was decent," I said. "I think there are some people who might consider what he says as being 'plain-spoken.'"

"'Plain-spoken' is saying things simply, without puffing them up. 'Plain-spoken' isn't cruel and indecent. He's the vice-president, for heaven's sake."

"I think there are people who think he will change."

Molly snorted. "That the office would make the man? No chance. You watch: he will deform the office."

"At least he's only the vice-president. That's a pretty ceremonial office."

"Only a heartbeat away," Molly said cheerily. "Has that baby had enough breakfast yet?" She pointed to my empty plate.

Molly served as Mother's food police deputy.

"She was hungry," I said.

Molly looked her question and I picked up our plates.

CHAPTER NINETEEN
Birthday

The day of Jules's party came and, with it, full-scale mayhem. The boys were out of their minds, each in his own way. Jules was anxious, Theo shrill and policing, Isaac and Jack jigging. Even self-sufficient Dylan's eyes were spinning in his head.

The cooking was proceeding in a sort of orderly chaos, with Clint at the center of it. The boys' birthdays were where he seized a chance to cook for them. It gave him so much pleasure and produced such dishes and cakes of beauty, we all wished he could do it more often.

He had the boys swirling around him, learning the art of manly cooking.

They had just ferried the sheet cake in a brigade formation to the dining room table when the doorbell started ringing.

Mother came in in her pink plaid suit, Cartier brooch emblazoned.

"I brought Delaney," she said. "He wanted to wish Jules a happy birthday. Under no circumstances is he allowed to open the door. He is out of costume."

It wasn't quite clear whether she wanted him to

have some free time or the costume, otherwise known as formal butler dress, made the role and it would be improper to function without it.

She sailed in her dignified way straight into the chaos swirling already through the kitchen, living, dining and sun rooms. She had said more than once that she wasn't sure why we held parties for the boys as she was pretty sure they themselves constituted one. But their chaos didn't blow her hair back ever. I could see her stop by the kitchen to check on Cint's creations. She gave him a nod of approval and he kissed the top of her immaculately coifed head, co-conspirators.

Then came the flood. Kids from Sidwell, the neighborhood, who knew where. Grateful parents jettisoned them from SUVs and Rolls straight down the loading ramp of the sidewalk, pausing only long enough to be sure they made it through the door, then jetting off with a spurt and look of "You're a better man than I, Gunga Din" in their eye. For such a security-conscious city there was a marked lack of care in their speedy departures.

The thing was I wasn't—a better man. I was flustered by my own kids more often than I cared to admit and the boys' birthdays were a thing to be endured, like labor. Which reminded me that there was another one, a girl, rolling and kicking her way into the world. I sent a quick prayer that little girls' pink and purple parties would be quieter.

But then I remembered my own girlhood and how

often the quiet whispering of girl groups was a cover for back-biting, one-ups-womanship and shaming. I dove into the friendly boy mayhem with more enthusiasm than I might have.

Clint was surveying the spread on the dining room table. It was hard for me to believe that I could find my husband any more hot and handsome than I did already, but seeing him in his crisp white shirt, one button undone at the neck and sleeves rolled precisely up, his black pants smooth across his butt, I was even more gone. I went up behind him and put my arms around him. He hugged my arms tight against his waist and continued to survey his culinary kingdom.

"Yep, I think it's all here," he said. He turned and pulled me in to him, turning us both sideways to the table. "What does milady think?"

"I think it's gorgeous," I said. I looked at the array, from delicate, carefully presented canapes for the adults—one place garnished with orchid blossoms for example—to the most perfect kid fare: chips and cheese, tiny pigs in a blanket, brownies, and, at the far end, gallons of lemonade in our non-soda pop house. "And a perfect balance for kids and for adults brave enough to enter the fray."

He leaned down and kissed me, long and deep, the taste of dark chocolate faintly on his tongue.

We stood like that, our arms around each other a long time, in the whirlwind time scheme of our house and life. I loved the feel of him, of course. But mostly I loved the deep rich smell of him—fresh and clean, the smell of light starch in his shirt, a very slight tang of man—of armpit and crotch—and an overlay of cinnamon that was somehow natural to him. And, that day, dark chocolate. I gave in to the headiness of it, a dizziness that might have been early pregnancy but felt more like early love. And delicious because just at that moment, I could lean into him, merge with his warmth, put my weight against the hard muscles of Clint and give up.

He took my weight entirely against him, turned me aslant as if my feet were on his, like when I danced with my father as a child.

I looked down at the table again and saw the sheet cake he'd made. It took a second to recognize the design of it and decipher the complex lettering. It was a spaceship and a Cylon from *Battlestar Galactica*, small figures of the President, Admiral Adama, and Starbuck scattered around the dark of space.

"Oh, Jules will love it," I said. *Battlestar Galactica* was his all-time favorite series. Quite a bit darker than *Star Wars*, of which he was also very fond—Clint and I decided its complexity and gravity suited Jules, whose optimism was not a result of ignoring the reality of the world.

Battlestar was as mythic as *Star Wars* but less binary. The tangle of power, good and evil, and technology was very adult and foretold a time where people would have to make unimaginable decisions with the trusty old weapons of honesty, bravery, fidelity. It made us realize not for the first time, how easy it was to underestimate children, to think that their youth meant innocence. At least this was true of Jules. Theo was no less complex. The twins might be buffered by their duality. And Dylan was his own little universe. But they were all going to go into a future where Clint and I could not follow. Could not protect them, other than to equip them with those rusty old values.

"It is so right," I said. Clint kissed me again.

Just then the tide washed our way and that was it for private time for us. The hordes descended on the table and left a litter of chips and brownies crumbs wherever it went after that.

The doorbell rang again and Mother went to answer, serene and not a hair or jewel out of place, despite the fact that she'd been immersed in the boy tide for some time.

"Oh, it's you," I heard her say. "Do come in."

It wasn't a very welcoming sound and there was a touch of unpleasant surprise to it.

I looked around the door to the hall so I could see the front door.

There stood Ana Trent, with Wolf at her knee. Wolf was in a blazer and carried a large, bright box. Ana herself was in jeans—albeit very stylish ones—which I had never seen her in before.

I looked around for my husband to see if he could explain this apparition—I hadn't invited her—but he was gone.

I sent Wolf in the directions of the mayhem after relieving him of the present. I took Ana's leather jacket and hung it on the coat rack. Neither of us attempted small talk.

"How is the life at Blair House?" I finally asked.

"Surely you of all people know I don't live there."

"No, I didn't know that."

"I didn't want Wolf's routine disturbed in the middle of the school year."

"That makes all the sense in the world," I said. "Does Adam mind not having the trappings of office?"

"Adam? Oh, Adam has moved to the Blair House," she said.

"Of course, he would," I said. "Silly me."

"Silly?" she said.

"To think he would stay where you and Wolf are."

"We live more separately all the time," she said. "I want you to know that."

"The traditional marital connections do seem to be missing," I said. "And you have some strange ones outside of the marriage."

"If you mean Viktor Rasputin, my family knew his family. That is all."

"Before the thaw, I take it."

"Long before the thaw," she said.

I took it that she meant ancient history. Which would have to be quite ancient—Montenegro's ties to Russia were as complex and conflicted as all of eastern Europe's to Turkey, Western Europe, and Russia.

"And then there is any possible connection to my husband," I said.

"Clint was kind enough to extend an invitation to Wolf because I told him how much it would mean to him. Wolf is very fond of Jules."

"What's not to like about Jules?" I said." He's the world's nicest person, not just kid."

Ana smiled what seemed like a genuine smile of recognition for my eldest's goodness. But it vanished almost instantly.

"We may not be here much longer," she said. It was close to a whisper.

"What do you mean?" I asked roughly. "You just got here." But then I understood her meaning. "Your husband just became vice president. Where would you go?"

"I've said too much," Ana said. "Forget I said anything at all."

She turned her head toward the sunroom where the tide of children was involved in some sort of game. I saw that chiseled profile again, so much more Slavic than any colonial presidential wife silhouette, so much more exotic. And, on closer inspection, the lines so much deeper, the ancientness of her culture etched dangerously deep into her skin. She picked up the birthday box and walked past me with it. When I looked down the length of the dark hall she'd entered, I saw Clint standing there.

I was too stunned by her revelation of leaving to ask where she was when Clint had extended the birthday invitation. The CIA? Her cool, calm Kalorama home? I didn't even know he had her contact information.

The birthday party went the usual route: everyone was having a lot of fun—more and more of it. Organized games were long since abandoned. The doors to the garden were open to increase the size of the loop the boys and girls described through the house. The younger brothers had friends over too so that the whole scene was complicated by mixing age groups. The older ones were universally good natured, being Jules' friends, but their very mass and energy caused them to knock down younger ones from time to time. When the cake and ice cream and accumulated sugar became the rocket fuel that they are, the whole thing reached a pitch and din that was hard to believe outside of a war zone. Ana was sighted in the midst of it all. At first, I thought she was trying to get a grip on Wolf, as protective as a mother of single cubs can be. But then I saw my mother beside her and I realized they were both enjoying it thoroughly.

Was it possible that they were egging the boys on just a little bit?

One mother showed up and stopped by to chastise me and Molly. We were leaning in the butler pantry door, looking as if we might be preparing to disappear into it if any youthful energy bombs detonated near us, drinking coffee to sustain our energy because we knew we'd need to be standing long after the party was over, cleaning up and supervising the calming process involving baths and the umpteenth millionth viewing of 101 Dalmatians.

"Why do you let them eat sugar?" the mother yelled. "They are wild now! It's the sugar!"

"What do you suggest instead?" Molly said. She projected her voice like a stage actress, from her diaphragm rather than yelling. "Kale chips and carrots?"

"That is what I serve at my parties," the mother said.

"What a great way to have leftovers," Molly said. In that English accent, it was hard for the woman to be sure there was an insult in there. First, she smiled as if complimented, then she wandered away, shaking her head a little, whether confused by Molly or just by the ear-shattering din.

Molly and I had a pretty good sense when a party might go over the top and end in fisticuffs or, the bugaboo of all parents of young children, biting. We signaled Clint who was more or less riding herd. His instincts for the level of childhood fun-into-hysteria were less refined so he relied on us to make the call.

When we gave him the throat-slash signal he began to round up the pack and little by little cut out and quieted down pairs until, though a child might have some cake in their hair when a parent arrived, they looked semi-civilized in the eye.

I saw Ana leaving—she said her thanks to Clint, I thought. I also thought it was possible she had some cake in her hair.

In bed that night the little girl in the making started raising a ruckus for the first time. Every pregnancy that quickening got earlier. I was distracted enough by the movement to miss the fact that Clint just got in bed, turned over, and went to sleep.

I started thinking the next day of ways to see Ana. I was dying to know how life as the Second Lady was going. And where she was going. She certainly looked no happier.

But the fact that she was the VPs wife made her that much harder to meet quietly. All those men in black around her. She must have done some fast talking to leave them outside at the birthday party.

I also, peripherally, wanted to know if she had an eye on my husband, or he on her. I wasn't sure how I was going to put that question, but I knew I wanted to have a run at it.

I wasn't going to ask Clint. For obvious reasons. Because I knew he wasn't interested in another woman—of course not.

Plus, you can never tell for sure when you're married to a spy. Deception is a way of life.

Six children wasn't a reason not to cheat—not in DC.

While I let the question about meeting Ana percolate, we entered the interregnum between Jules' birthday and Christmas wherein I just crossed my fingers that no virus wildfired through the school and sent the boys home early. Two weeks of nonstop boys was plenty without additional days added.

My girl was entering a growth spurt—I could tell because I got really sleepy. I walked Queenie after the boys went to school and then the three of us—dog, fetus, me—went back to bed. Molly was pretty quiet those days and even Mother seemed to slow down.

Mayhem seemed to have quieted down in the political world. What else could go wrong? Connie Edgerton was in some plush facility and her husband and children had retreated to Illinois to ride out her storm. Adam Trent was behaving, as much as was possible. There was no question that he meant to cause a ruckus, whether as a trickster or out of sheer love of the attention that goes with chaos. But he seemed to be willing to let go of it for the holiday season.

Molly and I did our shopping and ordering in the sunroom with a pot of tea between us.

The traditions of the season unfolded. Molly and I put up a real tree. People in my neighborhood often had several trees—artificial for the most part and the children's tree out of sight somewhere. Our one tree was in the living room for all to see, with all the children's gaudy, handmade ornaments prominently displayed. I loved the wreath made of pasta glued on a paper plate and painted glossy green Jules had made in pre-K.

The school, or course, was all about multiple holidays—Hanukkah, Christmas Kwanzaa—all of which had to be celebrated before the holiday break, so there was a lot of sugar going on.

We would have the family Christmas at my house and then Mother would give a party on boxing Day. Preparations were going forward for both, but, since neither aspired to reach the heights of my Halloween party or Mother's Thanksgiving (for which, mercies), they required relatively little attention.

Nevertheless, it felt a little manic. Maybe it was just me—but everyone seemed overstimulated and giddy just under the surface. I think the best word might have been "antic." All of this was overlaid by my colossal fatigue. None of my babies had ever made me sick, but they sure could drive me to stupendous salsa-consumption and a practically never-ending nap.

CHAPTER TWENTY

Christmas

"Have you seen Clint?" I asked Molly. It was the day before the kids got out of school.

"No, I haven't," Molly said. "But I might have easily missed him. He's mostly been home late and gone early lately."

"For about a month now—really since Thanksgiving," I said. I looked at the fridge calendar, which of course wasn't magneted to the fridge anymore. "Why can't they make magnetic stainless steel?"

"Harder than making a new nuclear weapon, it seems," Molly agreed. We were both aggrieved that an entire organizational system went by the wayside with the introduction of stainless steel appliances.

"I think it's possible I was asleep for much of that month," I said.

"Could have been all of it."

I looked to see if she was berating me.

"The babies take you that way," she reassured me.

"This one is starting to make herself known," I said. "I can already feel her."

"Her?" Molly said.

"I'm sure it's a girl," I said. "I don't know why I'm sure. I just am. Won't Clint be hopeless as a girl-dad? He might even get goofy.'

Molly smiled at me, at my goofy love for my husband—and, just possibly, at my conviction about the gender.

"We'll have to track him down first," I added. "Were there any dishes from his dinner or breakfast?"

"None that I saw. But he has been known to put his dishes in the machine."

"I'm going to have to get on him about eating. I think he's losing weight."

"Not as much as the President," Molly said. "He looks terrible."

"Speaking of missing—I don't think I've seen him in a few days."

"I don't know," Molly said.

She said it calmly enough and almost anything said in a English accent sounds more calm to me, but there was a look of real concern on her face that worried me.

"I'm going to check the bedroom—see what clothes Clint is wearing."

I went up the stairs thumbing his number into my phone on the way. I tried not to call him too often because he was busy, I didn't want to alarm him unnecessarily in case he was always worried a boy had gotten hurt, plus I hated the sound of his voicemail when I really wanted the deep timbre of his voice.

No clothes in the hamper. No steam in the bath. Were a few more clothes missing? And where was his small suitcase?

Clint often kept the suitcase packed and ready to go—often at the office---because he could have to jet at a moment's notice. So that wasn't such a big deal.

So why was my heart bouncing and fluttering? Was that the baby or anxiety?

For one thing I might have been subconsciously tuned in to the news.

Molly came up the stairs in a sort of dignified hurry.

"Quick, turn on the news," she said.

I turned on WAMU on my iPad.

"The President has been hospitalized at Walter Reed," Kojo Nnamdi was saying in his dignified way. "We do not have any more details. We do not believe that there was a shooting incident as we have had no such reports. At this time, the speculation is that the president was taken ill at his home and taken to the hospital. We will report further as we receive details. In the meantime, we will continue our conversation with George W. Bush's ethics officer but will ask if he can speak to the process that would now be put into place in the case of the President being taken ill as the President seems to have been."

"Well," Kojo," said the lawyer in his slow and carefully considered way, "That possibility is covered by the 25th Amendment which, as you know, was passed in Congress when it became clear that Woodrow Wilson had suffered a debilitating stroke and it was, in fact, his wife who was making presidential decisions for months so that President's illness wouldn't become public."

"As I understand it, the 25th Amendment calls for the succession to be the same as in the case of the death of the president."

"Yes, the Vice President acts as President until the President recovers or another election takes place."

Molly and I stared at each other. We raced down the stairs—Molly got out in front—to the TV, which we kept only one of, in the sunroom.

Sure enough, big as life, Adam Trent was looking somber from time to time when someone reminded him of the seriousness of the situation. But then the true Adam would break out and there would be a look of sheer glee.

The most powerful nation in the world was his.

Let the mayhem begin.

Molly poured us each a small sherry to calm our fears.

We turned off the news when the boys were coming home. A friends' mom with a bus-sized SUV had volunteered to bring them. I didn't know exactly what people think an agent's wife does, but, clearly, some thought I'd have a lot to do in a situation like this.

But I didn't. I didn't have nearly enough to do. For one thing we'd never had a situation like this—or, more accurately, know it when we did have. For another, I was typical of most spies' wives in that it wasn't a home business—I wasn't his partner—and in fact I was completely clueless what he was doing. And, lest we forget, I didn't even know where he was.

We wanted to limit the boys' exposure to the level and hype and hysteria that could easily sweep DC, so we left the TV off, made hot dogs and Ye Olde Kraft Macaroni & Cheese, and the boys and I made a heap on the gigantic sofa that was our refuge in any storm.

Molly made a discreet check in with the news on her TV from time to time then returned to her knitting.

By the time the boys went up for bed, we knew that the President was in critical but stable condition at Walter Reed with an undisclosed illness, that Adam Trent was installed in the Oval Office and had temporarily moved to the White House. Ana Trent was nowhere to be seen.

I went to say goodnight to the boys.

"Why aren't you milling about and calling people?" Jack asked.

"What?"

"That is what you do when you are upset," he said complacently.

How many of my numbers did these kids have? And where had he learned the phrase "milling about"?

"Good question," I said. "I think I'll go do that."

"I'm hearing what you're hearing," Mother said. "Nothing more. Your father is out making the rounds to see if anyone knows more. What about Clint? Surely he can tell you something."

"Actually, no. He is a master compartmentalizer, as you know well. Plus, also he isn't here."

"Oh?"

Did Mother's voice sound just a little panicky? A little more worried than she usually permitted?

"He often vanishes—you know that. He gets called away."

"Of course, he does. And there is quite a lot to get called away to."

"I've got to go to sleep now, Mother," I said. I was overcome by a wave of sleepiness that almost knocked me out before I could get off the phone.

I slept. Molly had the kids up and off to their last day of school before I woke up. She had the cookies made for the holiday party I'd take to school later in the morning. Then the boys would be home for the holiday, after only a half day of school. We spent our coffee time riveted to the TV where the hosts on MSNBC went over and over what we already did and didn't know. Father Bream had showed up at the back door just when we were sitting down to glue ourselves to the TV. The President was in the hospital with an undisclosed illness. Adam Trent was acting president for the time being.

"Breaking news: Acting President Trent has rolled back some banking and environmental regulations overnight. Here is the list of executive orders he has signed overnight."

They went on to list a series of possibly 50 executive orders signed by the previous president that provided consumer and environmental protections. There were a few that protected civil rights thrown in there.

"Can he do that?" Mika Brezinski said.

"What has been executive ordered can be unexecutive ordered," Joe Scarborough replied.

Molly and I looked at each other.

Mika said, "This just in. Acting President Trent has lifted all sanctions put in place after the incursions into the Crimea."

She and Joe just stared at each other. I'd never seen morning show hosts speechless.

"Was this what they were always after?" Molly said.

"Must have been, "I said. "But who do we mean by that?"

"Adam and his Russian friends?" Molly said.

"Are they friends? And are the Russian oligarchs? They all seem to be just rich, corrupt people. Do they just have something on Trent?"

"Same difference," Molly said, using an Americanism. "He will do what they want either way."

"But how does he know what they want? How do they communicate? People have been watching Adam for years, thinking he was Russia-friendly. No one has ever found anything."

"Wasn't there a questionable meeting with his chief of staff and the Russians?"

"Is Adam Trent smart enough to run a spy operation?"

"Back in the Cold War days, I remember the Soviets were always looking for people in the West they could use. They were looking for two kinds of people," Molly said.

"What were they?" I asked.

"One group was made up of the 'fellow travelers'—people who believed what they believed," Molly said.

"And the other?" I asked.

"Oh, I remember this," Father Bream laughed.

"They were called 'useful idiots,'" Molly said.

We all got a slightly evil laugh over this, right up until it turned sad and scary.

"But there isn't any Soviet Union anymore," I said. "And the former eastern bloc nations don't have an ideology to believe in."

"So, they've gone back to what they believed in before, where everyone goes who doesn't have something to believe in," Molly said.

"And what is that?" I turned to Father Bream. "Even you couldn't say it was God."

"Nationalism," Bream said. "Pure nationalism."

"And money," Molly added.

I was mesmerized for a moment, like the listener to Marlow's story as he spun the tale of the heart of darkness while their boat made its way down the Thames.

"But what does that have to do with us, with America right now? The country is doing better than ever before—more or less at peace, strong economy—problems galore but none that even comes close to what people are dealing with in, say the Middle East," I said.

"And, thus, ripe for the picking," Molly said.

"A sense of danger can easily be planted in the soil of complacency," Bream added.

"But we *do* believe in something larger—we have laws and a Constitution," I said.

"I believe I quote Dr. Franklin when I say, 'Here is your Republic, if we can keep it.,'" Bream said.

I helped Molly and Bream clean up. There would be mayhem enough when the boys were home for two weeks without us getting sloppy now.

I wondered again about the two of them—Molly and Father Bream. Of a similar age, one English, one Irish, they were both very smart, very well-read. And they both had chosen a life of service. I wondered, not for the first time, if my husband were the only spy in the house.

Though the boys provided the din of distraction once they were home for the holidays, I didn't forget for a second that my husband was missing. The level of anxiety was going up everywhere. Mine rose with it.

Adam Tent was everywhere—corking off about everything—saying outrageous things about people and institutions that were normally sacrosanct. He refused to do normal things like show his tax return or divest himself of personal interests in business that profited from the government. He backed measures that ran the deficit up wildly and clearly benefited only the rich and famous. By all accounts, he behaved like a bad-tempered boy behind the scenes and treated everyone badly.

Although there were few who were shocked enough to protest madly—they might have been believing that he would be gone soon—many people accepted him as what he said he was: a man of the people, fighting for the little guy.

Then the firings began.

One head of Justice went, many staff members were ploughed under. The head of the CIA was fired and one of Trent's pals appointed.

Congress shaped up into a collective deer in the headlights. They seemed to have no idea of what their role was or Trent's was; everyone had apparently forgotten what limits were, never mind checks and balances.

One day I did escape to make a quick trip to Dean and Delucca's to freshen the snack supply and my boots just kept on walking, taking me to Bream's office.

The smell of old books and, somewhere, deep in the bones of the room, good Scotch whisky, the warmth of worn Orientals and cracked leather armchair—even the dust—brought a sense of calm, of timelessness, of the fleetingness of the anxiety of the moment and the depth of the enduring, the eternal—all combined to give me a sudden and profound sense of peace.

Bream was having none of it.

He was pacing, fretting.

"It's not good, not good," he said. "Something is truly rotten."

"What do you mean?"

"Trent—the chaos, the ease with which he is knocking it all down."

"But what if, as he says, that is a constructive thing in the long run: to tear down the façade, show what's fake and not serving."

"Oh, come on, Agatha, surely you aren't fooled too?"

"What do you mean?"

"He knows what to say to anyone—that is his gift—he knows what will open the door a crack with that particular person."

"To let what in?"

"Doubt. The termite of all that is worthwhile. Small but very, very effective. Hard to see and harder to eradicate."

"But doubt—questioning authority in particular—in necessary to prevent authoritarianism," I said. The baby gave me a swift kick, whether of agreement or dis—I wasn't sure.

"And also allowing all points of view equally, with no more discernment, allows fractures that lets authoritarianism in. People behave irrationally. We know that. They make choices that aren't right, aren't even in their own best interest."

"So, doubt is good if it's based in some sort of rational thought—in some framework that is itself reliable."

"We also know from our work that people are irrational but also predictable."

"The cashews," I said.

"Exactly," Bream said. "People in general find it much

easier to make a good choice when the choices are limited—when the bowl of cashews is taken away before people's dinner appetites are ruined."

"It's easier to make good choices when they are limited to mostly good ones."

"One reason 'free love' ended up being destructive to the social fabric as a whole."

"It might be true that the choice between marriage and abstinence was too restrictive, but there might also have been something to say in favor of holding a family to some order of stability. But we are straying from economics."

"Except insofar as in every case the parent who has the children in the case of divorce is worse off financially not only for that time but for their lifetime," Father Bream pointed out.

"True," I said.

"But that is also straying from the political, which is where we started."

"What does our work tell us about the present situation?" I asked.

"I'm not entirely sure, except there are clearly economic motives behind everything Trent is doing. While he blows smoke about the common man he is enriching the wealthy and undermining the underpinnings of democracy. Though there never has been real equality here, there has always been free speech and freedom of the press, both of which tend to level the inequalities and both of which he is bullying out of credibility."

"There is also power at play here. Roughly equal power was supposed to be practiced among the three branches of government, but when the whole goal of two of them is simply taking more of profits from cashew sales for themselves personally, then the ground rules are being violated."

"And the third branch is now in play. The question is, then, who benefits?"

"The wealthy, clearly," I said, knowing full well that I was one of them.

"I think there is even more to it than that, though," Bream said, feeling his way through. "If we take power to be seized under cover of chaos and division, who benefits?"

"He's a hyena," I said suddenly. "Not a wolf or a lion. Trent is a hyena—killing fresh meat and scavenging as well."

"It's the Russians who benefit," Bream said after a moment.

My girl gave me a good swift kick, then. There was no doubt this time of her displeasure.

"Where is Clint?" Bream said. All the urgency and anxiety had returned to his voice.

The days passed in that blur that they do when kids are around. There were trips to the park and to the gym. Molly and I snuck out for shopping runs—whether for more groceries or toys. But mostly there was the mind-boggling routine of getting the boys up, dressed, fed, exhausted, rested, entertained, fed, exhausted, entertained, fed, exhausted. There were mountains of clothes to be reworn, rewashed, refolded, and reput away. The food to be cooked and the dishes to be washed. Though Mother and Father often took a contingent of boys off to Evermay to romp in the huge yard there, it didn't seem like there were any fewer at home. Delaney came over sometimes to run the boys through the military drills that delighted and exhausted them. I was prepared to use nefarious means to lure him over daily, but my mother could always out-nefarious me, so I gave that idea up before I got started.

And always there was no Clint.

At first it didn't seem that weird. Of course, he was gone often. He often didn't tell me he was going, never where he was going or when he would be back. It was an article of faith that he'd gone on business, because he had to, and he would return.

But as the days went by and there was no sign and no word, it started to feel stranger and stranger.

Especially as we got closer to actual Christmas, we all started to feel our nerves jangle. Molly knew better than to ask if I'd heard anything. Mother looked more and more like a bird of prey in her silence, ready to pounce on any hint of information.

As the days went by, I found myself watching the back wall, imagining Clint vaulting over it again, back into our lives, my waiting arms, my waiting body.

But there was no sign of him. The wall remained unbreached, the ivy covering it turned brown and withered as the weather became colder and colder.

The swamp underlying Washington always seemed to make DC colder than other places as arctic air moved in in waves. There was no snow yet, but the cold was intense. It got in your bones and I started to spend anytime I wasn't riding herd in my soaking tub. Mother knew to put me next to the woodburning fireplace whenever I was over there, her incubating granddaughter needing the warmth only burning wood can give.

But the absence only grew, like the silence on the other end of a dead telephone line or the sense of lifelessness that grew on you as you realized a house was completely empty.

On Christmas Eve the anxiety reached fever pitch. The boys—well, most of them—clamored for Clint, their boy souls craving him, deeply discontent without him.

All the adults kept saying the same things--he's at work, he'll be back, we aren't always sure when that will be, are we? But he always comes.

We depended on the past to serve as prologue, but Christmas Eve roared to its conclusion—last minute shopping for stocking stuffers, the usual chaos of clothes and food, and then a showing up at Christmas Mass at

Trinity Chapel, Clint's church, where Bream was giving the service.

It was quite something to get all five boys dressed, to church, and then through the service without having to retreat to the "cry room" where they could yell all they wanted. This was the first year we were trying to go public— Clint didn't usually care whether we went to church or not, but Christmas was different. Even my parents and Jamie went with Molly, me, and the whole gang.

Clint had invited his family to come from West Virginia in the first years we were married, but they demurred, sent gifts for each of the boys as they came but never made an effort to visit. Clint went to see them from time to time.

On that bitterly cold Christmas Eve, I wondered if it was remotely possible that he was there, at home in the small, dark, rural Catholic church in the dark crags of beautiful, wild West Virginia, on retreat like his parents from the worldly, the glitter, the power of DC where I sat with the welter of boys, next to my parents who came to show solidarity, my mother in her not-faux fur coat.

Of course, he wasn't.

We wrangled the boys to the Chinese restaurant, one of the few open on Christmas Eve.

No matter where he was in the world, I knew for a fact that he would rather be with us, with me.

Wouldn't he?

When I was alone at midnight, wrapping the last of the presents, waiting for the Pope to come on, Jules showed up.

He wasn't a good sleeper under the best of circumstances-of which these weren't. While the other boys showed their anxiety outwardly, Jules became quieter and more solemn.

He came down and sat next to me. I knew he would talk when he was ready.

"The President died," he said.

"What?" I said. "Where did you hear that?"

"On FaceBook. Everyone is talking about it."

"Except the Pope, apparently."

I switched channels and Jules and I sat together, my arms around Jules. Queenie had followed him downstairs and clambered up on the other side of him.

"Word has come from Walter Reed that the President has succumbed to his illness. Although there has been no official word about the nature of the disease, it is believed to have been possibly a rapidly progressing form of cancer or, alternatively, something to which he was exposed in his foreign travels. We will know more in the coming days."

The reporter was standing outside the gates of the Walter Reed campus.

"Back to you," he said to the news anchor.

Jules and I looked at each other, then back at the TV.

Adam Trent was on. He was in the Oval Office, sitting in the President's chair. There were people behind him—all his people.

He spoke, but it sounded like word salad to me. He was trying to look solemn and presidential. But he really looked like the cat who ate the Constitutional canary.

Jules and I looked at each other again. Was it possible for us to be any closer to each other? I felt like I might need to weld him to me while the world spun.

"Where is your wife?" a report called to him. "Where is the First Lady?"

Adam shrugged in that way ignorant bullies do. He made it so in his mind that there was nothing wrong with a missing wife.

I wondered if he had killed her. Or disappeared her. He looked so much like a thug at that moment. I wondered what I'd been thinking at the Halloween Party, how I could possibly have thought he had the cleverness of the trickster.

Oh, he had it—but only a superficial level of it. As Bream said, he had the capacity to ferret out what people wanted to hear and the cunning to know how to say it long enough to create doubt.

What was his secret? How was it possible to act with such cunning, all the while having only one agenda: self-aggrandizement that depended on crushing others?

He had no doubt. That was his secret. The narrative he had told himself was so deeply compelling there was no room for questioning it, for critique. And anyone who could be made to doubt could be convinced that Adam was right, could be duped.

But who was duping Adam? I had such a powerful sense right then that Adam's particular skill set—or lack thereof: the rigid lack of critique, the baseless confidence—were being used by someone or something else for their gain.

The Useful Idiot, as Molly said.

But no trickster. He lacked the wisdom of the trickster—knowledge of the end goal, of why he was destroying, of the ultimate consequences. He didn't have the attention span to see that far ahead. But someone did.

Someone who wouldn't even need to be convinced of anything.

Could Adam have become one of their most useful idiots? How could they have gotten to him? As a powerful politician he would be under constant scrutiny for who he spent time with.

Was there anyone in that gang behind him who could be feeding him messages or propaganda?

Was that what Clint was working on? Had he gone to find out how the Russians were puppeteering the president in the U.S.?

Had they had anything to do with the President's death?

How would that be possible? No one was allowed near him, except the very few—the aides, the Cabinet members, the family.

"Dad," Jules said.

That was all he said. Then he collapsed even closer to me, if that was possible.

To call that Christmas subdued would be a vast ironic understatement. All of us, my parents included, looked and acted like people who had been hit by a large Freightliner and pitched to the side of the road.

At least now it was the entire country who looked like that.

The boys other than Jules and possibly Dylan who had such highly attuned sensors nothing went by them might not have felt the impact of the President's death—we didn't turn on the news that day—if Clint had been home. But the double-barreled nature of the change knocked us all to our knees.

Bream, Molly, and Delaney were all there along with Mother and Father and Jamie to watch the kids tear through the wrapping I'd only just gotten on, rip through their stockings, and dive into the egg, bacon, grits, and cinnamon roll breakfast Molly and Bream had put on.

As the boys took over different parts of the house and yard to build (Jules), imaginarily fly (Theo), kick (Jack), paint (Isaac), "read" (Dylan), and Queenie patrolled them all, the adults settled into the living room to drink coffee, some with generous additions of Irish cream.

"None for you, my dear," my father said as he topped off coffee cups with the warming liquid. "Not that Quakers are supposed to anyway."

"Mothers-to-be certainly not. I know, Father," I said. "No problem. Though it seems like a good thing to be slightly stupefied. I think pregnancy has already taken care of that."

"As if life hadn't already," Mother said. "I remember as a young woman feeling that sense of unreality when Kennedy died."

"It was quite awful, wasn't it?" Molly said. "Even in England we watched it over and over."

We all stopped. We could all see it in our mind's eye, but no one could talk about it.

The baby took one long lazy drift across the front of my belly as if drawing her hand across water.

"Wow," I said involuntarily.

"What is it?" Bream said, looking around.

"Nothing," I said. "At least nothing visible. The baby. She just made her presence known." Molly and I looked at each other. Mother wouldn't be that interested.

But I knew I was already into the long conversation with my baby, the call and response of motherhood, the intensely private dialogue between the two of us: *I am, I am*, the baby would say.

Are you? I am waiting. Could you let me get some sleep? Don't step on my bladder again. Are you coming yet," I would answer.

"So where is Ana?" Bream said. He, Molly, and Mother all looked at me.

"I saw her once," Father answered. "She looked immaculate as always, but she wasn't holding the Bible for Trent to be sworn in, that was for sure. The Attorney General did that."

We all saw Jackie Kennedy standing next to Lyndon Johnson while someone held the Bible for Lyndon, still in her blood-stained pink suit on Air Force One.

"And what about Ana Trent?" Mother said as if we'd all acknowledged the shared vision. "Has anyone seen her?"

No one had. And no one had seen Clint either, but there wasn't a soul in that living room who was going to say so.

The day wore on—dinner was delicious, but I don't remember what it was. We took the boys out for a walk after to burn off some of the sugar. We ended up at Evermay and Mother had hot chocolate served.

Christmas got the leaden feel as the day wore on, the excitement and appetites sated, the very slight sense of dream for the return of routine.

But this one had both a national and a personal leadenness that felt like it might be settling in for the long haul.

"Funny how we always take a Christmas walk," Father said. "As if we were English."

"Some of us are, of course," Molly said.

"Has the Queen already given her speech?" Bream asked.

"Long ago. Probably already posted on YouTube," Delaney said.

"Speaking of English," Mother said. "I wonder how your grandmother is."

"Should we call?"

"It's late there," Mother said. "She'll either be in bed or at the pub."

Mother and her mother were by no means estranged.

They just didn't seem to need to connect often. And Grandmaman seemed to have gone native, at least to the extent that she'd lowered her upper-class standards enough to embrace the neighborhood pub habit of ordinary Londoners.

"I think you should leave the boys here tonight," Mother said. They were happily ensconced in her playroom—tucked discreetly away next to the kitchen. "And I think you should call Mother tomorrow."

"Okay, that sounds good," I said, though in truth I already felt bereft at not having the boys nearby.

"Which?" Mother said.

"Both," I said. "And I'm glad to call Grandmaman, but why do you sound so urgent?"

She didn't answer.

Molly stayed at Evermay too to watch TV with Delaney. Bream and I walked home. He got in his car though as we approached the house.

"You deserve a little time to yourself," he said. "And I need some."

I laughed. He loved my boisterous crew but in measured doses.

"Good night, Bream," I said. And we both laughed, thinking I might as well have said, "Good night, Moon."

I went into my castle and made a tour of it. I always checked the doors, of course, but on the extraordinarily rare occasion I was home entirely alone I checked everything, starting at the tower room. Not trusting the alarm system, I looked behind curtains and under beds.

I checked showers and laundry hampers. I gave the tower and its deep, Atlantis peace a once over and even walked the basement perimeter, claiming my space, my fiefdom.

I had no weapon, didn't even carry my phone with me. I wasn't trained in self-defense and had no real tools to negotiate with. I had a feeling behavioral economics wouldn't help in a face off with a burglar or a terrorist. Plus, I was forty and pregnant. So, my patrol was purely metaphor.

Except that Queenie went with me. She was glad I was home, happy to go on a mission. But then she became very serious. She sniffed where I couldn't go. She had a little worried frown between her brows. She took it seriously.

She gave me peace.

Or such as there was to be had.

I lay on our bed and drifted off to sleep.

But I awoke minutes later as if someone had called my name.

I was as awake as I'd ever been in my life, alert and peering into the darkness.

Queenie, once asleep on Clint's side of the bed, woke up and shot her ears forward.

We looked at each other.

We knew no one was there.

No one we either dreaded or desired.

CHAPTER TWENTY ONE

Winter

The next period of time was a really weird interregnum. It consumed the most of my second trimester. New Year's came and went, along with the President's funeral and Adam's inauguration.

Both were cold and low key, although Adam tried to make the inauguration look bigger than it was. He seemed to be quiet for a while after that, if you ignored how people under him were packing lower judiciary seats under his cover. He did try to make several anti-immigration moves that appeals courts blocked and happily cancelled more executive orders that protected consumers and students or controlled big banks' or corporations' freedom to steal regular people's money. He was either learning the ropes, becoming presidential, or frustrated by the limits of the office imposed on him and figuring out how to get around them, depending on your news source.

There was no Ana.

Mostly, people were too stunned to make much comment. Trent moved into the White House and set up a sort of carnival staff so that there were enough hijinks and gaffes to keep the media busy. If anyone pointed out the absence of the First Lady or First Son, it was with a sense of embarrassment, a discretion when it came to mentioning the radiation of their absence.

Trent himself seemed lost for a moment, as if the sound feed in his ear had faded.

But we were pretty absorbed with our own little world at my house. The boys were subdued over the long holiday, but they mostly got used to their dad's absence. It wasn't at all unusual to have him gone—just not for this long or this mysteriously. We stuck religiously to our routine— the mundane savior of sanity—and life went on.

The exception to the first generalization was Jules. Though he was glad enough to go back to school where he excelled, he never stopped looking for Clint, still checking the coat rack, the closet, and our room as soon as he got home.

The other exception was Dylan. He motored along through the holiday in his self-contained way, but when it came time to go back to school, he dragged his feet, came home several days with feigned illnesses, and always looked regretful when he had to leave me.

His reason—and I had no reason to doubt his veracity—was that he, like Jack before him was worried about me, worried that I would be lonely.

The truth was that I was lonely.

Molly, Bream, Father, Mother—I loved them all and they did their best. But if I couldn't have Clint, having one or more of my sons close to me was the next best thing, and after them, Queenie. They were the only things that warmed the arctic chill even slightly. Without them I might have just slowed down and stopped, slid into the void.

The baby girl, of course, helped. Except insofar as our deep conversation, our call and response, was so absorbing, the listening so intense, there were times it must have looked like hibernation.

Somehow, we all slept through January. It looked like February was going that way too. I heard from Clint's boss from time to time, but it was so cryptic I couldn't make any sense of what he was saying. He did or didn't know where Clint was. He couldn't tell me—but I could tell him. I always got off the calls more confused than before. I wondered if it was necessary to speak disinformation if you worked for the CIA. Did the man deliberately confuse his own wife as completely as he did me?

Molly, of course, was life-saving. Though she didn't ask me any annoyingly useless questions like had I heard anything or how I was, she was always there with a cup of hot Builder's tea, a square meal when I couldn't eat anything and wouldn't have if I'd had to make it myself.

Molly and I went to the movies when the boys were at Evermay and we shopped for little outfits in pink and salmon and teal. She was as convinced as I was that the baby was a girl. Or else she was humoring me.

I wasn't going to have amniocentesis. I'd had it with Dylan and he'd ended up with a needle mark in the back of his fat baby calf. So we were going to roll with this one, no matter what shape she was in.

Mother went with me to pre-natal visits. It was good of her to go. It would have been lonely to have no one there.

Though being with Mother could sometimes seem like a fairly isolating experience. She wasn't one to ooh or ahh. She asked no-nonsense questions of the doctor and nailed her down on the risks childbirth involved for a woman my age.

"The fact that it's her sixth," said the doctor, "is a good indication that all will go well. They have so far and Agatha knows better than to take chances. If need be, we will do a Caesarean again, but there is no reason to think it will be necessary."

"Yes, well," Mother said. "On the one hand, six seems excessive. But you're right—she should be able to handle it by now."

The doctor gave me a sympathetic eye roll.

I did notice the slightest glimmer of wet eye in Mother when the doctor put the stethoscope on my belly and we heard the baby's heartbeat go, "whang, whang, whang" about as loud as it could get.

Not even Mother had the nerve to raise the issue of Clint's long, unexplained absence, though. I could see she wanted to, but she also didn't want to hear my answer, so she didn't go there.

Jules did, though.

It was Jules who broke the ice jam.

"You'll have to go, Mom," he said.

"What?" I said.

I was in bed, where I usually was when not required elsewhere. Jules had appeared in my doorway, deep lines forming between his eyebrows that made him look related to Queenie.

"He's lying. All the time now," he said. He climbed onto Clint's side of the bed and opened the iPad he'd brought with him. He started a YouTube video of Adam Trent giving a talk about his greatness and the fragility of America, how he was the one to save it. He spoke again about the terrible state of the economy, how America was everyone's patsy, how weak we were, how threatened.

"He's saying it over and over," Jules said after a few of these, including the State of Union. "People are going to start believing him."

"Well, I do know from behavioral economics that people are predictably irrational all the time. They believe things that aren't true if they trust the person saying them, whether deserved or not."

"And they are told repeatedly," Jules said.

"They will believe anything," I summarized. I was trying to adjust to the idea that my oldest son might have become a colleague.

"Same with you," he said.

"What are you talking about?"

"You're telling yourself you can't do anything about Dad. Because of us. Because of the baby. Because he's a spy. But Dad is the only person I know who could help people doubt Adam Trent. You have to try."

What, he was turning into an oracle too?

"What am I supposed to do?" I asked testing the depths of his oracularity.

"That's for you to figure out," he said. "I'm only six."

"I don't know what I believe anymore," I said to Bream in his study. It was the day before Valentine's Day. I knew my son was right, but I had no idea what to do.

"If you knew what to believe, what would you do?" Bream asked.

"Don't the beliefs come first, then the actions?"

"In a way. But we know from our work that beliefs can be wrong and lead to wrong actions. The tendency is always to confirm what you already believe."

"Endowment effect."

"Also confirmation bias."

"Which takes us right back to our problem—how do you know what you believe is a good thing or a bad thing? People believe in Trent. I believe in Clint. Who is to say who is right? The possibilities seem infinite and undecidable."

"Thaler tells us that the best model is the roadside produce stand."

"Where the produce is available and the prices listed, but no one is there to enforce right behavior?"

"And don't forget the money box with a small opening."

"And that is nailed to the stand."

"Thus the nudge. Freedom within limits."

"Which some say risks paternalism—limits freedom."

"Which may not be such a bad thing given how liable people are to make bad choices, given too many of them."

"Which takes us back to the famous parental question: not what t-shirt do you want to wear but do you want the blue one or the green one."

"There is such a thing as right and wrong. It's right to pay for what you get—not just seize it without payment.

"Choice within limits—someone *could* choose to steal the produce, but they are prevented from taking the money. Losing what produce is there is far less harmful to the farmer than losing the income."

"But what are my choices here?"

"Do you go after him or do you wait here?"

I was stunned by the simplicity of the question.

Was it possible it was that easy? I felt myself rising up out of the fog of too many questions—the confusion of babble that had kept me immobilized.

If it was that simple—do I go or do I wait—then it was simple.

Of course, I wasn't going to wait.

"I think you just gave me a giant Thaler nudge," I said.

"Even pregnant?" Bream said.

"Even pregnant."

"That's more like you." Bream was beaming. There was only a tiny crease between his brows.

"I just have no idea where," I said.

"You'll figure it out," the man of faith said before I could deflate.

"I'm going after Clint," I said to my parents at Evermay.
My father was instantly alarmed.

"But you're pregnant," he said. "And have kids. And
where in the world you even look?"

"She'll figure it out," Mother said, cool, eagle-eyed.
Mother had far more austere faith in me than I did.

It took a couple of weeks, but by the end of February I
was ready to go.

"The boys are as organized as they'll ever be," I said to
Molly as we went over the last details.

"I'll pick them up today from school as usual," she
said. "They've already said good-bye, so they won't be
surprised you're not here."

"They all know I'm going to Grandmaman's in London.
Most of them have been there the last time we went.
Hopefully they'll think I'm just there to do the museums
and shop with their great-grandmother before the baby
comes."

"I saw Jules Google-earthing Grandmaman's house."

"He remembers being there, I'm pretty sure."

"The other boys might not."

"And Dylan wasn't even born yet. I think he intuits the
real reason I'm going anyway."

"If anyone could, it would be Dylan. Did you ever get in touch with anyone at the CIA?"

"I didn't tell them I was going to look for Clint. I just gave them one more chance to tell me what they know."

"And?"

"Nothing. He's on assignment—or not. They will let me know when they can where he is and when he'll be back. Or not. The usual word salad."

"You still have the feeling they don't know?"

"Very strongly."

"And you also don't know."

"Not a clue."

"So, your plan is?"

"Go to London and hang out with Grandmaman."

"And then?"

"Feel my way through from there, like in a dark room where you know someone is, but you don't know where."

"Or, actually, who."

"That too," I said.

Molly dropped me off at Dulles without further ado. She, my parents, Father Bream, and Delaney were in charge of the boys until I got back. But I didn't have a return ticket. I was going to stay there until I got an answer. Or the baby's due date got too close. Airlines wouldn't let you fly too late in pregnancy so I planned to be back by Easter at the very latest. My girl was due in the middle of May. She was a discernible presence as I boarded the bus to get on the plane—her existence an active bulge under the Delft blue big silk shirt. Mother had insisted on footing the bill for first class so we didn't have to squeeze into a regular seat—which, at the end of the second trimester, would have already been a significant problem.

"You'd better not get a whole lot bigger for the return trip," I said to her mentally. "Because even business class seats aren't big enough for small whales."

My boys had all been whoppers, but I was optimistic she would be at least reasonably petite.

Grandmaman, Mother's mother, had sent the car to Heathrow for me and I was swept off in style to her house in Knightsbridge. The driver bore no resemblance to Delany in terms of friendliness and kept the glass between us closed.

Just as well, I thought. I needed to get back to sleep. I'd slept all the way over and still felt sleepy there.

As we motored into the city from Heathrow I saw the little row houses with the tiny backyards give way to more and more urban neighborhoods then to neighborhoods with women in colorful clothes and headscarves, and finally into the city which always felt like another home to me—the buildings of reasonable height and motorways passable—right up until you realized everyone was going the wrong way and that you had to pass through security to drive to your destination inside London.

Grandmaman lived around the corner from Harrod's,

which was my location point for everything in the city. I had a mental line drawn from it to Trafalgar Square and everything existed in orientation to those two points.

Grandmaman herself lived outside of any lines.

Born of English stock who had gone to the colonies, she had married another member of the First Families of Virginia, had a career as a star of Virginia society, and then pulled up stakes as soon as Mother married and went back to England.

She and Grandfather were still married, and, as far as I knew, on good terms, but they were also separated by an ocean which, I imagined, could help any two strong personalities get along better.

When her one chick had flown, Grandmaman was done, in her mind, with all family obligations.

She did come over to my wedding, where she played the role of Queen Mother to the hilt. She much preferred that role to the "Grandmother" role that she had never played. When we visited her *en masse* she had a nanny hired and stowed the children in the top floor nursery. I had to admit there was something heavenly about that way of life.

Children were meant to be neither seen nor heard. On that visit I'd seen her look simply bewildered more than once on outings to Hyde Park with the whole gang of us where even the extra rent-a-nannies had a time keeping my gang—only two ambulatory at the time and the twins in a double stroller—from climbing the gates of Kensington Palace.

Grandmaman, as she was known to me and my brother, stood austerely at the top of the steps to her home. The silent chauffeur delivered my baggage to the butler who stood beside her and, taking the suitcase, promptly vanished.

Grandmaman extended her hand.

I drew her into a hug. Where I come from, we don't put up with much frostiness. She held back for a second, then returned my hug.

"My dear," she said, glancing discreetly at my open coat, "let's get your feet up."

"I'd rather walk around, Grandmaman," I said. "If I sit down right now I'm going to fall back to sleep."

"Blair," she called into the house, "could you hold the tea, please? We'll have it in the library in half an hour."

We went through the house and out the back door, straight into the garden. Though in the center of London, you'd never have known it, as the garden was terraced downwards and there was a sense of absolute privacy when you got to any of the high brick walls.

"How are you, my dear?" Grandmaman said. "How was the trip? And all those dear children?"

"The flight was fine," I said. "And the boys are thriving."

"Including the one . . . still on board?" Grandmaman would avoid the word "pregnant" at all costs.

We walked around the edge of the garden and down the brick walkways at a pretty good clip. When you said "walk" to Grandmaman, she took you up on it.

"Yes, though this one is a girl," I said.

"This modern thing—knowing your baby's gender," Grandmaman said, with clear implication.

"Well, to be accurate, I don't know it, as in having genetic tests done, but I 'know' in a different way."

Grandmaman's face was clearly having none of that nonsense.

"And that handsome husband of yours?" Grandmaman said. Here was a subject in which she clearly had more interest. "What is the news on him?"

"You did take a shine to him when we were here, didn't you?" I teased her.

"Hard not to," she said with more of a twinkle than I'd seen in her so far. "Handsome, kind, a great dad, dashing—and knows right from wrong."

"All in one," I said. "As I said when I called, he was on assignment right before Christmas and we haven't heard since."

"And you thought you'd come over and see if he were in Europe," she said.

"Though I don't have any idea how."

"I might have some," Grandmaman said.

"Some what?"

"Some ideas."

You couldn't have astonished me more.

Inside again, our tour of the early bulbs blooming done, Grandmaman steered me straight into her library.

We had come through the back doors and she'd made one stop outside the dining room as she went through it and pushed open the green baize door to tell whoever was in there to bring the tea. She had returned to steer me by the elbow, passing through the green room to get there.

I'd been a little light-headed outside—the reason for Grandmaman's unwonted elbow-holding—and she wanted me in the security of her remote study, I surmised.

The problem was that getting there took us through a room that demonstrated what was always shocking to me about English décor—the overwhelm of it: framed pictures floor to ceiling, the most vibrant, saturated colors (cerise dining room, vivid yellow kitchen, turquoise living room the sea green room, and finally the pumpkin study).

I knew the intensity of the colors was a result of paint archaeology—taking the house back to the original colors from lantern and candle days, when the saturation of color would simply have made it visible in the gloaming.

But the statuary, the marble knickknacks, the rugs of rich design—all gave an American eye—no matter how colorful her own palette was, was trained to the neutral and stripped—a sense of vertigo.

Or else, I was just jet-lagged, pregnant, shocked that my grandmother who had always been in my mind, pretty strictly statuary herself, had "connections" to the world of spying or politics or the underworld—it was often hard to tell one from another.

"You're missing him, I expect," Grandmaman said. "Your husband."

Which was probably the most accurate explanation.

We sat on the settee in her library, surrounded by jam-packed bookshelves, busts on plinths flanking the windows, and a sphinx. A fire burned in the fireplace in front of us.

Anonymous hands delivered tea and Grandmaman served. When I had sufficient hot, milky tea down me, Grandmaman turned to me.

"How much do you know, dear?"

"Very little," I said. "I'm a spy's wife. For all I know, he has another family in Montenegro."

It came out with such bitterness, we were both taken aback.

"Well, we don't think so," Grandmaman said. Was that the royal "we"? She poured more tea. Her dress was silk and it sliced rather than rustling. Somehow the austerity of the sound and the confidence of the gestures reassured me as much as the sweet milky tea did.

"No," I said. "We don't actually think so. I'm not sure even Clint, who loves our children, would want *two* families' worth."

Grandmaman looked for a second like she thought this might have been in poor taste, especially as I had to adjust the elastic on my skinny leg maternity jeans right then. But then she loosened up and rolled her eyes heavenward.

"Heaven forfend," she said. "In any case, you need to know for a fact."

"Yes, I do," I said. And I knew then that I did. I didn't know where he was or what he was doing. I didn't know if he had another family or if he'd just run off with the exotic First Lady. I didn't know if he had 10 children or merely the six that were ours. I didn't know if he was on his own business or that of our country. I didn't know if he was alive or dead.

But I knew I needed to know. Whether he wanted me to or not. Whether I could ever know or not. Though it might have seemed like a losing proposition—to come to Europe, where the knowledge of evil was so much deeper, longer, more layered, to come six months pregnant, to leave my boys to chase a spy, their father— all that smacked of futility, a sure way to lose.

But, perhaps like trading down in the NFL draft or choosing to go for a first down rather than a safe field goal, the moves that looked either stupid or risky in the moment or both could win in the long run.

"Yes," I said to Grandmaman. "I need to know."

She had given me the space to confirm this choice, to let the DNA she had passed down to me through Mother surface, and now she was all business.

"Good," she said. "You'll get your rest tonight. Then you'll go to the Banquet House in the morning. My friends will meet you in the hall itself. They already know the situation. They'll tell you what they can."

"So, Grandmaman," I said. "I had no idea you were involved with MI-6."

"I'm not, directly."

"But?"

"You don't think anyone in the diplomatic corps has

no connection, do you?"

"You were in the diplomatic corps?"

"Your grandfather," she said.

"He wasn't either."

"You don't think anyone with wealth and power isn't connected, do you?"

"Well, I guess not," I said. That—and the tea cakes— gave me so much food for thought that I felt immediately overwhelmed with the need to sleep.

Grandmaman saw my eyes roll back in my head. She gently got me up and steered me toward my bedroom on the top floor.

I was truly grateful for this bedroom, where I'd spent many girlhood summers, was painted a very restful clotted cream. Until then I didn't realize I could feel so passionate about neutral.

CHAPTER TWENTY TWO
London

In the morning I took a black cab to the Banqueting House which, to my consternation, was closed. The sign on the door said it was closed for scheduled conservation. Just as I started to turn back toward the cab, the door opened. Just as well, as the cab had vanished.

The person who opened the door was anonymity itself—nothing distinguishing at all about his appearance. Nor did he ask who I was or what I wanted.

As if in a magical castle straight out of Beauty and the Beast, doors opened to me by invisible hands, or, to be accurate, nondescript ones.

I was ushered up to the magnificent Banquet Hall itself, covered on every wall and all down the immense ceiling by monumental canvasses by Rubens, commissioned and brought to England rolled up in tubes by James I to decorate his feasting hall. The excess and grandeur were stunning.

A man waited for me at the far end of the hall, dwarfed by the canvasses all around him, made even more nondescript by his unremarkable grey suit, black-rimmed glasses, and a close-trimmed haircut.

I joined him and we began to walk the room, as if we were tourists, though no one else was there and the building was closed.

Plus the price of admission for either of us might have been unspeakable.

"I understand you are in need of information about the Russian connection," he said in a voice designed to bore anyone listening. I assumed that our walking would also frustrate anyone trying to hear what we said.

"I need to know as much as possible about what my husband was investigating when he disappeared before Christmas."

"Of course. As I'm sure you know, he was looking at the connection between Adam Trent and Russia."

"Rumors have gone around for years that Trent was involved with the Russians."

"It is common knowledge that Trent's business success was largely due to wealthy Russians."

"I have five children under the age of seven. I might have missed some history there. When did the Russians get rich? I thought they were more or less still struggling out of the repressions and restrictions of the Soviet era."

"Some 'struggled out' very quickly and made a lot of money, mostly in oil."

"Like Saudi Arabia?"

"Since 2005 they are neck and neck for production."

"And I take it glasnost didn't exactly come about."

"The ideals that were dreamed about in the 1980s fell apart in the 1990s. Factionalism and infighting took over.

As the possibility for wealth increased, the probability that it would be widely shared plummeted."

This seemed an improbably poetic way for Mr. MI-6 to describe it, but, I could tell by looking at his face, plummet they did.

"If there is an analogy," my anonymous poet-advisor went on, "it would be that the people returned to a state of near-feudalism, with the oligarchs taking the place of the aristocracy.

"And then the president appeared," he continued. "Trained in Soviet-era spying techniques and master of the long game, it seems that he found a way not only to control Russia, but to reach into Europe and then all the way into America as well."

"You are surely not claiming that that part has anything to do with Adam Trent?"

"The direct connection has never been found," he said, reverting to type. "He is suspiciously unwilling to reign in any interference from what was formerly an enemy of that state."

"But isn't that just good business—a changing world, progress?"

"Only if you discount all the ways in which the obligations Trent has could be used as leverage."

"But how could that leverage be applied? Trent has been suspect for years. Surely he is being watched—surveilled—at all times."

"Look at the timeline."

"What timeline?"

"For Trent's political aspirations, the Russian president's

ascension to power, and the mysterious appearance of Ana Trent in America."

"What?" I stopped at the foot of the Banqueting Hall. "What in the world could Ana have to do with it?"

"That is what we don't know. We do know that she appeared in America within a year of Trent's announcement that he would run for Congress."

"Wasn't he still married then?"

"Yes, to his second wife. Ana became a friend of hers. Not long after, Trent was divorced. And not long after that he and Ana were dating."

"But, all told, that is almost 20 years ago."

"As we said, a long game," Mr. Nondescript said.

"What about the other people around him who have Russian connections? Aren't they more likely the conduit, if there is one?"

"His brother is also deeply in debt to the Russians, and, of course, his chief of staff. We don't know how he got a security clearance."

"Well, there you are. He could be the one."

"He has been under surveillance for years. It has only gotten more intense since Trent ascended."

Another poetic turn. No sign of Mr. Unremarkable noticing.

"Are you trying to tell me that Ana Trent—who, I'm sure you know, has been a friend of mine—had anything to do with the Vice President stepping down? Or, God forbid, the President dying?"

"We know that she was out of Montenegro for several years before she came to the U.S. She might have been in

Russia. The Russian president desperately wants control of Montenegro for its access to the Adriatic. He might have identified Ana as a conduit to that. And then he had a much better game for her to play—to be the poisoned chalice for his biggest prize. That is what both MI6 and the CIA were trying to find out."

"What was Clint doing?"

"He was trying to find out who was behind her. Was she being given orders from Russia."

"Where is he?"

"We don't know," he said. I stumbled and he took my elbow, kept us moving. "He vanished from all our screens just after New Years."

"Where was he?"

"In the Alps."

"Where was she?"

"Also the Alps. Italian Switzerland, to be precise."

"The same place?"

"Close."

I might as well have been Charles I leaving the Banqueting House without his head for all the thought I was capable of having as I retraced my steps, got in the black cab waiting for me outside, summoned by those magic hands, and went home to Grandmaman.

They say the last things the king saw as he left this life on his way to beheading for losing the Civil War were the Rubens paintings, paying the price for that rich and gilded life.

I gave the paintings one last look as I left the building and the belief system I'd know before I went in behind.

CHAPTER TWENTY THREE
Switzerland

The next weeks were occupied with research, preparation, and making sure Molly and Mother had a full set of instructions for the boys—as if either of them needed one. Between those tasks were trips to the Victoria & Albert Museum in a sort of ritualistic routine of self-soothing by visiting the pre-Raphaelites home décor, the porcelain, the Rubens room there, and the museum cafeteria.

In the late hours of night when I was sleepless and there was nothing more to prepare, I wrote the article Bream and I had previewed. In it, I used the choices that parents have for styles of parenting as a model. One choice was to be the traditional, stern parent with a set of rules to be adhered. That one could be called "authoritarian" or "paternalistic." If another was to allow free choice to the child, expecting their innocence to guide then to good choices, that was the "permissive" or "libertarian" model of parenting. If the traditional form had prevailed until, say, late 20th century, and the permissive had held sway from late 20th through early 21st century, then the effects of both could be studied fairly extensively.

Clearly, the authoritarian models had created a lot of havoc—often, unhappy, driven children who were haunted by conformity all their lives, whether making traditional choices or rebelling against them. The freedom of choice model that was probably my natural one as it followed my more or less hippie way of thinking also, it turned out, had some big flaws. The children raised under this rubric had often ended up lost and confused, anxious and driven by perfectionism that was boundless because no one had defined clear goals for them.

The non-binary way of parenting turned out to be somewhere not in between, not a merging of the two, but something completely different: authoritative parenting. In this model, the parents made a choice first, limiting the child's choices to ones that would ultimately be to his benefit. Then the child was allowed to choose.

The difference could be illustrated in clothing:

Model 1: You must wear the red t-shirt because I said so.

Model 2: What t-shirt would you like to wear today?

Model 3: Would you like to wear the green t-shirt or the blue t-shirt today?

My old wrangle with the problem of who made the choice and by what standards was resolved in this model by seeing the parent as making a pre-selection based on what would be in the child's interests in the future—neither the present pleasure of anything goes nor the ironbound choice of "you must because I say so." But a longer-range view of what, historically, is the best idea: it is good to wear clothes. And then a view to the future:

how can my knowledge of the past best help my child's future. The confusion of so many choices leading to opting out of choosing is avoided, as well as the rigidity of only one possibility.

It wasn't a perfect system and depended very much on the parents' good judgment—on their character. But it was as good as it got, as far as I could see.

I sent the article off to Father Bream.

I finally left, taking the Chunnel under the Channel and to Geneva, where I picked up my rental car.

Grandmaman had listened to me and directed my research. She had helped me plan the trip and get the tickets. She didn't try to stop me. She would have gone with me if she could have. She knew as well as I did that plane travel was out—too visible in so many ways.

How could someone I'd known, someone who had been in my home, whose child had played with my children, have done what MI 6 suspected of her? How could she have disabled the vice-president? And by such nefarious, sneaky means. Could she possibly have pushed Connie Edgerton over the edge? Was there a poison that could cause mental illness? She was certainly right there at the dinner when she went. And the President? It still wasn't clear what he had died of. Could she have had anything to do with that?

Just before I left word began to come out of America

that Adam Trent was losing power, stumbling. Or his stumbles were catching up with him.

I, like most people, had seen her as a victim, as trapped in a loveless marriage, with a difficult and bullying man.

But what if that wasn't the case? What if she were the one pulling the strings? And what if someone else was pulling her strings?

And what did my husband know? What did he have to do with her? And where was he?

I rented a car in Geneva and headed for the Italian alps. I'd gone to school Switzerland and wanted the soothing effect of that tiny, tight jewel of a country. I wanted the illusion of control.

The baby had been lulled to sleep by all the activity, but she was waking up and making her presence known. Somehow or another she'd grown gigantic while I was touring the British Museum and the Victoria and Albert and waiting to hear any news about my husband. She must have liked all those pot pies I ate in the Museum cafeteria almost every day.

It was a surprise when I did get news—not about Clint but about Ana. She had turned up back in Italian Switzerland, near Lugano, for reasons MI-6 apparently didn't understand.

And for reasons I certainly didn't know, both MI 6 and the CIA wanted me to know.

Maybe I was being manipulated—or maybe they just thought I should know. It only took one short Skype call with Jules to know beyond a shadow of a doubt I was going to go.

Jules said everything there was fine—which Molly affirmed—and they just needed me *and* Dad home, emphasis on the conjunction. And, oh yes, the baby. Jules hadn't been overly enthusiastic about a fifth sibling, even a girl, and struggled to politely consider her in the equation.

I didn't want a driver or a train. I wanted the comfort of my own car—a black Mercedes SUV—and the autonomy of coming or going as I pleased, like any real American. At least everyone in Switzerland drove on the right side of the road.

Driving along Lac Leman—Lake Geneva to outsiders—was magical. April in Paris had nothing on April in Switzerland. We had skied there when I was young at Chamonix. I remembered the bitter cold of it—such a complete domination by cold and snow and wind that you couldn't even for a moment imagine that humans had somehow conquered weather. We could only cooperate with it—or take shelter.

But April there was beautiful, and mild, and a place as it can only when it has, again, gotten through the worst, the most biting northern winds—La Bise—the most terrible west winds—Le Fern—and lived to sell another round of spring flowers.

I drove along the northern edge of the Lake. It was stunningly beautiful, sparkling at the feet of the Alps. I drove past Lausanne, stopping for a quick raclette though I knew the cheese and potato dish might stay right at the top of my stomach, balanced on top of my girl's feet.

I drove on to Montreux, then up, up in the Italian Swiss Alps. I thought for a moment that the car, for all its power, might not make it through the San Gottardo Pass where it was decidedly still winter.

But we got across and down.

It was evening when I arrived in Lugano.

A medieval town, Lugano. Italian, yes, but Swiss Italian, so clean, orderly, a bit darker than French Swiss cities, being in the shadow of the immense mountains. The de Medicis might have felt at home there.

Why Ana Trent would be there, I didn't know. I got the answer from MI 6 via Grandmaman: she wasn't.

She was outside Lugano, in a tiny town up in the hills, where her family had owned a house for many years.

As the sun disappeared to the West, taking with it anything left of the familiar, I got back in the car and drove up the tiny twisting road to Fata Morgana.

Ana was easy to find. She was in the living room of her house, an old villa, with archways everywhere, a sense of hidden passageways. She was waiting for me, as surely as I had been looking for her.

"Come in," she said. She looked lovely, as always, and more suited to this strange, dark house than she ever had been to Kalorama.

I sat across from her in a winged chair, the terracotta walls around us, the large Moroccan design tiles on the floor between us, and a spread of exquisite Italian fresh food on the low table before us.

Ana was stretched out on the sapphire settee in a long silk gown of deep ocean green.

"Please eat," she said. "I am thinking you are starving."

I was. I hesitated.

"I didn't poison it," she said. "I didn't even poison Connie, so what would be the point of killing you?"

"Since we are coming straight to the point, where is Clint?" I loaded antipasto, two thin slices of baguette, and a generous dip of herbed olive oil and dug in.

"I'll get to that," she said.

"Where is Wolf?" I said.

"He is with my parents in Montenegro," she said. She drank from a tall silver goblet with stones encrusted on it.

"Why?" I said.

"I am thinking you mean why did I do it," she said. "Let's start with what did I do.

"I was chosen and trained for the job because I had these assets," she said, one long elegant hand gesturing toward her shining hair, her exotically beautiful face, her model's body. "At first I was only to try to influence the president of Montenegro to ally with Russia to open up the Adriatic to him."

We both knew who she meant by "him."

"But it was clear that I had more capacity. Just about then Adam began to bluster in the American press about running for political office. At the same time his businesses were failing. He was, how you say, a sitting duck? It is so easy to manipulate losers who have an ego they don't deserve."

"And it was easy to lure him away from his wife," I said.

"Child's play," Ana said. "American woman—they take their husbands' so personally, so much a matter of their ego. They treat them like a possession, an accessory that must behave up to their standard, or be punished," she said. "American husbands are very easy pickings."

Would Clint have been easy pickings? Did I treat him like an accessory? I couldn't bear to think about that then.

"What did you do to Connie Edgerton?"

"She was so close to the edge. That too was child's play—to push her over."

"And the President?"

"Plutonium. A weapon of choice."

I put down my plate.

"You poisoned him with plutonium?" I said.

"No, Adam did it. I was just cover for its delivery."

"Like all the directions to Adam what to do, how to disrupt."

"He is a natural agent of chaos," she said. "For people who have nothing inside, it is how they make it look like there is someone powerful in there. It is their method of disguise."

"Camouflage for the emptiness, the chaos they themselves feel."

"If they can get other people to feel it, then they have successfully sent their own misery, their fear of annihilation, outside."

"But, why, Ana? Why do this? Why did you choose this path? Your country has no real allegiance to Russia. It is one of the success stories, an emerging democracy in the Balkans."

"Yes, we have never been part of the Russian empire, though we have from time to time been an ally. I was born in Yugoslavia, which was, of course, part of the eastern European bloc. But Tito and Stalin had not gotten along, so it was not always a close relationship. Before the Revolution, it had been split between the Italians and the Ottomans."

"So why join with the Russians?"

"Because I saw the war—the terrible fighting among people with the same blood but who had fractured, set against one another, destroyed each other with the most terrible cruelty."

"And so unity with an authoritarian is better?"

"You can see it coming again in your own country, dear Agatha," Ana said with great urgency, with pain. "The terrible division growing, people gathering against each other—this time the left and the right, each coalescing into their own bubbles, feeding their own fears, taking more extreme positions, and refusing to talk to each other—reacting, always reacting to the latest news cycle, the sound bite, forgetting what is good and central and unifying!"

She might have made an interesting politician herself.

But as it was, she betrayed her country—and mine.

"But, why, Ana?" I said again. "I don't understand why?"

"You do not understand yet, my friend?"

"No, I don't."

"Democracy—freedom—that is a ridiculous idea. It is so fragile, so easily destroyed! People have to believe in it for it to work—and people are so easily led astray."

"You don't believe in the essential goodness of people—the ability to make good decisions?"

"No, and you don't either. You did not see what we did in the war, but still you understand. Most Americans are so naïve. It is a lovely quality—but it makes your people very easy to deceive, like children. When there are too many choices and no central belief, it is all too easy to bring your people down."

"But there are other possibilities—freedom within clear limits. Did you never tell Wolf he could wear the green or the blue t-shirt—not just pick any of too many or tell him he had to wear the blue one?"

"Who will decide the two choices, Agatha? You are arguing the same thing I am. There has to be someone making the decisions, a central authority that you trust."

"But people should be able to choose that authority," I said. "That is what representative democracy is all about." I could feel for myself that there was a big hole in this argument.

"You think people *en masse* are going to make a good choice, when individuals cannot? People cannot even decide to eat healthy food or take exercise when they know they will feel better."

"They think someone else will fix this—that the next

diet fad or surgery will fix the chaos their own poor choices created," I said.

"You see, Agatha, you do agree with me," Ana said. "When people cannot take responsibility for themselves, someone else must."

I felt I was sliding into a logical trap Ana had set for me, but I couldn't for the life of me see the flaw in her reasoning just then and started to doubt my own argument in the article I'd written.

"But you are arguing for going backwards—to feudalism, monarchy."

"Was that so bad, given the alternatives we explored in the past century?"

"Wait," I said suddenly. "What is your whole name?"

Ana began to laugh.

"You have guessed!" she said with delight.

"'Anastasia,'" I said. "The last child of the last tsar."

"I am not, of course, the original one, who died with her family at the hands of the Communists. No, but I bear her name."

That explained a lot—the royal bearing, the aura of untouchability.

But being royal—or thinking she was—did that make her any less caged, less a victim? Did not Rapunzel's beauty also get her imprisoned in a tower?

"What about Clint?" I finally said.

She smiled an appreciative smile that turned sad.

"He convinced me to stop," she said.

"When?"

"At Jules' party. He spoke of Wolf. Of what would be his future. That was it. I stopped. I took Wolf and left. He gave me a nudge. But, really, Agatha, it was you. You with your stubborn belief in your husband, your family. Your willingness to take long-term risks like having a lot of children while guarding the present moment by choosing fidelity."

That was more than I could fathom at the moment, so instead I asked, "Aren't you in danger?"

"I think not. I am still more valuable alive."

"And Clint came too?"

She looked confused, then she laughed. "Oh, that would be so great! Then I would feel like there was no danger," she said. "But that would never be. Do you not know loyalty when you see it? That is why I believe him when he said I should stop. He is one of those—very rare—people who does believe in your country, who knows there is a right and a wrong. If everyone believed— and acted—as he does, your representational democracy just might work. But, no, now everyone—on the left and the right—believes that everything is possible, all points of view are true. They are not."

"You haven't seen him since the party?"

"Oh, yes, he came here and asked me questions. Then he left and went east, behind the old Iron Curtain. He had to finish the job. There were others who could puppeteer Adam after I left. Your husband had to cut the Master's strings. Did you not feel that he has done that?"

Suddenly I knew that was true. Adam had lost air like a

popped balloon over the past two weeks. If anyone could have done that, it would have been Clint. I should have known that. On some level, deep in my dark and restless soul, I felt a spark of faith. Ana's argument foundered on the rock of the time-tested values of truthfulness, fidelity, and good character.

I slept that night in a velvet covered four-poster bed at Ana's and woke to an empty house. There was food waiting for me and my car in front of the door.

I got as far as Lausanne when, as I stopped to go to the bathroom, my water broke. I barely made it to the hospital in Lausanne before the baby came.

A week later, back home among my boys, parents, brother, Molly, and Delaney, we held the baptism at Trinity Church, Father Bream presiding. Molly drove the two older boys home in her Vette.

We named the baby Clint Wells, Junior. Because of course he was a boy all along.

We called him Junior so he wouldn't be confused with his father if he came home. When he came home.

ABOUT THE AUTHOR

Ginger Moran

A published and award-winning writer, teacher, and book mentor, Ginger Moran lives and writes in Maryland. She has Bachelor's and Master's degrees in English from the University of Virginia and a Ph.D. in Creative Writing from the University of Houston. She has published in salon.com, Oxford American, the Virginia Quarterly Review, among other journals and magazines. Her first novel, The Algebra of Snow, was nominated for a Pushcart Editor's Choice Award.

ACKNOWLEDGMENTS
Thank You

I'd like to thank, among many others who have been with me on this long journey, my parents, Chic and Fer Moran, for conveying their love of politics and society, my sons, Julian and Baird Lantry, for listening to me think this book through and reviewing the text, to my cousin Katharine for inside info, my friend Zvezdana for a Yugoslavian culture lesson, to my dear friends Rebecca Foster and Nancy Ford for their close reading, Jeb Bonner and Elizabeth Cating for the party protocol and food, to my friend and colleague John H. Matthews who was in on the beginning and the end, my friend and colleague Ed Hutchison who toured me through Georgetown, to the teachers of Behavioral Economics such as Richard Thaler whose work I hope I haven't mangled too badly, and the American founding fathers and mothers, who gave us the gift of representative democracy, should we choose to preserve it. My profound love and gratitude to my companion DixieGrace, who went with me on this journey over 16 years and lives on as Queenie.

Made in the USA
Columbia, SC
29 December 2020